Promise at Refuge Point

DONNA ALWARD

Copyright

Please Note

Cover by Ecila Media

Acknowledgements

When I started writing this book, I went to my FB fan group, Donna Alward's Amazing Readers, for help coming up with a hero name. The deal was the winner would get a shout out in the acknowledgements, so many thanks to Nancy Urtz in honor of her 7-year-old grandson Jax Howell! When she mentioned Jax, I knew it was the right fit, and Jax Brodie came to life in my head.

Thank you, Nancy!

Contents

Chapter One   1

Chapter Two   13

Chapter Three   30

Chapter Four   52

Chapter Five   68

Chapter Six   81

Chapter Seven   99

Chapter Eight   118

Chapter Nine   132

Chapter Ten   154

Chapter Eleven   174

Chapter Twelve   186

Chapter Thirteen   200

Chapter Fourteen   218

Chapter Fifteen   231

Chapter Sixteen   252

Chapter Seventeen   267

Chapter Eighteen   279

Chapter Nineteen   291

Epilogue   308

Preview   311

About the Author   321

Chapter One

Summer Arnold stared at Sally Jenkins and willed herself not to cry. "You…you've already sold? Signed the papers?"

Sally nodded, her eyes also filling with tears, but her face didn't reflect the same anguish that was currently crushing Summer's chest. "I have, Summer. I'm sorry. I know this means you're out of a job, but it's time I retired."

Summer liked Sally. She liked this job, even if it was scooping ice cream and supervising teenagers which sometimes felt like herding cats. Sally's Dairy Shack was a summertime fixture in Jewell Cove. People lined up to have a double scoop and sit at the picnic tables along the wharf, listening to the lap-lap of the waves and the cry of the gulls over Penobscot Bay. Summer's "career" had consisted of working seasonal jobs for years, and every July and August, she worked at Sally's. Only it wasn't Sally's any longer.

Summer hadn't even known retirement was a discussion that was happening, though perhaps she should have. Sally was no spring chicken. But she wasn't exactly old, either. And now Summer wondered how she was going to make her rent, let alone put money aside for tuition. She'd decided to go back to school in the fall, to do something more with her life. She'd paid her application fee to the nearby community college and had been accepted into the paralegal program. But none of that would work if she didn't have a job from June through the end of August.

She should have known better than to get her hopes up. When Sally had called asking to meet for coffee at Breezes Café, Summer had foolishly thought that maybe an offer to manage the dairy bar was forthcoming—maybe even a raise. Instead, she was being shown the door.

Conversations swirled around them, but for once Summer wasn't interested in people-watching. "I could have managed this for you, Sally. You didn't need to sell it." She failed to keep the disappointment out of her voice, and Sally's crow's feet deepened as she frowned. But Summer knew she had the experience to do the job well. Honestly, it stung that Sally hadn't asked. Sally certainly could have taken a step back from the business if she wanted to have more time to herself.

Sally sighed. "I know you're disappointed, Summer. I hated having to tell you. But the truth is, I needed to sell the business to fund my retirement. It'll likely be closed for a good part of the season, as the new owners renovate."

"Renovate for what?"

Sally's gaze slid away. "A gift shop."

Summer looked down, crushed. Another gift shop tourist trap, selling the ubiquitous tchotchkes and saltwater taffy and everything with stupid lobsters on it, spelled *lobstah*. The mass-produced kind of gift shop, no doubt, that stocked up on magnets and keychains and T-shirts. It might have been all right if it was something like Jess ran up at Treasures. That was all local goods and consignment from nearby artisans and craftspeople. True souvenirs from a gorgeous little town on Maine's midcoast, as well as art supplies and evening classes for the townies and activities for the kids. But losing Sally's meant losing yet another business that catered to the townspeople and replacing it with one that provided cheap goods to the transient tourists that came and went three months of the year, maybe four if the weather was good and the "peepers" came in search of the splendor of fall colors.

The more immediate problem was that it meant no job for her. She would finish at the elementary school in two weeks and had nothing else lined up. Her school job was only part time. She was a lunchroom supervisor for two hours a day each day, then worked for three hours in the afterschool program. Twenty-five hours per week. She barely made ends meet. Scooping ice cream was just over minimum wage money, but it had always been more weekly hours, plus tips.

June first was in three days. Sally always reopened on June first. Now Summer had less than two weeks to find something else. And the stupid thing was, most of the summer jobs were already spoken for. Students had started applying weeks ago in anticipation of positions going fast. Sally's reluctance to tell Summer the truth had put her in a doubly awkward position.

And yet, as she looked at the woman who'd been her employer for... oh, at least eight summers now, she didn't have it in her heart to be angry. Sally had always been so good to her, and Summer treasured their relationship. She knew what it was like to be alone; she'd spent the majority of her childhood on the fringes. It made her extra thankful for the friendships she had now.

"Don't worry, I'll find something else," Summer said quietly. "And of course you've earned the right to retire. And to sell the business. I'm just disappointed, Sal, that's all."

"I know, honey, I know. If I hear of anything I'll give you a shout. Promise."

"I should go, then," Summer said, staring at the half-full coffee cup that she'd abandoned on the table the moment Sally had given her the bad news. She reached for her wallet, but Sally put her hand over Summer's.

"I got this, Summer. It's the least I can do."

"Thanks," Summer answered, not even putting up the usual argument of "you don't have to do that," and "oh, it's all right, I can get this one." All she wanted now was to go home to her little apartment, pour herself a glass of the wine she'd been saving for Saturday night, and feel sorry for herself.

She exited Breezes with a heavy sigh. The May evening was sunny but cool; the wind off the water held a chill that said summer wasn't here quite yet. Summer put her purse strap over her shoulder and wrapped her arms around herself as she made her way home to the apartment on the second floor of an old captain's house overlooking the harbor.

Along the way she glanced in at the businesses lining the waterfront, checking for Help Wanted signs just in case. There was nothing at the coffee and tea store, Leaf and Grind, and nothing showing at Bubbles, the boutique featuring locally made soaps and essential oils. The art gallery, The Three Fishermen, was already closed for the evening, and she knew the owners ran it with a very small staff. There was always waiting tables, she supposed, or dipping fish and clams at Battered Up.

This was exactly why she wanted to go back to school. She was ready to be challenged. Ready to stop floating through life. She was going to be thirty-two soon, and she'd let her upbringing dictate far too much of her life, thinking she couldn't reach for more. That she didn't deserve it.

The moment her comfort zone became a rut, she'd known she had to do something.

First school, and maybe a better job. And then maybe a place better than her cramped apartment. She'd open the windows tonight and let in the cool air, but within a month when the humidity and heat descended, that second floor would be hot as balls, even with the breeze off the ocean. The only thing hotter was the third floor apartment, and her neighbors had installed one of those window air conditioners on the backside of the house that didn't face the street. They kept cool, and Summer got to listen to the rattle and rumble of the A/C that Fred down at the hardware store called a "window shaker."

Despite the racket, Summer had considered splurging on one of those and getting Tom Arseneault to install it. Unlikely she could do that now. Not while she was unemployed. Her old fan at the foot of the bed would have to do.

She was nearly home when a voice called her name and she looked up. It was Abby Arseneault, Tom's wife, who'd moved to Jewell Cove a few years back when she'd inherited her Aunt Marian's house. "Summer! Hi!"

Summer pasted on a smile she didn't quite feel. "Hey, Abby. What are you doing in town?"

Abby grinned. "Oh, I was picking up a prescription and some diaper cream at the drugstore before it closed." She lifted up her cloth tote as if to demonstrate. "You?"

Summer sighed. "Coffee with Sally at Breezes. She's sold the business. No Dairy Shack this year."

Abby gaped. "What? I didn't even know it was up for sale! Wow, the grapevine really let us down, huh?" Her eyes suddenly registered understanding. "Oh, hon. That means no job for you this summer, doesn't it?"

"Yeah." Summer sighed again. "I'm trying to not feel too sorry for myself, but hell. I'm disappointed. I mean, I'll have the school job again in the fall..." She looked at kind, sympathetic Abby. She considered Abby a good friend, and she'd been dying to say something about her plans for weeks. "Do you want to come in for a glass of wine? I could use a sounding board for a few minutes. But not if you're busy…" She didn't want to be a nuisance or bring someone else down with her troubles. They were hers to manage, after all. They always had been.

"I can handle that. Tom's got the baby at home while I run a few errands. I'll just send him a text. But I'll pass on the wine since I'm driving." She grinned. "And still breastfeeding."

They climbed the outside steps to the second floor and Summer's door. She opened it and stepped inside. Lord, it was stifling in here. "Hang on while I open a window and turn on the fan," she said, hustling to the kitchen to lift the window above the sink. A pedestal fan sat in the living room and she turned it on, creating some air movement. "It was raining when I left this morning, and I haven't been home since." Indeed, her dinner had been the half cup of coffee at Breezes. She'd lost her appetite.

"This is a cute spot," Abby replied. "You know, I don't think I've ever been inside before. I always see you around town. At Sally's. Or at Jess's craft classes, or whatever."

"It's kind of small. Not really great for entertaining."

Abby toed off her shoes and entered the living room. "It's cozy. And cute. I love the colors."

The apartment was painted the standard rental eggshell throughout, and Summer wasn't about to say it out loud, but all her furniture was thrift store finds. The sofa was red and plush, and she'd steam cleaned it and flipped the cushions over so the threadbare spots didn't show. There was a wing chair in orange with a scrape down one leg, and she'd found plump orange cushions at a discount department store in Houlton that she'd put on the sofa to tie the two together. The coffee table she'd grabbed at the church rummage sale for ten dollars, and on it sat a bowl filled with artificial, fat sunflowers. And the few prints on the wall she'd discovered on sale at Amazon, with the same red, orange, and yellow color scheme.

It was determinedly warm and cheerful, just the way she tried to live her life. But damn, sometimes it was hard to be positive.

She went to the fridge and grabbed Abby a soda, popping the top and pouring it into a glass before delivering it to the living room. Then she went back and took out her weekend bottle of Pinot Grigio. Moments later she joined Abby on the sofa, letting out a sigh as she sank into the old cushions.

They chatted for a few minutes about nothing in particular, until Abby said, "So what did you want to run past me?"

Summer cradled her glass, knowing her hands were warming the sweating bowl but not caring. "I'm registered for a paralegal course in the fall through the community college. It's not super expensive, and I'm able to do it online, so I don't need to travel." That had been a big concern, as Summer didn't own a car. She walked or biked anywhere she needed to go in Jewell Cove, and the odd time she went out of town she took the bus or rented a car. "But it does mean I can't work quite as many hours to make ends meet. I was planning to really economize during the summer and put extra away to help me with expenses, but without the summer job..." She took a long sip of wine. "I don't know how I'm going to make my rent, let alone put anything aside."

Abby nodded, turning on her cushion and putting one foot under her leg. "Definitely. In the short term, you can apply for unemployment insurance, right?"

Summer nodded. "I guess. I should have enough hours at the school to qualify."

"Which helps you in the short term, but not for the fall."

"I'm wondering if I should just forget about it. I mean..." It hurt her even to say it, but she had to consider that maybe her plans were going to change. "I have half of the tuition saved. I could use it to get through the summer, but then won't have anything to pay my tuition in September."

"What about student loans?"

Summer swallowed tightly as her stomach formed a knot. She'd always been super quiet about her upbringing, not wanting to air her sordid laundry to her adopted hometown. She remembered too much about not having money for groceries, for the electric bill. Remembered a few times someone had come to the door looking for money her mother had owed, and Summer hid in the closest. "I, uh... I have a thing about debt," she admitted. "The thought of taking out a loan scares the hell out of me."

Abby regarded her curiously, then took a drink of her soda. "Summer," she said gently, "what if a loan came from a friend?"

Summer shook her head, knowing exactly what Abby was suggesting. "I can't do that, Abby. But gosh, I thank you for the offer." And it wasn't like Abby couldn't afford it. She had inherited her Aunt Marian's substantial estate and her husband, Tom, was a top contractor on the midcoast. Still, Summer had always made her own way and she would this time, too. Relying on other people had only ever let her down.

"Well, you can't change your plans. Not when you're this close. The issue isn't about whether or not you go to school, it's about making ends meet during the summer months. Sadly, a lot of the seasonal jobs are taken." Abby frowned.

"I know. And other full-time jobs aren't going to want to hire me knowing I'll be leaving in September."

They sat in silence for a few moments. Suddenly Abby sat up and snapped her fingers. "I just had an idea. I don't know why I didn't think of it before! A production company is filming a documentary on Aquteg Island this summer. Some history buff with a shitload of money is bankrolling it. I bet there are jobs there. Let me ask around and see if there's a call for local jobs. When we were approached about it, the film schedule was for three months, ending mid-September. It would be perfect."

"About the island? Really?"

"Yes! Oh, and a bit of local history for context. About the founding families, that sort of thing."

The tiniest flicker of hope flared in Summer's chest, tempered only by a slight sense of unease. How deep was this company digging into the three men who'd settled here? And yet... the prospect of a three-month job made her feel a little bit lighter. "It *would* be perfect. Even if the pay is crap, if I can get full-time hours I can manage everything." She looked at Abby, who was smiling widely. "I don't want to get my hopes up." Nor would she be broadcasting any of her family history around town. No one knew her ties to the origins of Jewell Cove, and if she had her way, they never would.

"Oh, don't you worry about that," Abby said, her voice confident. "I'm the lone descendant of the Foster family who settled Jewell Cove, and my participation in the documentary is crucial. Leave it all to me."

Summer knew she should say no, that she shouldn't let her friend take advantage of her position like that. But it was Abby. Abby was sweet and kind and also knew how to get things done. Besides, she'd far rather Abby used her connections than accept a loan—at least then she'd be working for the money. "I won't take a loan, but... Well, if you hear of anything at all just let me know. I'm done at the school in two weeks. I'm free in the mornings for interviews. And it doesn't have to be the documentary thing either. Just... anything." The words "lone descendant" stuck in her brain. Abby was a Foster. Tom was an Arseneault, a descendant of Charles, who had a reputation as a blockade runner in the Civil War. But where were Edward Jewell's descendants? No one knew.

Nor would they. She'd be keeping that tidbit to herself. Edward Jewell hadn't been the paragon everyone thought he was.

Abby grinned. "Of course, I'll let you know if something comes up. Summer, I don't think you realize how much you *are* Jewell Cove. You work here, you volunteer here. Gosh, do you remember the first time we met at the candle-making workshop at Treasures? We had wine and you made some comment about Tom's good looks..."

Heat climbed Summer's cheeks. She did remember. It might have had something to do with him being sex on a stick...

Abby laughed. "Don't be embarrassed. You were right. He *is* sex on a stick. A blind woman would notice. What I'm saying is, you're loved here. People care about you and will help you if you let them. This is going to work out, I promise."

It seemed to Summer that Abby couldn't promise anything. Promises were made to be broken. Looking back, she couldn't think of one single promise that had ever been made to her that had worked out. But her friend's words touched her. She was loved? That was a surprise. She'd never really felt loved in her life, and for the most part, she'd made peace with it. Instead, she'd worked very hard at loving herself. She didn't need external validation. She never had. Waiting for it was an exercise in futility, and when it did arrive it could be ripped away as quickly as it had come.

And yet those words—*you're loved here*—sent something warm but terrifying through her. Like if she messed up somehow, it would be taken away. Just as her mother had been taken from her. And then her grandparents.

"You're the best, Abby," she said, and rose from the sofa to refill their drinks. At least she could hide in the kitchen, where Abby couldn't see how much she felt like a fraud.

Chapter Two

J ax sat behind the ancient desk and tapped his pen on the yellow pad of paper before him. Five applicants already this morning and none of them were standing out as anyone special. His next interviewee was five minutes late. He appreciated punctuality and getting off on the right foot. His dad had always said that being on time meant arriving fifteen minutes early. That the next person was behind schedule didn't bode well. And he only had the six interviews. He supposed he'd have to choose one.

The outer door to the house slammed and footsteps rushed through the entry. He stood. The instructions to each applicant were to exit the mudroom, go through the kitchen, turn left at the hall, and then right into the makeshift office. There was a pause, a rustle of paper, and then more steps until a woman stepped into the open doorway.

"Mr. Brodie? Summer Arnold. I'm so sorry I'm late. I had some bicycle trouble."

He lifted an eyebrow. Her face was flushed from heat, exertion, or both, and little pieces of hair curled around her face, damp with sweat. She was attractive, though, with bright blue eyes and lips that just now curved into an adorable, sheepish smile. "To be honest, I should have been here twenty minutes ago, but my chain came off. I had to stop to put it on, then made another stop to wash my hands. It was either be a smidge late or shake your hand with grease on my fingers." She stepped forward and held out her hand. "Pleased to meet you."

He shook it automatically, still surprised by the whirlwind that had just taken over the office with her breezy presence. "You biked? All the way from town?"

"From Jewell Cove, yes. I don't own a car, but it's a nice bike ride just the same. Thankfully more down than up at the end of the day." She smiled again.

He guessed the woman—Summer—to be in her late twenties. Her hair was pulled back, but there was a purple stripe on the right side that was tucked into the braid she wore. She also wore sturdy flats, for biking, he supposed, and pants and a cute top with short sleeves and a ruffled collar. Professional, but serviceable. And that was actually a box checked as far as he was concerned. His assistant would be going with him to the film sites occasionally, and Aquteg Island was rough terrain in places. A woman who biked to work and wore sensible shoes was a good thing.

"Why don't you sit down, Ms. Arnold, and we'll get started?"

"Oh, certainly." She smiled again—or was it still—and took the seat across from him, perching on the edge of the chair with her posture straight. He glanced down at the resumé on his desk and remembered that this was the applicant whom Abby Arseneault had recommended. She'd used the words "reliable," "smart," and "hardworking." Her CV held a vast array of employment, from scooping ice cream to waiting tables, church secretary, and working at the school in the afterschool program.

Zero experience in film or television, or with research, even.

"Why do you want this job, Ms. Arnold?"

She met his gaze evenly. "I work at the school for nearly ten months of the year. Normally, I have a summer job that pays my bills during the break, but this year the business closed. I'm going back to school in the fall, and this seemed like an amazing opportunity. You're looking for someone for a short-term contract, and that's exactly what I'm looking for as well. I'm smart, I pick up things quickly, I can absolutely be a Jill of All Trades, so to speak." She shrugged. "Besides, I've lived in Jewell Cove my whole adult life. I can help you navigate the town and its people if you run into snags or need additional information. I can be your Girl Friday."

Cutesy movie references aside, she had a point. One of the applicants today was a film student. She'd be wasted in this job and would do better on the film crew. There might be something for her there, in the thick of things, as a paid intern. What he needed was someone to help with the day-to-day, and honestly, a lot of it domestic in nature. "You'd be acting in a rather broad role here. A mix of housekeeper and personal assistant, whatever is required at the time. It requires flexibility and good time management skills."

"If you check my resumé, you'll see I've worked hospitality housekeeping in the past and I'm a bit of a neat freak, so that's not a problem. I'm a fair cook, though if you're expecting a personal chef I'm not it. I'm good at time management, though. Most of my life I've had to juggle more than one job, and if you've ever had to manage thirty elementary school kids, you'll know that flexibility and being good in a crisis comes with the territory." She grimaced. "Or at least it should, if you know what I mean."

He was tempted to laugh. Summer Arnold said what she thought, and he liked that. Too many people, when they found out who he was, tripped all over themselves to say the right thing. Or maybe she didn't realize who he was. Either way, it was refreshing.

She looked around her. "I've never been inside this house before. It's nicer than I expected."

He agreed. The owner was a lawyer who'd practiced in Jewell Cove before joining a lucrative practice in Portland. Now he leased the house—which was connected to the now-defunct lighthouse—as a short-term rental, like so many were doing these days. "The owner apparently did a massive reno a few years ago. I think Abby Arseneault's husband's company did the work."

"He's an excellent contractor," Summer said, still looking around. "He restored their house, you know. The original Foster mansion on Blackberry Hill."

"Yes, I know," he replied. "Abby has been very helpful with researching the island." His first visit to the mansion had left him slightly in awe. Tom Arseneault was talented, and Abby had decorated it beautifully.

Summer turned her attention back to him. "Mr. Brodie, I know my qualifications aren't academic. But I do know Jewell Cove, and I know its people. Whatever you need, I can point you in the right direction. You'll get quality work for the best price so you can stay within your production budget."

He appreciated that, because even though this was a pet project of his, and he was definitely able to bankroll it himself, there was no sense wasting money, either. And perhaps she really didn't know who he was if she thought such things were a concern. He liked that. He was used to being used. Leveraged, simply on the basis of his name and his fortune. Or rather, his parents' fortune. That he'd chosen a different path from his parents wasn't exactly a bone of contention as much as puzzling for them. His money was family money. He felt guilty using it when he'd made it clear that he had no intention of joining the family business, a fact all the more disappointing since he was now the only Brodie capable of doing so. Not that his parents reminded him of it—at least not overtly. They didn't have to. He was all too aware he'd refused to follow in the family footsteps.

"When can you start?" he found himself asking, not sure when he'd actually come to a decision.

"I finish at the school at the end of the week. I'm available after that." She hesitated, a small frown twisting her lips as if she tasted something bad. "Might I ask what I can expect as far as pay?"She should have asked for terms before giving her availability, but Jax wasn't about to use it to his advantage. He named an hourly wage, told her that payroll was every two weeks, and that he'd pay overtime if she ended up working more than forty hours a week.

Her eyes widened. "Is there a contract I should sign or something?"

She really was so disingenuous. He thought back to her resumé. She'd worked lots of jobs, all local, presumably for people she knew. Negotiating wasn't something she probably did very often. He loved these small towns where everyone knew everyone. The kind where deals were struck over coffee or maybe a beer at the local pub—which he'd discovered to his delight was called The Rusty Fern. Towns where neighbors helped each other. He'd always been jealous of that way of life, even as he'd grown up surrounded by privilege. It was partly why he'd decided to rent here for four months—to get away from Philly and Brodie Biotech. Having a world class surgeon for a mother only added to the prestige that came with the Brodie name. And here he was, a lecturer and fledgling filmmaker with a tiny production company. He felt like he never quite fit in. Square peg in a round hole and all that.

"Yes, there's a contract, but I'll have that sent over from HR. Is email okay?"

She nodded. "So... you're offering me the job."

He probably should tell her he was going to deliberate among the candidates, but what was the point? He already knew she'd be the best fit. Her description of being a Girl Friday was pretty accurate, really, though the classic movie reference had surprised him, and he was certainly no Cary Grant. He needed someone to keep the house going—it was quite large, really—and help with the odd jobs that cropped up during his day.

"I'm offering you the job. But look over the contract first, and make sure everything is in order before you accept."

"I will." She looked at her watch. "I have a half hour before I need to bike back to the school for work. Could you maybe give me a tour? I've been on the grounds before, though not for ages, and I've never been inside the house or the lighthouse, for that matter."

Jax didn't see why not. "I can give you the nickel tour. Would you like a coffee or anything?" He'd figured out the Cadillac of coffee machines yesterday and wouldn't mind making himself another espresso.

"I'm more of a tea girl, but thank you." She smiled up at him. "And thank you for this opportunity. It's a lifesaver."

He laughed. "Don't tell me that. Always bargain from a position of power, Ms. Arnold."

Her cheeks pinkened. "You're so right. And please, call me Summer. I'm Miss Arnold at school and..." She shuddered.

"Well, imagine thirty kindergarten and first graders all trying to get your attention."

He laughed unexpectedly, thinking she was both artless and charming. It felt good to laugh; he hadn't been doing much of that lately, and the sudden lightness he felt buoyed him immensely. "All right. Summer, then." He rose from behind the desk as she also got up from her chair and then headed to the door. He stopped and spread his arm wide. "After you," he said, and when she brushed by, her scent trailed in her wake, a soft fragrance that reminded him of his grandmother's lily of the valley.

But, he remembered, lily of the valley was poisonous and could cause cardiac distress.

Good thing, then, that his heart was good and locked away. He had no time for relationships. He was too busy trying to prove to his parents that his path could still be an important one.

A job that would be easier if he could actually convince himself of it.

⁂

Summer tried to pretend that Jax Brodie wasn't incredibly attractive and charming. She'd entered the room to find him behind his desk and immediately started babbling about her stupid bike chain. He hadn't seemed to mind. And he'd offered her the job. Which was amazing, but she'd have to get over being flustered in his presence if they were to work together.

He got up from his chair and she noticed he wore faded jeans and a pair of Vans, of all things, with an untucked button down. His light brown hair was slightly on the shaggy side without looking sloppy; he simply gave off a relaxed vibe that she hadn't expected. He smiled easily, which sent little butterflies winging from the middle of her chest to her tummy. *Get a grip*, she told herself. *You're thirty-two freaking years old, not fifteen.*

"The house has only been here since the twenties," he was saying, leading her from the room, "but you probably know that already. The lighthouse itself was built in the 1880s. Of course, it's not used anymore."

"The Jewell Cove Historical Society has a whole thing about it," Summer replied, following him back down the hall to a spacious, modern kitchen she'd only glimpsed in her hurry to the office. "The coast guard maintained the light for a while, but now it's defunct."

"That's right. And the town took over the land but then sold it in 2008 to a private individual." He paused by a massive butcherblock in the middle of the kitchen. "I'm no lawyer, so I can't tell you how that all went down. But the man who bought it is a lawyer, so I'm assuming there were some interesting negotiations and regulatory hoops to jump through." He shrugged. "The historian in me wishes the history of Refuge Point was shared with the public. The other part of me is glad it's not a big tourist trap, and that it remains much the same as it always was—except the owner has done a fantastic job updating and maintaining it. No massive parking lots for buses, no cluttered gift shop."

Summer agreed with him wholeheartedly. "I know tourism is big business for the town, but the ice cream shop I used to work at is being replaced with another gift shop for tourists. There are enough of those, thanks." She met his gaze. "So, you're a historian and not a television exec?"

He laughed. "Both? But I'm a historian first. I'm a lecturer at Penn State, but I also own a small production company that works to bring lesser-known stories in American history to life."

It sounded pretty grand when he put it that way, and Summer found herself awed once again, not by his presence but by his brains. And who was she? A high school graduate, and barely that. She wasn't stupid. She knew that. But she wasn't educated, or well traveled. Heck, she'd hardly been out of Jewell Cove since she was eight years old. It was her little safe corner of the world and that was just how she liked it.

Safe. Secure. Constant. Even predictable. To her, that wasn't a failing. She'd never really had a surprise that was a good one.

"Come on," he said. "Let me show you the rest of the house."

She followed him through the two-storey house, upstairs where there were two bedrooms, each with their own updated bathroom and king-sized bed. While the house was old, the decoration was modern and beachy. Roman blinds the color of sand dunes adorned the windows looking over Penobscot Bay, the hue repeated in the area rugs on the floors. One room was decorated in white with accents the same pale green as beach grass. The other brought in shades of blue, making it feel airy and open. The blue room looked lived in; she assumed this was where Mr. Brodie—Jax—slept. There was a thick book on the night table and the bed was made but lacked that professional look from a cleaner. A pair of trousers were folded over the back of a chair in off-white upholstery. "Your room," she said, feeling like she was intruding.

"I try to keep things neat, so you won't have much to do here. But look at the view." He seemed to have no problem inviting her into the space, even though she felt odd entering. There were three windows on the back wall, and beyond the lighthouse stretched the ocean, as far as she could see. It glinted and sparkled in the sunlight, while sea birds darted and dipped on the wind.

"Wow. That's stunning. I have a small view of the harbor from my apartment, but nothing like this."

"A million-dollar view," he agreed. "Let me show you the rest."

They went back downstairs where Jax led her to a beautifully appointed living room, a powder room, a small dining room off the kitchen, and past his office again. "I was thinking I could set up a workstation for you in my office, or you're welcome to work elsewhere in the house. I'll provide you with a laptop to use so you can access all the spreadsheets and calendars you'll need. But where you work is up to you. It's wherever you're comfortable."

She got to come to work to this beautiful house every day. And would be working side-by-side with a man who looked like he should be on a magazine cover and not poring over dusty history books or standing in a stuffy lecture hall. And he was concerned about her comfort. There had to be something wrong with him somewhere. But why should she care? She was here for a few months to do a job. She didn't need to concern herself with his attributes or flaws. She just had to do the work, pay the rent, and get started on building herself the life she wanted.

She definitely didn't need to be in the same office as he was.

"Oh, I'll probably set up in the dining room, or maybe the living room. The view is quite lovely, and it's so open and inviting." She tried a smile. "If that's all right."

"Of course, it is." His smile suddenly widened. "Do you want to see the lighthouse?"

She took her phone out of her pocket and checked the time. She'd be cutting it close, and she could see the lighthouse another day, but he looked so excited, and his enthusiasm was contagious. "Quickly," she compromised. "I need to head back soon."

"You won't regret it."

He opened a door toward the back of the house that led into what felt like a long shed. It was more rustic than the rest of the house, with plain white walls and plank flooring beneath her feet. "No need to go outside, which would be handy for a lighthouse keeper in the winter. Can you imagine having to do that during a Nor'easter? Or a hurricane?"

She followed along until they reached the other door. He took a keyring out of his pocket, found the correct one, and inserted it into the door. It opened with a creak, and Jax led the way inside.

The first thing that Summer noticed was how dark it was. There was a solitary window to her right that let in a bit of light, but it was meager at best. And it was cool inside, cooler than she had anticipated. "The tower is made of iron and lined with brick," Jax said, his voice echoing in the cavernous space. "The owners also had everything cleared out. There was no need for anything to remain, really, since it's not operational."

"It's a bit eerie." Her voice echoed in the cavernous space, and goosebumps skittered over her skin, from the cool air, the haunting sound of their voices, and the darkness. She could almost hear the foghorn in her head, calling out to sailors at sea during bad weather. "But really cool."

"Do you want to go up?"

"Of course." She grinned, turning her head and looking up at him. "I've come this far. This is so neat. Most people only get to view the lighthouse from afar."

His smile was boyish as they made their way to the winding stairs that would take them to the platform. They were steep and winding, and Summer held on to the iron handrail until they reached another door. This one wasn't locked, and she turned the handle and entered the lantern room. The light was still encased in its glass dome, but no longer cast its glow out to sea. Instead, the entire structure of the lighthouse served as an old sentinel of days gone by. She could see for miles down the south coast, then further out to sea in a watery panorama. "God, this is stunning."

"Come out onto the gallery." Another door led to a deck outside, where the wind off the ocean whipped strands of hair out of her braid and made her catch her breath. Something expansive filled her chest, something wild and free and happy. Like how she felt when she was on the bow of a boat, feeling the spray from the waves mist over her face as the entire world opened up. It wasn't often she got out on the water, but when she did she tried to enjoy every single second.

"Are you sure I can't work up here?" she asked, lifting an eyebrow and teasing just a little. "What a view! I love it."

"Not sure how great the Wi-Fi signal is," Jax answered, chuckling. "It's something though, isn't it?" He came closer, close enough she could feel his body just behind hers as he pointed to the right at about forty-five degrees. "Can you see that speck out there? That's Aquteg. Lovers' Island. A rock in the ocean that harbors secrets and treasures."

She could barely make it out; perhaps it was time to get her sight tested again. But she saw a few clouds and then a dark smudge beneath them in the direction he was pointing. "Pirates and stowaways," she said, her chest tight from his nearness. The butterflies took wing again. Attraction to her new boss was inconvenient. And he wasn't being inappropriate. There was nothing intimate about his gesture. She was the one imagining atmosphere.

"A stop on the Underground Railroad," he confirmed. "Leaving from here to Canada."

"Hard to imagine that happening so close to little old Jewell Cove," Summer said, stepping back. She could smell his cologne—something subtle and woodsy—and needed to give herself some space. He might be surprised to know that she was well-versed on the history. And that it wasn't just pirates and stowaways that had shaped the area, but betrayal, too.

"That's what I mean, though," he said, taking her cue and turning so his back was against the rail. "All these little places, little towns like Jewell Cove that are off the beaten path, have significance. The founders of Jewell Cove had their own bit of scandal, didn't they?" He didn't wait for her to answer. "Some of the rumored treasure's been found, though it's highly probably there's more somewhere. And the tidal caves! The records found there tell us so much about the Underground Railroad and blockade running these men engaged in. Those documents were in rough shape and need to be cared for properly. That's not my area of expertise, though of course I've seen them as part of my research. Names, dates... we can actually put pieces together of families who fled and made it north. Then creating a story, and bringing that story to the world..." He turned and looked over the ocean again. "It's all I've ever wanted to do."

It was almost poetic. It was definitely a grand ambition, the kind that Summer had never allowed herself to dream of. Getting her bills paid, perhaps entering a career that was a bit more interesting and challenging was as far as she'd let herself go. What was the sense of flying in the clouds when the fall to earth was so devastating? What was the point of hoping for big and grand things when reality was far more practical?

No, the closest she ever got to flying was keeping her feet on the ground and the ocean breeze in her hair. That was enough. And she got the feeling that Jax wasn't a "feet on the ground" kind of guy. She didn't have to know his story to know that he led a very different kind of life from hers. Everything about him said comfort and confidence in living a life that was big and privileged. And that just wasn't her. Her sense of adventure equaled the purple stripe in her hair, her nose ring, and a few other quirks. Mostly, though, it was a face she put on for the world. She wasn't sure anyone truly knew who Summer Arnold really was.

But she knew. Even when she tried to forget. A scared little girl who played pretend. Pretending to be happy because if anyone knew the truth, they'd head in the other direction.

"I should be going. I'm due at the school soon and I'm going to have to re-do my hair." She laughed a little, forcing the sound, tucking a piece behind her ear which blew right back into her face again. "But thank you, Mr. Brodie. For the job and for the tour. If you can send me the contract that'd be great. We can work out my exact start date."

She held out her hand. It was good business practice to conclude a deal with a handshake, wasn't it? Jax smiled at her and fitted his palm against her, giving it a firm squeeze that sent her pulse racing as he held it just a tiny bit longer than what was appropriate.

"That sounds fine," he said. "But please, call me Jax. I'll have a contract sent over this afternoon. I'll see you out. I have a few calls to make, anyway."

She darted back inside and went straight to the lantern room door while he shut the gallery door behind them. His footsteps sounded behind hers down the spiral staircase, and she waited for him by the door to the walkway. Thankfully, he started chatting about lighter topics, like the best places to eat in Jewell Cove. By the time they reached the front door of the house, her heartrate was nearly back to normal. She needed this job, and she certainly didn't need anything resembling romance. The last thing she wanted was for there to be some sort of *atmosphere* between them.

"I'll be in touch soon," he said, seeing her to the front step.

"Thanks again." She smiled and gave a little wave before going to retrieve her bicycle. She was just about to mount the seat when she looked back, wondering if he was still standing there.

He wasn't. He'd gone back inside and shut the door, exactly like a boss should.

A boss. She shouldn't have to remind herself of that, but as she began to pedal across the point and to the road leading to the cove, her body echoed with the feel of him standing beside and just behind her, pointing out toward Lovers' Island.

Chapter Three

J ax hurried down the wharf toward what looked to be a fishing boat with the words *Mary's Delight* painted on her side. He had no idea who Mary was, but that was fine. As long as she got him out to Aquteg Island while the tide was in was all he cared about. With production just starting, he'd had yet to make a site visit, and the crew was trying to make the most of the nice weather by filming outside as much as possible. Even so, they were already a day or two behind schedule, due to a few unavoidable factors. Like one of the camera crew suddenly quitting and a few mechanical delays. It wasn't anything too out of the ordinary, but it wasn't how he liked projects to begin.

Still, he took a moment to stop and take a deep breath. The cove was calm, with little waves slapping lightly on the wood of the wharf, and the air was crisp and fresh as the sun peeked out from beneath a cloud. Jewell Cove was picturesque, there was no denying it. And all reports from the crew were that it had the hospitality to match. A happy crew made for a better production experience. They'd managed to book rooms at both the local motel and a B&B called Evergreen Inn; some were a little further out, staying in a hotel in nearby Brunswick. While tourism was naturally big business in the town, Jax was equally pleased that the production would contribute to the local economy—in accommodations, catering, transportation, and, once the documentary aired, increased visibility.

"Good mornin'," came the call from the boat, jolting Jax out of his thoughts and back to the task at hand. A man stood at the port side of the boat, a broad smile on his face. "You Brodie?"

"Yessir," Jax answered, stepping forward. "You're Sullivan, right?"

"Rick Sullivan. Come on aboard and we'll get you out to the island."

Jax's footsteps sounded hollow on the dock, but in a matter of moments he found himself on the deck of *Mary's Delight.* She wasn't a big boat, but big enough for the crew to transport their equipment and get back and forth. "Good morning," he said as he faced Sullivan. "Appreciate you making the extra trip today, Mr. Sullivan."

"Call me Rick," the man answered, grinning from beneath his ball cap. "And I'm happy to. Let me get the ropes and we'll get on our way."

As Rick turned to prepare to cast off, Jax realized that the man had a prosthetic. Despite it, he deftly dealt with the ropes and started toward the wheelhouse. "You wanna come in? Or stay out on deck?" Clearly the disability had no effect on Rick's competence in piloting the boat. He moved about, completely comfortable and confident.

"Out here, I think. At least for a bit." Jax didn't want to be antisocial, but it was a gorgeous morning and he found himself remembering how Summer had mentioned liking the feel of the ocean breeze in her hair. She was due to start her job in a few days, but he'd been thinking about her far too much in the days since her interview and that troubled him. Particularly since she was going to be in the house with him much of the time... just the two of them.

"Don't blame you," Rick said. "If it gets too blustery on the open water, come on in."

And with that, Rick disappeared and the engines chugged to life, the deck vibrating beneath Jax's feet.

The slow trip to exit the cove was breathtaking. Jax stood near the stern and got a good look at the town from the water. Cheerful buildings in bright colors rose from the harbor, the streets like steps leading up a hill. Wild roses bloomed along the shore, and birds swooped and dived, looking for breakfast. The air was crisp and cool off the water, and it seemed as if he could feel his blood pressure drop ten points just by stopping to breathe and enjoy the view. When the colors of the buildings blurred together, he moved to the bow, letting the brisk sea air blow his troubles away.

He couldn't wait to get to the site and see what was happening with the production. And yet he half wished he could just stay on the deck of the boat for the whole day and do nothing but listen to the waves and feel the sun on his face. He'd gone from his lecture schedule and exams to being full-on with the documentary with no break, and the planning for it had started long before April. They had a short window to get this year's show filmed and then off to postproduction. He sighed and tapped his hands on the rail, knowing no sea breeze could completely eradicate his anxiety. It would be great if he could mention good news during his next call with his folks. They were bound to ask how things were going, and each time Jax felt as if he had something to prove. That his choices weren't mistakes. That what he did was valuable.

It would have been so much easier if Matt were still here. His brother could have stepped into their father's shoes; he'd always been interested in science and math and robotics. Jax's refusal to become part of Brodie Biotech had been, if not rebellious, a statement on choosing his own life. His parents had never put up an argument, but that didn't mean they weren't disappointed. He knew they were. He had a hell of a lot of guilt about not continuing the family legacy. Not enough to change his mind, but guilt just the same. He could have been handed an empire, and he had turned it away. He had, in a sense, rejected his family and chosen himself, and it was real work to not feel selfish because of it.

He remained outside on the deck for twenty minutes or so, letting the wind blow away his troubles, but Rick had been right. The wind out on the open water was stronger—and colder—than it had been in the shelter of the cove, and as the boat nosed its way through the waves, spray came up over the bow. Jax went inside the wheelhouse and joined Rick, who was standing at the wheel, his body utterly relaxed, completely at home. He envied that feeling.

"So, *Mary's Delight* is yours?"

Rick nodded. "She is. Bought her from my buddy, Bryce—she's named after his wife. In the summer months I do some private charters, and while she's not as sleek and new as some other boats, my family does use it as a pleasure boat." He looked over at Jax and grinned. "My wife and daughter and I take her for jaunts down the coast, do some fishing, that kind of thing."

"But you're not a fisherman yourself?"

Rick shook his head. "Naw. Fishing for a living is a tough life." He lifted his arm. "Got this blown off a few years ago when I was in the service. Felt sorry for myself for a while, but then my wife came along and shook some sense into me." His eyes lit up when he spoke of his wife. "She owns Treasures, the shop up on Lilac Lane. Can't miss it. It's purple." He laughed. "Anyway, I help make ends meet as an artist. And the charters I do in the summer keeps the boat paying for itself."

"Sounds... idyllic."

"Pret' near. Thanks to you, this summer I'll be in the money, so to speak. I'm thinking I'll treat Jess and our daughter to a family vacation somewhere warm this winter. Maybe Mexico.

Before we add another kid to the family." He grinned. "Might be a bit too late for that, actually."

They hit a particularly rough wave, and the boat shuddered a little as it hit the bottom of the swell. "Weather coming in the next few days," Rick said, changing the subject. "Things are getting a little rough ahead of it. If you're the queasy type, being out in the fresh air and staring at the horizon will help. It's not so rough that you can't be on deck."

"I'm fine." He gave a chuckle. "Actually, my mom comes from just outside Baltimore. I spent a lot of time on the Chesapeake as a kid."

"That's a gorgeous area. Where's home now?"

"Philly."

Rick laughed. "I'll take Jewell Cove any day of the week."

"I can understand why. It's a great little town."

Rick adjusted the throttle slightly and then looked over. "Mr. Brodie…"

"Jax, please."

"Jax," he amended. Rick's face took on a serious expression that gave Jax a sense of unease. He didn't think it was anything with the boat; they were still chugging along despite the bit of chop.

Rick looked over at him. "Listen, I asked Abby not to say anything in her interviews, but there's something you should know about me."

"Oh?"

"The Aquteg Island treasure? I have a piece of it."

Jax frowned. "All artifacts were to be appropriately documented when they were removed from the island."

"It's not from the island. It's..." Rick hesitated. "I've looked into you, what you do, and how you do it. I've also been talking to your crew over the past week. You have to understand that I've kept part of my private life private for a long time now. But I think I can trust you with it. Or maybe it's just time it stopped being a secret."

Jax lifted his eyebrows. "I'm intrigued."

"Well, the truth is, I was adopted. You already know about Abby's Aunt Marian, and the Foster family story. Well, I was the last child adopted when Marian stopped hosting unwed mothers. More than that, it turns out I'm actually Abby's cousin. And we figured it out because my adopted mother left me a necklace in a safe deposit box. A necklace that was part of the original treasure."

Jax stepped back, surprised at the revelation. "You mean it had been handed down?"

"Yes," Rick answered. "I'm descended from that same Foster line. There was a picture with the necklace in it, and we pieced things together." He eased back on the throttle. "We're coming up to the island soon. But if you want to talk to me about it, I'll tell you what I know. It's a part of the history of this place, you know? Finding out I was adopted was tough, but my mother loved me. I know that for sure. Nothing can take that away."

"I'll be damned."

Rick laughed. "Won't we all? Anyway, I hear Summer Arnold is coming to work for you starting Monday. If she's managing your calendar or anything, tell her to give me a call. We can figure out something with our schedules."

"You can bet I'll do that." Whatever they discovered, and whether Rick wanted to appear on camera or not, they could make it work and add it into the story they were telling. Jax wished he'd known earlier and could have planned for it, but there was no reason they couldn't juggle a few things around. Inevitably surprises and new information cropped up in every production.

The dock on Aquteg was much smaller than anything on the mainland, and not in nearly as good a shape. The first time Jax had come here, he'd been struck by the wildness, and today was no different. One of the conditions of filming was to disturb the landscape as little as possible. The crew might have access to the entire area, but there was nothing motorized. Everything was carried on and packed out. About three hundred yards inland there was a basic staging area, but otherwise the crew stayed on the marked paths.

When it was time to film on the other side of the island, by the caves, the crew and equipment were limited to whatever could be carried on a small zodiac while *Mary's Delight* anchored further out.

As Jax disembarked and strode up the dock, he briefly wondered if Summer had ever been on the island, and if she'd like to visit it during one of their filming days. It might be fun to bring her over to see what it was like. Filming was actually quite unglamorous, but always interesting. Plus the island was stunning, a natural gem in the vast Atlantic, and on a sunny day like today, the water held the same mysterious blue as her eyes.

He wondered why he spent so much time thinking about her. Certainly, she was memorable, with her chattiness and animated expressions and the colored stripes in her hair, twisted in her thick braid. Still, she'd been nothing but professional. He had too—outwardly. That didn't mean he wasn't affected by her, only that he wouldn't let on. The last thing he needed was any sort of tension between them. That had happened once before, and he'd vowed never again. His best friend in the faculty, Tyler, had given him serious side-eye and told him *you never shit where you eat.* Crass, but accurate. It just created problems.

Rick came up beside him towing a rollaway cooler. "This wasn't ready when we came out earlier," he said to Jax. "The catering for lunch from Breezes. You want me to wait for you to take you back?"

Jax considered, then shook his head. He needed to be here, to oversee what was happening with the production. It wouldn't hurt him to spend the day, help where he could, see how it was all coming together. He'd set up the production company, but he also liked being the boots on the ground, so to speak. To make sure everything was going to plan.

"I'll come back with the rest of the crew," he decided. "No sense in you making more trips than necessary."

"Sounds good. Enjoy your day. I'll be back at five thirty." They wrapped for the day at five, took a half hour to pack up and lock the staging area, and then it was another thirty to forty minutes return to Jewell Cove. By six everyone was pretty tired, and sometimes Jax like to have update meetings to ensure everything was on schedule.

As he wheeled the cooler up the path toward the top of the island, he thought about the craziness of the summer and wondered if he'd ever actually take time off between spring and fall semesters. His arm already ached from tugging the heavy cooler, and he stopped for a few moments, took a deep breath, and looked out at the view and the vastness of it all. Rick's boat was already turned toward home, and here, in the space between civilization and his film crew, he felt almost... lost.

Then he turned around and started back up the hill again, giving the cooler a firm pull to get the small wheels started. He wasn't lost. He was exactly where he wanted to be. And if he felt a little unsettled, so what? He just had to keep one foot in front of the other. The feeling would pass, and everything would get back to normal again.

Problem was, he no longer understood what normal even looked like.

Mid-June brought the last day of school. It always ended with a celebratory potluck in the staff room, and then all the teachers finished tearing down their rooms for the year, removing the spring and summer items to make room for the back to school and fall-themed decorations that would be added in late August. Summer stayed behind to help the other support staff tidy since there were no kids in the afterschool program today. And when everything was cleaned and packed away, she and a handful of teaching assistants headed to The Rusty Fern for a well-earned first-of-summer drink.

Last summer "The Fern" had finally got on board with the latest trend and got approval for an outdoor patio. When the five of them arrived, they immediately chose a table outside. "And what can I get you ladies to start?" the waitress asked.

"I already know what I want," Summer said, ready to enjoy the three days she had before beginning work for Jax Brodie. "I'll have one of those Strawberry Coladas, Tanya." It was really a pina colada with added strawberry daquiri mix, and it was delicious.

Everyone else ordered, and the chatter began, mostly about the end of the school year, which teachers were leaving, and, a bit more quietly, which kids they were glad to see the back of until September.

They were nearly finished their second round—normally Summer would limit herself to one, but the new job meant she could splurge this once—when the door opened and Jax walked in. Becky nudged her arm and leaned forward. "Lookee there, girls. That's him, right Summer? The guy you're going to be working for. The documentary dude."

There was no reason at all that just seeing him, his hair all windblown and his butt in another pair of faded jeans, should make her body heat. But it did, and she deliberately took a long drink of her colada and hid behind her glass. "That's him," she confirmed, forcing herself to look away so she wouldn't get caught staring.

"What's his name? John? Jack?"

"I heard he's loaded."

"He'd have to be to rent up at Refuge Point. What's it like inside, Summer?"

"His name is Jax, and it's been renovated beautifully."

"Jacks? Like with an s? Weird."

Summer shook her head. "No, J-a-x." She spelled it out. "He seems nice. I'll find out on Monday when I actually start work. Hey, did any of you want nachos or anything?" She tried to change the subject.

"Well, you're lucky is all I'm sayin'. He's hot."

At that moment Jax looked over, and Summer hoped to God he hadn't heard Cindy's last words. Her face flamed—it wasn't the sun since they were under the umbrella—and she hid behind her glass again.

"He's coming over here," Becky whispered, nudging her arm again. For Pete's sake, could she be any more obvious?

"Hello, ladies. Summer." His gaze stuck on her, and she managed a smile.

"Hi, Mr. Brodie."

He started to laugh. "Just Jax is fine. I just wanted to say hello, but I don't want to disturb what looks like a fun girls' night."

"It's the last day of school," Cindy said, holding out her hand. "Hi. I'm Cindy. This is Becky and Emma and Carly, and you obviously know Summer."

He shook her hand graciously, all while holding a beer with condensation forming on the outside of the glass. "Nice to meet you all. I'm not much of a cook, so I stopped in for a beer and a bite before heading back to the lighthouse. Enjoy your evening." His gaze lingered on Summer a little longer than necessary, and she bit down on her lip.

"Oh, we're just finishing up. I've got to get home to the kids," Cindy explained, reaching for her purse. Summer sent her a dark look, but Cindy ignored it completely.

"Oh, me too," Carly said. "I mean, not about the kids, but I told my boyfriend I'd be home by seven."

Emma said nothing, but also reached for her handbag. Summer knew exactly what they were doing and wished they weren't, but she couldn't exactly say anything in front of Jax, could she?

Carly had paid for the previous round, so there was no tab to settle. They just up and left, leaving Summer sitting and Jax standing awkwardly by the side of the table. Summer swallowed and did the polite thing. "Do you want to sit down?"

"Are you sure?" His gaze delved into hers. "They weren't exactly subtle."

Summer shrugged and ignored the fizzing in her veins that came from his simple nearness. "You're my boss. I'm pretty sure we can be civil while you have a burger."

"If you're sure..."

"Take a seat, Jax."

He put his beer down and took what had been Emma's seat. The waitress returned and cleared away the empty glasses. Summer's stomach growled; she'd eaten very little at the potluck and she'd had two drinks on an empty stomach. "Hey, Tanya, could I have a sparkling water and the black bean burger?"

"Sure thing, Summer."

When they were left alone again, Summer looked up and attempted a smile. "You've got a windblown look about you. Out on the water today?"

"I went out to the island where they're filming. Rick Sullivan said there's weather coming in. It was a bit choppy."

"It can get rough in between the two pieces of land," Summer offered. "If you go a bit south of there, though, there's good fishing. I've gone a few times. And there are whale watching tours, too." She knew she was prattling on but couldn't seem to stop, just like she had when they'd first met in his office. "And in the summer, there are a fair number of great whites in the area. If you find seals, you're gonna find sharks."

"They do seem to be moving farther north, don't they?"

"Up past Nova Scotia, even," she added, then thought of how silly it was they were talking about sharks. "I like watching the Shark Week stuff," she confessed.

"Do you go out on the water often?"

She shook her head. "Not really. I've gone with friends a few times if they're doing a day out on the boat, but honestly, past summers I've been working at the Dairy Shack. It didn't leave me much time to spend days on the water."

"Maybe we can change that this summer," he suggested with a smile. "If you come out to the site with me now and then. It's a really nice trip. A little over half an hour, but better than nothing."

Right. Work. Not a day off, social, run-away-to-the-beach kind of thing. She could imagine what that might be like though, for the two of them to escape for a day. She'd wear a cover up over her favorite bikini. He'd wear board shorts and a T-shirt, and they'd feel the salty breeze in their hair as they zipped out into the Atlantic. She'd pack a picnic, maybe, and they'd drop anchor and nibble on lunch and soak in the sun and maybe they'd—

"One deluxe burger platter, one black bean burger and fries. And ketchup." Tanya put the food down on the table, interrupting what had been the most delicious part of Summer's daydream. Jax thanked Tanya and she zipped off again, leaving them alone once more.

Summer pushed the fantasy firmly away. He was her boss. BOSS. She had to remember that, and it might help if she changed the subject.

"So, history. Have you always been a history buff? How did you get into producing documentaries?"

He picked up a French fry and popped it in his mouth. After chewing, he said, "Actually yes, I've always loved history. Do you remember those Magic Treehouse books from when you were a kid? I always loved the ones that went into the past, like the Egyptian mummies or the Titanic. My brother would want to watch cartoons and I'd be on the History channel looking for documentaries."

"You have a brother. What's his name?"

Jax's face clouded and she saw him swallow before he looked up at her. "I had a brother. His name was Matthew. He was eighteen months older than me."

"Had..." Summer saw the grief etched on Jax's face and felt the pain of it in her chest. "What happened? If you don't want to answer, that's fine, but if you want to talk about it..."

He shook his head. "I don't talk about him much. Or enough, really. We were really close. But he got sick when he was eleven, a kind of childhood cancer. He died three days after his twelfth birthday."

"Oh, Jax, I'm so sorry. How horrible for you and your parents. I can't imagine how hard that would have been." Her own childhood had been a nightmare a lot of the time, but the pain of losing a sibling had to be devastating.

"It was. Still is, sometimes." He brightened a little. "Anyway, we were talking about history. I really enjoyed it all through school and did my undergrad at Dartmouth. I wanted to get away from my folks, and they wanted me close by. I think losing Matt made them hold on a little too tight. Dartmouth was close but not too close, if you know what I mean. Then I did my grad school at Yale, and I've gone back to Penn State to work."

He picked up his burger and took a big bite, while Summer sat in awe. He was so smart, so educated. Nothing but the Ivy League for him. And clearly, he came from money. No living at home and going to state schools and he didn't appear to be swimming in student debt. Meanwhile, she was struggling to put together a year of community college tuition. They couldn't be more different.

As if he read her mind, he wiped his mouth with a napkin and asked, "What about you? What is there to know about Summer Arnold?"

She should have expected the topic would come up at some point. Those who knew her in Jewell Cove didn't ask, and she didn't make a habit of volunteering information about her past and her family even though she knew there must be rumors. *What family*, she thought briefly, pushing away the sadness that always came on the back of that kind of thought. Everyone was gone now, and before that she'd had a pretty messed-up childhood. There was very little of it she cherished. Her early years were ones she thought of with pain, not nostalgia.

"Me? Oh, well. Only child, came to live with my grandparents here in Jewell Cove when I was nine and never left." She played with a French fry, swirling it through her ketchup. "Both have passed on, though, so now it's just me."

"Oh, I'm sorry. Where did you live before, then?"

She waved the fry, trying to be nonchalant, but a little ketchup flew off and onto her napkin. Embarrassment flickered but she carried on, determined to be as breezy as possible. "Oh, here and there. I don't remember much."

Which was a baldfaced lie. She remembered a lot—and wished she didn't. Nor did she wish to delve into the topic of her parents. How did you explain a father who'd gone to prison and a mother who was a junkie? It was a miracle she'd ended up where she was, really. But it was too much to share, and too heavy for a casual conversation at The Rusty Fern.

Instead, she deftly changed the topic. "So, what led you to go from history professor to owner of a production company?"

His face lit up; clearly this was a topic he loved talking about. "It was all the documentaries I watched as a kid, and all the interesting things I learned as a historian. I wanted to bring those two worlds together."

The subject change was successful, and they spent the next twenty minutes eating and talking about his work. She'd seen a few of his documentaries listed on her streaming menu, she realized. But what really struck her was how he'd found something he was passionate about. Something that really jazzed him up and he found fulfilling. She'd never had that. Wasn't even sure where she'd go looking for it. Her life had been a constant search for stability and making ends meet. Survival. It wasn't the kind of thing that lit her up. It just was. For a long time, it had been enough. Not anymore, though. The past few years she'd started to feel like she could reach for happiness, rather than settling for the necessities of life.

"Are you all right?" Jax's voice interrupted her thoughts. "You looked kind of glum all of a sudden."

"Oh!" She brightened with an effort. "I'm probably just tired. Last day of school and all, and I had a few drinks before you got here. I think my body is winding down even though it's early."

"I shouldn't have kept you and talked so much," he said. "I got a little carried away."

"I enjoyed it," she replied truthfully. "And I got a better idea of the man I'm working for."

His gaze met hers, and even in her fatigue, awareness rippled through her. This attraction was the first time she'd felt drawn to a man in a long time, and it was both exciting and awkward. The last man she'd been interested in was Josh Collins, but he was remarried now and happy as a clam. She and Josh had gone on one single date, which really wasn't a date at all. They'd gone for coffee, and he'd been honest about his non-feelings for her. She'd gone along with him, blaming matchmakers for shoving them together, but deep down she'd been, if not crushed, disappointed. Josh was a good man, exceptionally handsome, funny, nice. But he'd wanted Lizzy Howard, another of Jewell Cove's doctors. Someone with education and aspirations.

That wasn't her.

"And did I meet your approval?"

Her thoughts slid back to Jax. His voice had lowered a little, become intimate, and she couldn't help it. Her gaze dropped to his lips and then back up when she realized what she'd done. "As long as you sign my paychecks every two weeks, you sure do." She tried to make it sound flippant, like teasing, but it didn't come out that way. Instead the moment extended, the ripple of attraction spreading outward from her tummy to her fingertips, making her tingle all over.

"Can I get you anything else?"

Tanya's interruption was either perfectly timed or horribly so. The moment broke, and Summer turned her head and blinked, looking up. "Oh! No, thank you, Tanya. I couldn't eat another bite."

"I'm finished as well," Jax said. "Great burger. And one bill, please."

"No," Summer interrupted. "I can get my own."

"We'll call it a working dinner," he said, nodding at Tanya before she headed away with their dirty dishes. "After all, you got to learn a lot about the company."

And about him. Except she hadn't asked what had happened after his brother died. She was curious, but to ask meant opening herself up to the same sort of personal questions, and that was the last thing she wanted. Jax researched for a living. She didn't want to talk about her dysfunctional upbringing, and the only other thing interesting about her—and what no one knew—was that she was descended from Edward Jewell. That wasn't something she wanted broadcast, either. There was a lot of shame in her family. Generations of it. She'd done some digging of her own and had been aghast at the actions of the town namesake. He certainly didn't deserve to have his statue standing in Memorial Square.

The evening was starting to cool, and as Jax paid the bill, Summer reached for her tote bag and wished she had a sweater inside for the walk home. They exited the patio and paused, another awkward silence taking over. "Well, thank you for dinner. And I guess I'll see you Monday."

"Right, Monday." Jax put his hands in his pockets and rocked on his feet. "Are you all right to get home? Do you have your bike?"

She laughed, easing the tension. "No, it's only a ten-minute walk. I'm fine."

"Oh, of course." Goodness, he appeared nervous, too. Which was surprising to her. He didn't strike her as the kind of man who ever felt awkward or out of place.

"Goodnight, Jax. I'll see you Monday morning."

"Goodnight, then."

She turned and walked away but was dying to glance back around to see if he was still standing there. She wouldn't though. Tingles and ripples and all other foolishness aside, he was her boss. He was out of her league. He was only in Jewell Cove for the summer. Three very strong reasons why even flirting would be a mistake.

She had a good life here. Good friends, good neighbors. A place to live, food on the table. It was the most security she'd ever had in her life, including when she'd lived with her grandparents. Jax was like a shooting star—bright and glowing but gone again in a tail of fire. Instead, as she walked home in the chilly June evening, she was grateful for the life she had. Maybe it wasn't much, but she'd built it herself and built it honestly. And she'd keep building. This job was another rung on the ladder. And she'd be damned if she'd let a crush on her boss mess that up.

Chapter Four

Summer had hoped that Monday would be bright and sunny and indicative of a new and shiny start to her job. Instead, she woke up to fog swirling around the harbor, and when she checked her weather app, the forecast was cloudy with intermittent showers.

She stood by the bed and assessed her clothing choices. It was still supposed to be warm, so she didn't want anything too heavy. A line echoed through her mind: *dress for the job you want, not the job you have.* Her job at the school was at lunch and afterschool and her "uniform" generally consisted of good jeans, cute tops, and comfortable shoes since she was either on her feet, chasing kids, or cleaning up messes. Her paralegal job, though, when she was finished her program, would be much more businesslike. And while her job for Jax included domestic chores, she was also going to be doing administrative work.

If she wanted to be taken seriously, perhaps she should start with herself.

She still had to bike, though, so she chose dark gray pants with a cute top in a pink, charcoal, and white pattern. She put makeup on, too, hoping it would stay in place during the ride uphill to the lighthouse. Finally, she tamed her hair, streaks and all, into a "messy" bun that she could tuck beneath the hood of her raincoat.

After her usual breakfast of yogurt and fruit, she tucked her wallet, keys, an apple, and a vegan protein bar into her day pack. Thirty minutes before she was due at Refuge Point, she was on her bike, raincoat protecting her against the misty fog, waterproof pack on her shoulders.

The humidity was killer, and the raincoat didn't breathe, so by the time she reached the lighthouse she felt like a stick of melted string cheese. She took a moment to push down her hood and smooth her hair, but what she really needed was the air conditioning inside to cool off. The door was still locked, so she knocked and waited for Jax to answer.

He did, holding a cup of coffee in one hand and bearing a brilliant smile.

"Good morning!" He stepped aside, making room for her to enter. "Gloomy outside, but I've got coffee. Oh wait. You don't drink it. I have tea. Somewhere."

She laughed, wondering how he managed to seem to be a ray of sunshine on such a dreary day. "I'd love some tea. But first, is there somewhere I can hang my coat?"

"Of course! Sorry. There's a closet just there." He pointed to a door on her left. "I hope you don't mind that I set some stuff up on the kitchen table. I thought it would be easier there, with more room for today. Since I'm going to be showing you the ropes, so to speak."

"Kitchen's fine," she called from inside the closet. Having her jacket off was such a relief, and she fluttered her top a few times to feel a little less sticky. She picked up her pack by a strap, rolled her shoulders, and headed toward the kitchen and the sound of water running.

He was standing at the sink, filling a kettle.

"Oh, I can do that! I don't expect you to make me tea. I'm the one who is supposed to be doing this stuff for you."

He looked over as he shut off the tap. "I'm not that kind of boss," he said, plugging the kettle into an outlet. "I'm used to working at the university. If I want coffee, I get it myself. Everyone pitches in. It's... collaborative."

He looked so earnest. There were moments he totally gave off this relaxed, easy-going vibe. And then other times he seemed so intense. She wondered why. Oddly enough, she also liked both sides of him.

"That being said," he continued, "I'm not a great cook and I put in long days, so your help with the household stuff is appreciated. But I can still make tea." He sent her a winning smile, which made her feel warm all over again.

She put her pack on an extra chair and had a look at what he'd set out on the table. There was a laptop, mouse, and mousepad ready for her, plus a moleskine notebook and a selection of pens in different colors. There was also a cellphone and a keyring with two keys on it. He caught her staring at it and said, "Spare keys to the house. One for the front door, and the other goes from the shed to the lighthouse. Not that you'll need that one, really. But I didn't want to split up the keys and chance losing one."

"Oh. I...yes. Keys."

"There might be days I'm at the site or doing business away from my office. You can still get in, do what you need to do. It only makes sense."

It did. Absolutely. Still, she hadn't expected it.

He put the tea on the table and the held out a hand, gesturing toward a chair. "Ready to get started?"

"Oh. Yeah. I mean, of course."

Dressing for the job she wanted didn't do much good if she continued to sound like a moron. She cleared her throat and slid into the chair in front of the laptop.

Her nerves disappeared as she concentrated on just keeping up. As they sipped their tea and coffee, Jax gave her the login information and a basic tour of the applications he used. There was a neat project management app that tracked deadlines and tasks, which looked like a jumbled mess. He had spreadsheets upon spreadsheets that detailed budgets, resources, research. While her head was still spinning, he brought up his personal calendar that showed meetings, calls, engagements. "One thing you won't have to worry about is any accounting," he said. "I have a CPA for that, and I do the payroll. Other than recording stuff in the spreadsheet, of course, so I can get a run-down on where we sit at any point during the project."

She was just getting her feet beneath her when he continued on, explaining the ins and outs of what needed to be done as far as the day-to-day production. She'd had no idea how much a producer did. She'd always thought that a producer's job was to come up with financing and that was it. But not Jax. He was the filmmaker, too. He set up the interviews, did the research, worked hand in hand with the writing staff, which he told her consisted of exactly two people, of which he was one. There were also permits to acquire and releases to be signed by any participants. Every evening he looked at the day's footage. And while it would take time for the documentary to be ready for release, he was already working on promotion and marketing plans.

She was dizzy thinking of it all and wondered if the sheer volume of work—since he didn't have a production assistant other than her—contributed to the moments of strain she saw around his eyes when he wasn't being his jovial self.

They took a break around eleven, standing to stretch and take their cups to the dishwasher. "I hope you're not too over-whelmed," he said, smiling.

"I am a bit. But I'll get the hang of it." She hoped, anyway. The project management app looked to have a lot more features than he was using, and she was pretty sure she could tidy that up after a few tutorials. It was spreadsheets that worried her. She didn't have a lot of experience with them, and the last thing she wanted to do was mess anything up. She had no idea how much work went into filming a one-hour show like this one. Or how a crew could spend an entire day to only get a few minutes of usable footage. Until this morning, she didn't even know what B-roll was.

She'd grabbed some water and was just taking her protein bar from her pack when he spoke up behind her again.

"I did up a list of things I need done right away," he said, handing over the notebook. "I have to run over to do a prelim interview with Rick Sullivan." He sighed. "The weather today meant we lost a day of filming. Cloud we can manage. Fog, though?" He shook his head. "I've got the crew sitting in their hotel rooms having an unexpected day off."

And time was money, she realized.

"I can manage," she said brightly, sounding far more confident than she felt. But if he were gone for the afternoon, she could have time to work through everything they'd gone over this morning, on her own time, without him looking over her shoulder. That had been disconcerting—and distracting.

"The cell phone is for you," he added, nodding toward it. "My number is programmed in, so if anything comes up and you have to reach me, you'll be able to."

She glanced over the list. It was all business tasks until the last item. In his precise hand, he'd written "Can you make dinner?" and used a question mark instead of simply giving a directive.

"Dinner? I don't know what you like."

"I'm not fussy. Have a look in the fridge and see what you think."

Before she could answer, he gave a flash of a smile and disappeared out the door, leaving her gaping in his wake.

Summer took a moment to drink some water and nibble on her bar. Jax was a study in contradictions. In some ways he was incredibly easy going. He dressed comfortably, smiled a lot, seemed to be happy eating anything without being particular. On the other hand, though, he was wound pretty tightly. When it had anything to do with work—the labor of love he kept talking about—she got the impression he was in a constant state of crisis management. Perhaps he didn't mind since he was so passionate about it. And it was only for the summer...

Except she bet that in the middle of his teaching schedule at the university, he'd be already planning the next year's project.

Before settling in to work, she went to the fridge and opened it up, looking for something she could make for his meal later. She found a handful of fresh vegetables, sodas, a few condiments, coffee cream, and cheese in the fridge, and some chicken, salmon, frozen waffles, and a frozen lasagna in the freezer. The cupboards didn't reveal a lot to work with either. Some pasta and a packet of brown rice.

Another glance in the fridge and she found a small jar of garlic, one of ginger, a bottle of maple syrup, and a few packets of soy sauce, presumably left from Chinese takeout. It was enough that she could glaze some salmon and bake it, make some rice, and steam some carrots. He needed groceries, and she decided she was going to take ten minutes this afternoon to make him a list. Especially if he expected her to prepare things. The frozen lasagna was a big tell, and so were the single-serving condiments. He shouldn't live on processed food all summer.

Once the salmon was out of the freezer and marinating in a covered dish, Summer sat back before the laptop and started working through her list of tasks. Thankfully he'd kept them simple for her first day, and rather than call and interrupt his interview, anything she didn't quite understand she put aside to ask him about when he was home. What she was quickly learning, however, was that his involvement in the documentary was total. Every decision had to have his final say. Looking at his notes and files, she realized that what she was staring at wasn't just oversight. It was micromanaging. No wonder he looked stressed all the time.

Moreover, a study of the funding showed that a good portion of the money put into the film was from his own trust fund. Why? Why would he do that when he could apply for funding and grants?

The man was a mystery, wasn't he? And here she was, in close quarters with him for the next three months.

She hadn't even realized that four hours had passed when he opened the door again and entered the kitchen. She looked up, her eyes dazed from staring at the laptop for so long. "Oh. You're back."

"Don't sound so excited," he joked, hanging up his coat. "Did you make out all right?"

She sat back in her chair with a sigh. "Other than being certain I'm going to see rows and columns in my sleep tonight, I did okay." She smiled at him. "I did leave a few things that I had questions about. Maybe we can go over them before I start dinner and head home."

"Of course. I can do my stuff later tonight."

The word *workaholic* flitted through her brain, but it was none of her business. She flipped the page in her notebook back and went to the first of three items she'd left incomplete.

Jax was incredibly helpful, but when he leaned over her shoulder and pointed at a column in her spreadsheet, it was hard to focus. He smelled good, like fresh sea air and some sort of woodsy cologne and fabric softener, the scents heightened by the dampness outside. His arm brushed against her shoulder, and she bit down on her lip, forcing herself to look at the laptop and not turn her head to look up at him. He didn't seem frustrated with her for not picking it all up on the first day, and was patient as they worked their way through crunching the data he needed. She definitely could use a tutorial or two.

When he stood back, she missed the subtle heat of his body close to hers. This was ridiculous. She was more professional than this, wasn't she? Besides, it wasn't like her to get flustered by a man. She was the calm one, the chill one, the one who never appeared to worry, embraced a simple lifestyle, went with the flow.

At least that was the face she showed the world. And she did try. She practiced gratitude. Focused on what she had rather than what she didn't. Had learned it was okay to depend solely on herself and that she was worth caring for. It had taken years for her to bolster her self-worth. And yet every time Jax Brodie got within six inches of her personal space, all her Zen flew right out the window.

It made her uncomfortable, that's what. Even if she kind of liked it at the same time. So she scooted out of her chair—on the side furthest away from Jax—and hurried to busy herself in the kitchen, finding what she needed to prepare his dinner.

"What can I do to help?" he asked, standing by looking helpless.

She laughed a little, but it sounded tight. "From the look of your refrigerator, you don't cook much. Tonight's pretty simple. But I did make you a grocery list for some staples if you're going to need me to cook regularly."

"I can give you a credit card so you can do it," he suggested.

"There's more than I can carry back on my bike," she pointed out, placing the salmon fillet on a baking pan. "But you can just go to the grocery store here in town. They carry almost everything."

He frowned, then swiped his phone and stared at it. "I'm scheduled to be on site tomorrow if the weather shifts. I can't go."

She busied her hands with peeling carrots, trying to think of an alternate plan. "Well, maybe I can drop you at the wharf and then pick you up at the end of the day. You can just call when you're back. It only takes ten minutes to get there. If you don't mind me driving your car, that is."

"That would work." He looked relieved. "Actually, it would be a big help. There are a few other errands that need running, if you don't mind?"

"Make a list. And actually, rather than me bike out here super early, why don't I just meet you at the waterfront? You can give me the keys then. I'm assuming the boat leaves early."

"Seven thirty," he agreed, nodding. "Yeah, that sounds like a plan." He sniffed the air. "What are you making?"

"Maple ginger salmon and rice and carrots." She chopped the last carrot, added water to the steamer, and put the pot on the stove. "Why don't you write out that list of errands now, while it's finishing, and then I'll hit the road?"

He'd grabbed her notebook and started jotting things down with her pen, but he halted and looked up. "You could stay. It looks like there's more than enough food."

He looked so hopeful, and she wondered why. Was he lonely? She could imagine it, being up here at the lighthouse, away from the town, no neighbors close by. It was beautiful but it was isolated, and he was new to town. She understood all of that and more. She knew that you could be in the middle of a crowd and still be lonely, be in a town you loved with people who cared and still feel isolated.

She was also his employee. And cooking dinner because it was oddly part of her job was one thing, but staying to eat was crossing a line, wasn't it? Perhaps it wouldn't be, except she already felt things when she looked at him. When she heard his voice or when he flashed a smile. And domestic scenes like cooking dinner and sharing meals together would only amplify those feelings.

She couldn't tell him any of that, though, so she fell back on practicalities. "Um... I'm actually vegetarian."

The surprise on his face was priceless and she started to chuckle. "I had a black bean burger the other night, do you remember?"

"Well sure, but sometimes people order stuff without being, you know, totally vegetarian. Or vegan. Oh no—the tea this morning. I put milk in it."

She grinned. "I'm not vegan. I eat some dairy and eggs. My summer job that I lost this year? The local ice cream shack where break time included free ice cream. Though I also like a good sorbet or the coconut-based stuff."

She tended to the stuff on the stove and then turned back. "It's fine, really. I'm happy to start your dinner at night and then head home for the day."

"It just seems foolish to cook two meals," he replied, going to the cupboard and taking out a plate and a glass for water.

Summer appreciated the consideration, but she'd been working menial jobs her whole adult life. She leaned against the counter and folded her arms, watching him fill his water glass at the fridge dispenser.

"You know, all kinds of people repeat tasks at home after they've finished work. Cooks. Servers, who go home and serve dinner to their families. Housekeepers. Handymen... and women. They do all those things for other people who are busy doing... other things, and then go home and do them for themselves."

He stared at her until the water ran over the top of his hand and he pulled back from the dispenser, spilling some on the floor. "Do you... think I'm a snob?"

Did she? She didn't want to. And deep down she didn't. But the truth was, he had a freaking trust fund. He worked in academia and a quick search today had shown her just what kind of business Brodie Biotech was. It didn't make him a bad person or mean he looked down on others, it just...

"No, not a snob," she said softly. "But perhaps a bit oblivious."

"To the plight of the common working man."

"Perhaps. Some people's realities are very different from yours, that's all. So going home and making myself dinner after cooking yours is truly no big deal. I've been doing this kind of thing since I was old enough to hold a job."

Silence fell over the kitchen, and then Summer moved to grab a dishtowel to wipe up the spilled water. She was just going to stand again when Jax reached out and put his hand on her wrist. Tingles radiated up her arm as she paused, wet towel in hand, and her gaze shot up to meet his.

"And how old were you when that happened?"

She swallowed tightly, unsure if she was most uncomfortable about the question or his hand on her arm. Perhaps uncomfortable wasn't the right word, because nothing about his touch was unpleasant. Just the opposite. And his eyes... the blue irises had little gold flecks in them, she noticed.

"Fourteen," she answered.

"Too young to legally work."

She shrugged and reluctantly pulled away from his grasp. "I worked at Gino's a few nights a week, writing down takeout orders and running the register. I got paid in cash until I was older, and then I moved on to retail. Too young to serve alcohol, you see."

They weren't touching anymore but she felt tethered by his gaze just the same.

"Fourteen... most girls that age are babysitting occasionally and going out and having fun."

"I did that. Both. Babysitting and friends." Always hanging out at their houses, not Summer's grandmother's. She'd been... ashamed. Her grandparents had tried, she supposed, but their house had been a hole.

"You needed the money?"

It was getting a little too close for comfort now, so she broke eye contact and returned to the stove, turning her back toward him as she lifted the lid on the rice. "This will be done in a few minutes. I really need to head home before the fog rolls in again."

She scooted past him to get her jacket from the front closet, then smiled as she packed up her backpack and hoisted it onto her shoulders. "I'll meet you at the wharf tomorrow morning, seven thirty sharp."

"I'm sorry I pried." His voice was earnest, apologetic. "I know it's none of my business."

"I don't talk about my childhood, really," she said firmly. "Ask anyone. Actually no, don't ask. I'm sure people in town think they know what it was like. But they don't. The main thing is, I'm here, and I've become a fully functioning adult. Which is good news for you because your organizational app is a hot mess and I made a good start at straightening it out."

Business. She had to keep it coming back to the business, instead of focusing on the understanding expression softening his face. He didn't know. He didn't.

But he did know pain. He'd been ten when he'd lost his brother, just a year older than she'd been when her mother had died, and her father was still in prison. Nine when she'd come to her grandparents with nothing but two grocery bags of clothing and one dingy stuffed dog that she still owned, buried at the top of her closet with her only other keepsakes. Jax had lost a brother. He didn't have to understand her to understand pain. She wished he didn't. No one deserved that.

"I'll see you in the morning, then," he said, letting her off the hook. She exhaled a full breath in relief.

"In the morning."

She went out and shut the door, retrieved her bike, and started down the hill. She'd got halfway to town when she realized she'd left the house keys behind. It didn't matter. He could bring them in the morning. She'd send him a text. That was far better than the tempting invitation to join him for dinner, and the danger of letting him in even further.

Chapter Five

Summer was at the wharf at seven twenty-five and discovered Jax was already there, along with a group of people she assumed were his crew and several watertight chests of what she also assumed was equipment. Jax was chatting to a group of maybe three, while others stood around sipping cups of steaming coffee from the Leaf and Grind coffee shop, which served fancier drinks than the "regular or decaf" offerings at the café. It was early but the fog had cleared, and the day was looking to be a nice one, so she was perplexed as to why no one seemed particularly smiley.

She hooked the strap of her purse over her shoulder, then made her way along the heavy wooden boardwalk to where Jax was standing so she could get the car keys. As she skirted around a group, she heard rumblings. "I don't know why he has to come along. Every time he does one of his site visits, it messes everything up."

She slowed her steps, trying to eavesdrop.

"I know. It's like Bryan has everything set for the day and he blows in and changes it all and then blows back out again."

Oh, dear.

How many of the crew felt that way? She knew now that Bryan was the director and could only guess that the "he" they spoke of was Jax. She glanced in his direction. He was gesticulating and smiling as he chatted to someone, who was nodding and smiling but not quite as enthusiastically as Jax. Jax was so likable, so she was a bit shocked to realize he might not be all that popular with his crew.

But then, if she was right about him micromanaging and holding on too tight...

She reached him and gave him a genuine smile. "Hi. Hope I'm not late."

Jax turned to look at her and warmth lit his eyes. "Good morning. No, you're right on time. Jeff, let me introduce my local assistant, Summer Arnold. My Girl Friday, so to speak."

"Hi," she said, smiling. It's nice to meet you."

"Likewise." He looked relieved at the interruption and took the moment to step back. "I'll see you on board, Jax. I should run this by Steph."

"Oh, sure. See you in a few."

Jax turned his full attention on Summer, and she felt an odd wave of sympathy. This was his passion, and to think that his team would rather he not be along was sad. But she wouldn't mention it. Maybe he knew and was working to fix the dynamic.

Or maybe he didn't, in which case she didn't want to burst his excited bubble or tell him something inaccurate because of something she'd overheard out of context.

"I brought the house keys like you asked and put them on the key ring to the car." He held out the cluster of keys. "And this is my credit card. A few minutes ago, I texted you the pin so you should be able to use it at the market."

She put both keys and card into her purse. "Did you make that list of errands?"

"I did." He reached inside his other pocket and withdrew a small piece of paper. Other than groceries, there was something to pick up at the post office, and then a drive to a shop in Portland where a piece of equipment had been repaired. "Is there an office supply store in Jewell Cove? I need toner and some new pens. I wrote down the model number for the toner and my preferred pen style."

"There's not, but I can find one in Portland while I'm picking up the part," she replied, taking the list. "Relax. I've got this. I'll be back to pick you up at... what time? Five thirty?"

"Yeah, or I can get one of the crew to run me out to the point. I'll message and let you know." Then he grinned again. "Come on. You can meet more of the crew."

He put his hand under her elbow and guided her along the wharf to the clusters of people, growing larger by the moment. "Anna, Colin? This is my assistant, Summer Arnold. Summer, Anna and Colin are two of my best camera people."

Anna shook her hand, then Colin. "We have a great intern with us this year, too. Luke. I think he's off flirting with Elise."

Summer laughed, while Jax frowned.

She nudged him with her elbow. "Lighten up," she murmured. "Summer workplace romances are sweet."

She'd no sooner said it and her cheeks flushed hot. If she had her way, would she and Jax have a "sweet summer romance"? She started asking questions about the documentary and the upcoming cave shoot to cover the moment.

She probably met ten or twelve people before the boat was loaded up and Rick was ready to set sail. The crew all went to board, and Summer smiled at Jax. "I'll see you later. I've got the phone if you think of anything else. Your car's in the lot?"

"It is. Drive carefully today."

"You mean don't scratch your BMW."

He grinned, but then it softened. "And don't scratch you, either. Have a good day."

He turned and jogged down the ramp that led to *Mary's Delight*, climbing aboard and greeting Rick Sullivan, who gave a brisk nod and prepared to leave the dock.

Summer didn't wait to see the boat off. Instead, she walked the short distance to Breezes, shaking off the warm feeling his words had left behind. She'd been up early this morning and decided to grab some breakfast while she waited for stores to open. The market didn't open until nine, and neither did the repair place in Portland. There was time to grab a veggie omelet before getting on with the rest of her day.

Breezes did a brisk business most mornings, and just before eight on a Tuesday was brisk. There were only two tables open, but she snagged one and ordered her breakfast and a large peppermint tea. As she sipped on it, waiting for her food, a group of women walked in, talking and laughing. Summer's heart took a leap. These were her friends—ones she didn't see quite as much in the summer as everyone's schedules seemed to fly in all directions. There was Abby, with her baby in her arms, and then Jess Sullivan, Rick's wife, who ran Treasures up on Lilac Lane. Josh's wife, Lizzie, was there too, with her best friend and Jewell's Cove's other GP, Charlene Yang. Charlie's husband, Dave, worked at the docks.

"Summer!" It was Jess who noticed her first. "Oh my gosh. We haven't seen you in so long!"

Summer smiled up at her. Jess's tummy was rounded slightly, and her whole face glowed, framed by luscious dark curls. "You're expecting again?"

"Second baby. We kept quiet until the first trimester was over, but by twelve weeks I was popping buttons. I'm at fourteen now. Showing a lot faster than I did with my first."

Her first wasn't quite a year old. They weren't wasting any time.

"Do you all want to sit down? There are three chairs here and we can sneak another one over."

"We'd love that," said Abby. "Lizzie, can you grab a chair?"

It took some maneuvering but soon they were all seated, cramped around the table, the chatter lively as they ordered coffee and pancakes and apparently Jess's baby wanted French Toast with peaches. Once everyone was settled, Abby turned her attention to Summer while she held her baby on her lap.

"So, how's the new job?" She added sugar to her coffee and gave it a stir. "You started yesterday, right?"

Summer nodded. "I did, and it's fine. There'll be a bit of a learning curve, but it's only for a couple of months."

"New job?" Charlie asked, lifting her mug of black decaf to her lips. Charlie was petite and efficient, her black hair pulled into a precise ponytail. She worked at the clinic with Josh as a GP, and sometimes it felt as if she'd always been a part of the town.

"I'm working for the guy producing the Lover's Island documentary. He's a prof out of Penn State, and they're doing a show on the treasure and the Underground Railroad connection."

"I've met him. He interviewed me about George and Jed Foster," Abby explained to the group. "Plus he wanted to talk to Tom about Charles Arseneault. It doesn't seem like there are any of Edward Jewell's family left around Jewell Cove. I'm sure he'd be interested in talking to them if there were. He seems very thorough."

That was one way to describe him. Attentive would be another. He did know how to focus. But Abby's words also made her stomach twist uneasily. There were good reasons to keep her childhood details to herself. She definitely didn't want Jax to pry too deeply into any connections she might have to his project. It wasn't like Edward's shame was hers, but she didn't want anyone digging into her life. There were skeletons she'd rather keep in the closet. It felt odd, knowing the people she was closest to knew so little about her, but she didn't want them to look at her differently. If her connection to Jewell came out, it was likely her secrets would, too. Better to remain silent.

"He's out at the site today, so I'm running errands. Honestly, it's a weird job. I'm a cross between an admin assistant and a housekeeper. Yesterday was all about spreadsheets and today is groceries and picking up a few things. But whatever." She smiled, perhaps a little too brightly. "It pays better than Sally's ever did, and I'm going back to school in the fall. I can use all the help I can get."

That pronouncement brought about another flurry of conversation, and Summer was happy to leave the topic of Jax behind and just hang out with her friends, eating a delicious breakfast and indulging in a second cup of tea. The last time they had all been together that she could think of was in April, when Jess had held an egg-dyeing class for Easter at the shop. Her classes generally ended with wine and charcuterie which made it a true girls' night out. Jess, Abby, and Lizzie were all related by the Collins family. The only one missing from the group was Jess's sister Sarah, whom Summer discovered was on a family camping trip to Acadia National Park.

"I've missed you guys," Summer said unexpectedly, and Jess reached over and squeezed her fingers.

"I know. June always gets a little crazy with end of school for you and Sarah, and then summer hits and regular schedules go out the window. We need to do this more! It doesn't have to be breakfast, either. In fact, our Fourth of July barbecue is coming up. Summer, you need to come. And this Jax guy is new to town. You can always bring him along. It must be pretty lonely out at Refuge Point."

"I haven't quite figured him out yet," Summer admitted. "Sometimes I think he likes the isolation, and then other times I think he really needs to be around people. Maybe it's a bit of both. I can always ask him. Heck, he's met some of you already. He knows Abby, Tom, and Rick, so it's not like everyone will be a stranger."

"You like him," Lizzie pronounced, and Summer shook her head, perhaps a bit too quickly.

"Not that way," she lied, though was attraction the same as liking? "And I've only known him a few days. But he's nice, and he's going to be in Jewell Cove for the entire summer, so I can always ask. Regardless, I'll come." She smiled. "It's always a fun time with the Collins and Arseneault gangs."

"Will you bring your homemade hummus? It's so good."

It was an easy request. "Of course, I will. I'll make homemade pita, too. Those are fun."

The conversation turned again, plus their food arrived. By the time eight-forty-five rolled around everyone was getting ready to leave for their respective jobs. Summer pulled out the keys and reluctantly stood, sad that the impromptu coffee klatch had to end. "I'm so glad you all came in this morning. So much nicer than eating alone."

"All you have to do is ask," Lizzie said, squeezing her arm. "Between work and Josh and my mom, sometimes I forget to be social. And then I am, and I promise myself it won't be so long next time. Josh tells me I'm still a workaholic."

"You've made outstanding progress," Abby chimed in. "Both you and Charlie have."

"It's a doctor thing," Charlie piped up. "Speaking of, my first appointment is in fifteen minutes. I'd better motor."

They went their separate ways, and Summer walked back to the marina parking lot and hit the button on the key fob, the beep guiding her to where Jax's car was parked. She stared at the sleek sedan for a few moments before opening the door and sliding into the soft leather driver's seat. She didn't have a car. She occasionally rented one if she wanted to go somewhere, but she always went for the cheap sub-compact option that was a lower rate and easy on gas. This, though... It was just a sedan, but it was loaded with options, no expense spared. She'd never driven anything like it in her life, and suddenly felt very strange about using it today.

There were times over the past few days when she'd felt as if she and Jax were on the same level, but then she was reminded how far apart they were in how they lived their lives. If he could afford to rent the Refuge Point property for an entire summer, what kind of place did he live in back in Pennsylvania? It certainly wouldn't be a one-bedroom second-floor apartment with no air conditioning. Her apartment was the nicest place she'd ever lived. He'd been born into wealth, from the sounds of it.

She started the car, the engine purring as she buckled her seatbelt and put it into reverse. She'd go to Portland first and do what needed to be done, then come back to Jewell Cove and get groceries before returning to the house on the point. It was early but already warming up, and she delighted in the climate controlled interior as she left the main road and headed toward the highway. A blissful sense of freedom shot through her as she accelerated and then hit the power button on the stereo. Classic rock filled the car, and she might have tried to change it only she needed her attention on the road, not trying to figure out the elaborate display on the dash. No matter. The very idea that she was being paid to drive a luxury car to run a few errands and food shop was crazy, and she intended to enjoy every moment. It was much preferred to fighting with spreadsheets.

Coastal Maine was gorgeous this time of year, and their consistent rain in May had everything full and lush. Wildflowers bloomed on the side of the road and cultivated ones in the baskets and planters outside homes and businesses in Portland. The aesthetic near the repair shop was more "concrete" than *Better Homes and Gardens*, as it was in an industrial area, and the Staples store was out by the airport. But she didn't mind. It was such a joy to get out of Jewell Cove for a few hours. She even stopped and grabbed a hibiscus iced tea at a drive through for the ride home.

By the time she got back to the house, it was nearly noon. She spent the next thirty minutes putting groceries away, then put the office supplies and box of repaired equipment in Jax's office.

It was quiet, orderly. A few papers were askew on the top of his desk, but it was clear that everything was organized and precise. She ran her fingertips over the top of the leather desk chair, then studied the photos he'd put on his desk. Interesting, that he'd bring family pictures when this rental was only a few months. She smiled a little as her gaze fell on one photo that had to be Jax and his older brother, sitting on a picnic table eating dripping popsicles. It was so typical of an ordinary upbringing, and she wished she'd had a sibling. But what if she'd been like Jax? What must it be like to have that sibling only to lose them forever? Maybe it was better to not have that kind of love at all than to lose it.

The other picture was of Jax in a graduation gown with a mortarboard on top of his sandy hair. The couple on either side of him were surely his parents, smiling for the camera on graduation day while he held up the embossed, thick paper of his degree.

She pulled out the chair and sat in it, studying the photos. Why these two? Clearly they represented something important. His brother, of course. And perhaps his biggest achievement? She wondered. Jax had at least three degrees now and was incredibly accomplished, so why this one?

It wasn't something she could ponder at length. She needed a snack, and then she needed to get to work. She pushed away from the desk and went back to the kitchen. Her laptop was still on the table, but her things were tidied and placed all together, unlike how she'd left them last night. Jax did like things a certain way, and yet he didn't seem to get upset or annoyed or anxious if they weren't. Yesterday there'd been things all over the table and dirty dishes on the countertop from making dinner, and he hadn't seemed to care. He really was an interesting paradox.

She opened the laptop and continued with the previous day's work while munching on an apple and eating a bowl of Greek yogurt. When her snack was done, she threw in a load of laundry that had been piled in a basket.

Just as she was about to return to her laptop, her phone rang, and she burst out laughing. He was the only one with the number—and he'd set her ringtone to Lionel Ritchie's "Hello".

"Hello?" she asked after she hit the answer button, and then started laughing again. "Jax, that ringtone. So funny."

She expected him to chuckle in return, or to offer her a warm reply. Instead, his words were clipped. "Summer, can you please pick me up in thirty minutes? I'm coming back a little early."

"Are you okay?" She asked it automatically, instead of simply answering "of course," and then rolled her eyes at herself.

"Yeah. Must go. Rick is waiting for me."

He ended the call and Summer stared down at the phone in her hand. He'd said he was okay, so maybe he was just rushed. But the clipped tones… they hadn't sounded rushed. They'd sounded annoyed. Maybe even angry. Had something happened during today's filming?

There wasn't enough time to delve into any of her work before she had to leave, so instead she did a quick survey of the house and tidied up anything that was out of place, wiping off counters and swapping out hand towels in the bathrooms for fresh and then throwing a load in the washer. Then she got back in his car and drove to the waterfront, parking and watching as Rick piloted the boat into the dock, Jax standing against the railing as if he couldn't wait to get on dry ground.

She could tell by his posture that he was in a bad mood. His body was stiff and his movements sharp as he disembarked and strode up the gangway. Summer got out of the car and moved around to the passenger side, certain he'd want to drive himself.

Jax didn't even say anything to her. Just shoved his pack in the trunk and got in the driver's side.

They were halfway up the hill toward the point when he finally let out a long, harsh breath. "Sorry. I figured it was better to be quiet than to open my mouth and start a rant."

Summer looked over, unperturbed. Something had happened that put him in a mood, but it had nothing to do with her. "You showed great restraint," she replied with a small smile. "I'd ask if it was a rough day, but I don't need to, do I?"

He shook his head, both his hands on the leather-wrapped wheel. "I suppose not."

And as he closed off his expression once more, Summer turned her head and looked out her window. She was not his girlfriend. She was not his therapist. Unless he chose to speak to her about what had gone wrong on the island, she would mind her own business.

For once.

Chapter Six

Jax let out a frustrated breath and slid his gaze over at Summer. She was completely unperturbed, looking out the window as he wound the car along the winding road leading to the lighthouse.

It wasn't every day he got kicked off his own set.

And yeah, he'd been in a bear of a mood when he'd got off the boat and into the car, and it wasn't her responsibility to fix any of that. He knew that absolutely.

And yet it bugged him that she could be so calm and cool. Speaking of great restraint.

"How did your day go?" he asked, attempting to sound normal, pretty sure he'd failed.

"Fine. Your fridge is stocked, post office run done, office supplies in your office, as well as the repaired light." She looked over at him and gave him that serene smile again. "I was just sitting down at my laptop when you called. And there's a load of laundry to put in the dryer."

"Sorry."

"Don't be. You're my boss. When you call, I go."

He snorted. "Not everyone feels that way," he muttered under his breath. The scene with Bryan today had been too much. It was one thing to have a conversation, and another to be dressed down in front of half the crew. When it was over, no one had met his gaze.

The lighthouse came into view and he let out another breath, beginning to feel calmer, less angry. The problem was, when the anger departed, disappointment took its place. In the five years he'd been doing this, he'd never had a day like today. Never had someone threaten to walk away from a project.

And there was not a soul to talk to about it. About his worries, about how let down he felt, even how afraid he was of...

Everything. If Summer asked, he was afraid he would tell her all about his fears, and there were a lot of them. Nearly all revolved around letting people down. But she wouldn't ask. And why would she? She'd been on the job for two days. They certainly weren't friends. But right now, Summer Arnold, with her purple striped hair and blue eyes and nose ring was the closest thing he had, and that too was sad.

They arrived and he parked the car, then slid the house keys off the ring and gave them back to her. "Here, so we don't forget them again," he said quietly, before getting out and shutting the door. He got his pack and followed Summer up the walk to the house, but when they went inside, Summer took the key in her hand and started down the hall to the lighthouse access.

"You coming?" she asked.

"Um, where are we going?"

"You'll see," she said, leading the way to the lighthouse.

He didn't question. What was in his head was the need to fix what happened today, to go over what they'd filmed so far, see where they might have gone wrong. The only reason he obeyed was because he at least recognized that Summer didn't deserve to be yelled at and he could take his frustration out later when she was gone for the day.

She led him up the winding stairs, through the lantern room, out onto the gallery. The wind whipped his hair off his face and he looked over at her. She'd closed her eyes and turned her face to the water, the very picture of calm and serenity. Without opening her eyes, she said, "Take a big breath in and let it out slowly. Close your eyes and turn your face to the sun."

He did, only because the turmoil inside him was so uncomfortable, and the soothing sound of her voice was the most pleasant thing he'd heard today.

His breathing slowed, and he let the sunlight bathe him with warmth and brightness. When he opened his eyes, she was looking at him, a kind expression softening her features. "Better?" she asked.

"Yeah," he answered. "Though I don't want it to be."

She laughed. "If you can pout about it, you're coming around. You're lucky to have this here. Anytime things get to be a lot, if I can find a spot outside to breathe deeply and feel... I don't know, the openness of nature, I relax. Whatever happened today, you can't deal with it or fix it until you chill out and are able to gain some perspective."

As much as he hated to admit it, she was right. "And how do you know all this?"

"Whether you're five or thirty-five, room to breathe and the calming effect of nature tends to work. Unless, of course, nature's what's trying to kill you." Summer grinned. "She's fickle that way."

He smiled back, something he wouldn't have been able to do five minutes ago. "Okay, so you're right. I was a little spooled up when I got back."

"A little? I thought you were about to crack your jaw, you were clenching so tight."

"Things were not good on the island today."

"I'm not surprised." She turned away again and rested her hands on the rail, looking out over the bay. "Not sure what happened, but people seemed a little restless this morning." She looked over her shoulder at him. "And a project like this, when strong personalities are involved, is apt to have a little conflict at some point in the process."

He considered that she was right. Bryan was damned good at his job, but he could be bullheaded. And yet the words Bryan had hurled at him had hit their mark. Meddling. Controlling. In the way.

"Hey," Summer said, and he discovered her hand on his arm and her gaze looking at him with concern. "What happened, anyway?"

Her hand felt too good there. If he were making missteps with this project, then thinking about his new assistant in anything but strictly professional terms would be a new and worse one. He tried to ignore her gentle touch and let out another breath.

"I had a difference of opinion with the director this afternoon," he admitted. "It got a bit heated, and a lot of the crew witnessed it."

"I see."

"I'm not sure our individual visions for this project are in sync." He gripped the railing to keep himself from reaching down for her hand.

"But he works for you, doesn't he?"

Jax realized he was clenching his teeth and tried to relax his jaw. "Well, yes. But..." He hesitated, feeling something that might be shame and definitely failure. "When your director says that either you leave or he walks, that sends a pretty clear message."

"Oh, Jax. I'm sorry."

She sounded genuinely sympathetic, as if she understood what he was feeling. But how could she? He loved teaching. Adored it. But he loved his documentaries too, and felt like they offered him a chance to make a mark in the world that might somehow compensate for what he'd turned down. Not to himself, but to his parents. He hated the idea that he'd disappointed them, even as he was determined to do what he loved.

Sometimes he felt like one big walking contradiction.

Summer leaned against the rail, staring out to sea, while a strand of hair whipped around the side of her face and stuck to her lip. She hooked a finger around it and tucked it behind her ear again, only for it to come loose and swirl around in the stiff breeze. She was so lovely. And kind. He was used to nice people, for the most part, anyway. But kindness was a little different. He'd had a bad day and she'd somehow known exactly what he needed: a change of perspective and a chance to talk. Without judgment.

After a while she asked, "What was your difference of opinion about?"

He sighed, leaning his arms against the iron railing next to her. "It's really about the balance of action to voice-over. Without getting into the finer points, Bryan thinks I'm controlling and interfering."

It stung just saying it.

She didn't look at him, just kept staring out to sea. "Is he right?"

He cringed as she asked, even as he respected her for it. He'd only known her a short time, but he'd already come to the conclusion that Summer Arnold was as insightful as she was beautiful, and as smart as she was unique. He liked her, a lot. When he had gone off in a spin, she was a calming presence.

Someone grounded was good to have as an assistant. And... well, perhaps as a friend, too.

Could they be friends? Right now they were speaking like friends, not as employer and employee. Of course, it was fine to get along at work; in fact it was preferable. As long as it wasn't anything more than that.

He looked at her profile, sighed. "He might be," he admitted.

A little smile teased the corner of her mouth and she turned around to face him now. "That must have been hard to admit. But knowing there is something to what Bryan is saying means you have a starting point for resolving what's going on."

"You mean admitting I'm wrong."

"Not necessarily." She smiled at him, her eyes crinkling at the corners. "It's more about considering *he's* not. Why did you hire him? And I mean him in particular."

This was an easy one to answer. "He does outstanding work. He did a series on the Salem Witch Trials a few years ago that was incredible."

"So, he's a good director, with a lot of experience?" "Yeah. He is."

"Then maybe, just maybe, you should trust him to do his job. You should trust all of them. Some of these people have worked for you before. Some are new, but I'm guessing you wouldn't have hired them if they didn't have stellar credentials."

Ugh, she was right. He was incredibly invested in the production, but that didn't mean he should be telling his crew how to do their jobs. He thought back to the last time he'd gone to the site and had taken over one of the cameras. It had been so fun, and he'd been able to get exactly the shots he wanted, but what message had that sent?

That he didn't trust his crew? That he thought he could do it better than them? A weight settled in his gut. It was highly possible that he was the one standing in the way of the show's success. Not the one swooping in to ensure its perfection.

"Jax, let me tell you a little story. I worked for a coffee shop once and the guy who owned it prided himself on getting his hands dirty. A lot of mornings he'd swoop in during our break-fast rush to 'help out,' but really, he got in the way of the systems we already had in place to keep things moving smoothly and efficiently and he slowed us down. His intentions were good, but he was the owner. We all would have preferred him to do owner stuff and let us do what we were good at—serving customers."

Ouch.

A gust of wind buffeted them, cool off the Atlantic. "Look," she said, softer. "It's clear you care about this project very much and just want it to succeed. I don't have to know what's driving you to know this matters to you. But sometimes, relinquishing control is not just necessary, it's healthy."

"I have a hard time relying on others," he admitted.

"Oh, you're preaching to the choir." She let out a soft laugh. "Most of my life, I haven't had anyone to rely on anyway—not my choice. I only have myself. But over the years I've come to realize that there are people in this town I can trust."

"It is a nice town," he admitted. He liked Jewell Cove, a lot. The people were friendly, the scenery picturesque, the shops quaint. When he took a break from his hectic pace and took a look around him, he realized the slower speed was actually quite relaxing. Or could be, if he let it.

"It is. Anyway, I'm just saying that maybe you keep on top of the production details but trust the people you hired to do their jobs and be a little more hands off."

He knew she was right, even as his brain rebelled against it. "I can try."

She chuckled, the sound warm on the sea breeze, and it made something swoop in his stomach, a little ripple of attraction, a little self-satisfaction at making her laugh, especially since they both knew "I can try" was a weak-ass reply. As if she already knew him when they barely knew each other at all.

"Let's go back down and I'll start dinner."

"Will you stay this time?" The invitation was out before he even thought about it.

Her gaze met his, a one-two punch to the gut. Oh, no. Just because she was kind, because she'd listened, didn't mean... No. Except it did. She'd swept into his office and life, fresh as a summer morning, bringing light and calm with her, and damned if he didn't like it.

"I could maybe stay."

"Good. And I'll take you home after."

It sounded absolutely harmless.

Summer wasn't sure what had possessed her to say yes to his invitation. Hadn't she already given herself the talk about blurring lines and keeping things businesslike? But today, she'd seen not only Jax's irritation but something more in his expression: rejection. This project meant a lot to him and someone had just told him he wasn't wanted or needed—at least for part of it.

Rejection... Yeah, this was something she was too familiar with. The feeling that she was not enough—and sometimes too much.

Add that into what she'd heard this morning, and she'd wanted to help him.

Now he'd asked her to stay for dinner—a dinner she was going to cook—and she'd agreed without thinking.

Their footsteps echoed dully on the steps descending the lighthouse, and then they made their way back to the main house again. Bless him, Jax tried to make some small talk about the town, and she followed along, but the whole time she was distracted by that last glance they'd shared up top. Their eyes had caught and heat had blazed through her belly to her core. It would have taken only a movement on his part and they might have done... what? Kiss? More? It had felt as if there was a string pulled taut between them, ready to snap.

Then again, maybe he hadn't felt it. She was certainly not going to make a move on her boss, no matter how tempting.

"I'll start dinner," she said as they entered the kitchen.

"Is there anything I can do to help?"

She needed him away for a bit, to allow her pulse to settle and common sense to return. "Naw, I'm good. You probably have some work to do. Maybe," she suggested, smiling a little, "you can catch up so you don't actually have to work after dinner. You could watch TV or read a book or something."

Or something...

"What? Not work?" He made a mock shocked expression. "I don't know what that means."

"I know. It's why I suggested it. Now scoot. Dinner isn't going to make itself."

Thankfully, he did scoot and headed toward his office, far less tense than he'd been when they first arrived home. Summer let out a breath, relieved for the reprieve. She went to the pantry and started gathering ingredients for a simple meal, one she could share in but hopefully Jax wouldn't find wanting without meat.

While rice was cooking, she rinsed and drained a can of black beans and started chopping vegetables. Before long, she had a nice, colorful array sautéing in a pan while she grated cheddar and found sour cream. She mixed everything together and let it cook a little longer so the flavors would sink in, and in the meantime built a simple salad. She called Jax forty minutes after he'd left the room, and he came in, a rewarding look of surprise on his face as he took in the salad and the burrito bowls.

"This looks amazing." He put a hand to his flat stomach. "Do you want to eat out on the patio? It's nice out. I'll grab some wine."

Dinner, wine, eating on the patio... this was feeling more and more like a date, even if she had done the cooking. Once more she thought she should say no, make this more utilitarian than special, but before she could think of the right words, he'd grabbed two glasses and a bottle of red from the wine rack.

Summer got a tray and put their bowls and the salad on it, and then followed him through the living room and out the French doors to the stone patio facing the coastline.

The chairs were stacked to the side to protect them from blowing over, so once Jax put down the wine he retrieved two while she set out their meal. Soon they were seated, he was pouring her a glass of wine, and she was handing him his fork and knife.

"This is much better than sitting inside alone," he remarked, putting the bottle down and letting out a sigh. "The whole workday I don't mind being alone, but when mealtime hits, it can get a bit lonely."

"And the evenings long," she agreed. "I live alone as well. And I don't mind it at all, but you're right." She took a sip of the rich red—delicious and not too jammy, not too dry. "There's something about dinner. You know families are sitting down together, and you're setting your table for one."

"I take it you're single, too."

She picked up her fork and laughed, though that floaty, nervous feeling from earlier had returned. "We didn't know that about each other, I guess. Since you said 'too' and all."

He considered his glass, running his fingers over the stem. "I was with someone, but we split last year."

"Do you still love her?" Immediately Summer knew she'd overstepped. "No, don't answer that. It's none of my business."

He merely smiled and scooped up a bite of the rice mixture. "It's no big secret. And no, I don't. I'm not sure I ever did. We had stuff in common, and I cared about her, certainly. In the end, I think she knew it. She broke it off and moved on." He took a bite, then nodded at her. "This is really good."

"It's just a vegetarian burrito bowl. Rice, beans, veggies, spices, some cheese and sour cream on top."

"Just because something is simple doesn't mean it's not wonderful. Thank you, Summer. I've eaten better the last two days than I have in a long while."

"You're welcome. All part of the job." She smiled thinly.

"Right," he said, growing suddenly distant, turning his head to look out over the water.

They ate in silence after that, a sliver of awkwardness creating a wedge between them. Why had she brought up the job and ruined the easy mood between them? Setting a boundary, perhaps? Or creating distance so she didn't have to worry about the fascination taking hold within her?

When the silence drew out, and the rice started tasting like sawdust in her mouth, she put down her fork. "Did I say something wrong?" she asked, even though she knew exactly what had caused the shift in mood.

He swallowed, then reached for his glass of wine and took a sip before answering. "No, Summer, you didn't. You're right, you do work for me. It's just... well, this afternoon felt a lot more like chatting with a friend, and I liked that. I forgot that you're on the payroll, that's all."

Now she felt like an idiot. Not that she'd been friend-zoned. She actually kind of liked that. That he'd considered her a friend gave her a warm, contented feeling. It was something she valued, because when people included her or called her their friend, it felt as if she had worth. She was incredibly self-sufficient, but it was still nice to know that there were other people out there who valued her.

"I did too." Her cheeks heated at the admission, and she hid behind her wine class. "I suppose there's no reason why we can't be friends, too. In fact, it's kind of nice that we get along so well. It would make seeing each other every day a bit of a trial if we didn't." She smiled, then, because her nerves were getting the best of her, reached for the wine bottle and refilled her glass.

"You see..." he began, then cleared his throat. "A few years back I had a relationship with a grad student in the department. I wasn't her PI, so it could have been worse. But it did make things awkward when we called things off. I tend to..." He frowned into his glass. "I'm a rule follower. I try to conduct myself with, well, integrity, I suppose. Anyway, that's why I'm annoyed with myself right now. I allowed myself to think of you in a way that wasn't as an employee. If I've crossed a line and made you uncomfortable, I'm sorry. It won't happen again."

She took a moment to digest what he'd said and how she felt about it. She kept coming back to the friend part. She wouldn't lie to herself and say she wasn't attracted to him. She was. Inconveniently so. But the bit where he'd said it felt like talking to a friend...that was the part that made her heart expand.

"It's all right, Jax," she replied softly. "You didn't cross a line. Sometimes it's good to get a fresh perspective. I'm glad you're comfortable enough with me to do that, after such a short time. Besides, can someone ever have too many friends? Why would I turn one away?"

But it wasn't just friends, was it? Not when he looked at her like he was doing now, his blue gaze focused intently on her face, as if he were hanging on every word. Not when her own gaze dipped momentarily to his lips, then slid away self-consciously while butterflies danced in her stomach.

He was only here for a few months. It wasn't like he'd be her boss forever. And why was she even worrying? He was fretting about talking about personal things, and that was all. He hadn't done anything inappropriate. He hadn't said anything or touched her or... anything. Her mind was only racing like this because she was the one with these thoughts in her head.

"You're sure? Because the last thing I want is to make you feel uncomfortable or do or say something inappropriate."

Whoever the woman had been in the history department, she'd left a mark on him. The concern in his gaze, the way his lips turned down the slightest bit told her that this was really important to him. "Were you reprimanded or something? Did dating her break any rules?"

He shook his head. "Not officially. I got well-meaning lectures from a few coworkers. You know, the whole 'don't shit where you eat' talk." He cringed at the vulgar phrase.

She laughed a little. "I've heard that one before. I'm sorry that happened to you. You really cared for her, huh?"

He straightened. "What makes you say that?"

Summer leaned back in her chair, trying to look casual while, for some reason, her heart was beating a little faster than normal. "It's clear that this really left a mark on you, and if it didn't professionally, then perhaps it did... emotionally."

He turned away again. Looked out over the darkening sea, the color deepening as the day waned and a few clouds scudded over the sky. "It did," he admitted. "It wasn't a long relationship, but I cared about her a lot."

Summer wondered why it ended. There had to be more than him being a workaholic, didn't there? Or perhaps not. Either way, it was none of her business.

And yet he'd confided in her today. A lot.

She lifted her wine glass for another deep drink while Jax rose and started gathering up the dishes. "I should get these in the dishwasher and get you home. Tomorrow's another workday. And I should talk to Bryan again, now that my head's a little cooler."

Message received: personal chit chat was over.

She stood and gathered up their napkins and glasses while he took the plates and bowls. Inside was warm, out of the brisk breeze; she hadn't even noticed how the air had begun to chill. Jax had opened the dishwasher and was putting dishes in. She joined him and added the glasses, then began to run water in the sink to wash the pot and skillet she'd used for the meal.

It all felt so domestic. When was the last time she had worked around a kitchen with a man? Years. It had been years, so long ago she barely remembered. Her dry spell could be considered a real drought at this point. And because Jewell Cove was small, the number of eligible men were few. In recent years her love life had consisted of short-term flings. Like a few summers ago and the architect who'd rented a place on the water, coming up on the weekends to sail and bring his friends and clients. She'd been working at Sally's but also working part time for the property management company who owned the beach house. There'd been an attraction, and they'd had a good time together, but it had only been fun. In that whole summer, she didn't think they'd had a conversation as intimate as the one she'd just shared with Jax.

It was twilight by the time Jax drove her back into town. She gave him directions to her address and opened her car door before he could have the chance to get out and do it for her. "I'll see you tomorrow," she said, giving a small wave and smile as she shut the door. Still, Jax waited until she'd climbed the outer stairs and had unlocked her door before driving away.

He was a gentleman. Principled. Maybe too principled. But as Summer sank onto her sofa with a sigh, she wondered what he would be like if he let go of the rules he held onto so tightly.

Chapter Seven

J ax was still in bed, his arms outside the covers and gaze fixed on the ceiling when his phone rang.

He rolled to his side and reached for it, swiping the screen and seeing his mother's face in the round circle in the middle. He answered and then pushed himself up to sitting as he put the phone to his ear.

"Morning, Mom," he said, his voice gritty from sleep... or lack of.

"Good morning, sunshine." Sandra Brodie's voice was warm and smooth, as if it weren't an ungodly early hour. "Are you still in bed?"

"Of course not," he lied. "I've been up for hours." That was almost the truth. He'd had a hard time getting to sleep last night, thinking about the project, and more than that, thinking about Summer. The way she'd looked across the table last night, sipping on her wine, listening to him as if she were really interested.

"...wanted to get you before I have to leave for the hospital." He was jolted back into the conversation. "You haven't forgotten, have you?"

Forgotten what? He closed his eyes and scrambled to think of what she might be talking about. "Of course not." His brain started going through his schedule, week by week—

"Don't forget it's black tie. And you can bring a guest, of course. Being there as a family is important, Jax. I know you won't let us down."

Of course. He remembered now, even though he would have preferred not to. The new pediatric oncology wing that Brodie Biotech had funded was to be dedicated in Matthew's memory. His brother would be immortalized, helping children beat cancer even after his death.

And Jax was up here in Maine, making what his father had once called his "little pictures." He'd apologized for it, but the words couldn't be taken back, nor the sting they left behind.

"Jax? Are you still there?"

"Sorry Mom, of course I am. I'll have my assistant double check my calendar and make my travel arrangements."

"You're not driving?"

"I can't afford much time off." The wheels of guilt turned in his chest, twisting his complicated feelings. "I can fly down and then fly back the next day. We're on a tight production schedule."

"I see. We had hoped we might have a visit with you. As soon as exams finished, you left for Maine. We live so close together and hardly see you."

Guilt, guilt, guilt.

"Maybe I can stay the night in the city, and we can do brunch on Sunday? Then I can fly back in the afternoon."

"Oh, that would be wonderful. Why don't I make a reservation at the Logan? I do love their brunch."

"That would be fine, Mom." The event was a few weeks away. He had time to get his head together before then. To plan what he'd say and to prepare himself to smile and shake hands and be content with being the second son.

Still, the idea of walking into the hospital and standing to the side during speeches and ribbon cutting... he hated these official kinds of events. There was always a lot of handshaking and congratulating each other in the world his parents inhabited. Sometimes it didn't seem as genuine as it should.

And then he felt guilty feeling that way about his folks, who were lovely people and undeserving of that criticism. Somehow, this kind of conversation always turned him into a crank.

"All right, must go. I've got consultations all morning. Have a good day, honey."

"You too, Mom. I'll see you soon."

Even though he didn't want to. Or if he did, he'd rather it was just normal family stuff. Like watching football and eating nachos in front of the big screen TV in the den, or grilling steaks on the barbecue and having a beer while the kids next door played in their pool. But his childhood had never really been that way. It had been occasion after occasion. Relaxing had always been on some sort of social itinerary, he realized as they ended the call. Scheduled in between events.

He sank back into the crisp cotton sheets and thought about yesterday. Going up the lighthouse instead of working had felt irresponsible and unhelpful. And yet it had turned out to be incredibly productive in sorting out what had gone wrong and what needed fixing—even if he didn't know how to fix it. Summer had done that for him. And last night, their dinner on the patio... it had been so relaxing and easy. Well, mostly easy. Sometimes this *atmosphere* seemed to form around them, making things, well, not really awkward, but definitely not comfortable. As if they were totally aware of each other, and yet very guarded in their conversation.

Self protection, he realized. Caution. Perhaps because it *did* feel easy.

He looked at his phone and realized it was nearly time for his alarm to go off anyway. He'd slept restlessly last night, thinking about her. Trying not to think about her, but picturing her face, the deep blue of her eyes, the warm, blond strands of her hair and the streak of purple down one side. Even her nose ring, which intrigued him to no end. There was an originality to Summer Arnold that was utterly alluring. And as he'd laid in the dark, he'd allowed his mind to go where he hadn't dared: he'd imagined kissing her, holding her in his arms. Never in his life had he developed a fascination for someone so quickly and that was super unsettling.

Remembering caused other problems, so he turned off the alarm before it could blare a good morning and got up to take a cold shower. He was dressed and in the kitchen making coffee when he looked out the window and noticed Summer pedaling up the incline in her raincoat.

She parked her bike under the eaves and he opened the door for her, abashed at being so unthinking. "Summer, I'm so sorry. I should have come to pick you up this morning. You shouldn't have to bike in this weather."

Summer carefully unzipped her coat and reached for a coat hanger. "Do you mind if I hang this on the closet knob? It'll dry better that way."

"Of course. Let me take your pack."

The backpack was covered in droplets, but the waterproof material kept them from soaking in. He gave it a little shake over the doormat. He'd been so distracted by his call with his mother and then his shower that he hadn't even noticed the weather. Not just a little shower, but a full-on steady rain. It was a thirty-minute bike ride from her place to here.

They moved into the kitchen, but it was immediately apparent that Summer's socks were wet by the footprints she left on the tile. "Hang on," he said, turning toward the stairs and his bedroom. He spun back. "Is anything other than your socks wet? I can lend you something. A T-shirt, or a pair of sweats or something." He pictured her in his clothes and nearly needed another cold shower. Why was the thought of her all soft and snug in fleece so enticing?

"I'm afraid the bottom of my pants are wet, too, but they'll dry easily. At least the raincoat covers my butt." She laughed and gave a shrug.

Her words only made his eyes stray to her pants, where he could just make out the difference in shade between dry and wet. "I'll be right back." The words sounded choked as he left the room and bounded up the stairs.

When he returned a few moments later, she'd fixed his coffee and put the kettle on. "After yesterday's lovely weather, it's a bit raw out there. Your coffee's ready and I'm going to make a cup of tea, and then I'll get started."

"I brought you some socks and a pair of sweats. It'll make quite the fashion statement, but it won't take long for your clothes to dry." He held them out, hoping his face wasn't turning red. He'd kept his cool last night, but he'd indulged in those thoughts of her in the dark, and now he felt awkward as hell.

She just smiled, though, and took the items from his hand. "Thanks. I'll be right back. If the kettle pops, can you pour my tea?"

Thank goodness one of them was acting normal.

When she returned she looked adorable. Her blue summer sweater didn't match his gray sweats, and they were too big so they hung on her, but she was smiling and honestly, when she smiled like that, would anyone truly notice what she was wearing? "Your tea is steeping," he advised, and reached for his coffee cup. "I'm going to be working in my office this morning, and then hopefully having a meeting with Bryan this afternoon." He grimaced. "Finding a way forward is a top priority. But I do have a request to add to your list for the day."

"Oh?" Summer flipped open the lid on her laptop and hit the power button.

"In a few weeks I have to go to Philadelphia for a family commitment. Could you book me a flight on the Saturday morning, then back on Sunday afternoon?"

"Of course." She sat down, putting her tea beside her. "Quick trip, though. You sure you don't want to take a few days?"

He shook his head. "No. There's stuff to do here."

Her fingers hesitated over the keyboard and she turned halfway around so she could meet his gaze. "But you haven't seen your parents in weeks, have you? I'm sure they'd like to spend time with you."

His parents would be overjoyed if he announced he was coming for two nights. Part of him would be, too. But the other part of him, the Jax that constantly needed to prove himself, felt that he needed to be here, working.

"Hey, what's wrong?" she asked, getting up from the table. "You look like someone just kicked you in the shins."

He cleared the grimace from his face. "I just don't enjoy these official engagements. It's black tie, dedicating a new pediatric oncology wing in my brother's memory. It's just not my idea of a fun time."

Her brows pulled together. "But what a lovely way to memorialize your brother. I mean, of course it can't bring him back, but think of how many children will be helped. I think it's incredible they're able to do something like that."

Instead of placating, her words added to his annoyance. "Yeah, I know all that. Which is why I feel like a total asshole for not wanting to go."

The wrinkles in her brow smoothed, giving way to a puzzled expression. "So why don't you want to go? The real reason—because I don't believe it's because you have to wear a tux."

He waited so long that she took the coffee from his hand, put it down on the table, and pulled out a chair. "Okay. Sit and talk through this with me while I pull up the travel site."

"This isn't in your job description," he pointed out.

"Maybe not, but we kind of established that we're friends, right? So, tell me why you'd rather be here working than spending a weekend with your parents. Because from what little you've said, it's not that you don't get along."

"No, we get along fine. And my mother would love your suggestion. She was disappointed I'm not staying longer." The guilt wound through him again. "It's totally me. I'm the one who—" He rose abruptly. "It doesn't matter. If you can book me Saturday morning, and back Sunday afternoon, that's all I need."

"I will because that *is* in my job description." She turned around to face the laptop again and started clicking on the keys.

While she waited for her search to load, she lifted her cup of tea and took a sip, completely unruffled.

He sighed.

"Okay," he said, sitting down again. "The thing is, I told you that my parents have never made me feel at all bad about not following in their footsteps. Either in the business or in medicine. But that doesn't mean I don't feel it. Or that… I mean, if Matt had lived, he probably would have. And I was given the opportunity, and I threw it away for something *I* wanted."

"I see." She clicked on a box and then turned his way. "And I suppose what you wanted was unimportant?"

"Well, no, I—"

"Or you were supposed to live your life for someone else?"

He blinked. "Dammit, Summer—"

She smiled. "Right. But just because you know these things doesn't make the feelings go away."

She was so damned perceptive. It was like she could see right into his head all the time, and it was unsettling. He didn't think he was so transparent, but it was a talent Summer seemed to have.

She went back to the website and finished making the purchase with his corporate card. "Okay, that's done and I've had the itinerary confirmation sent to your email. Do you need me to book you a hotel as well? A car?"

"Ideally I'd like a room at the hotel where the gala is, and I can find that info for you. But I could do with a car for the day. I'll have to drive out to the house to get my tux. Plus then I won't have to worry about calling an Uber or using a car service."

"I'll add that on, then."

"Thank you, Summer."

"Of course."

But he meant for more than taking care of the details. She'd listened to him, responded, but hadn't hounded him or made it seem like this huge deal. It was like she... well. It was like she accepted who he was without trying to talk him out of it or change him or urge him to be better. Instead she'd quite rightly stated that what he knew in his head didn't always translate to his heart.

He wanted to tell her all that, but he didn't, too. They were already getting closer than they should; at least on his part they were. He doubted she'd laid in the dark late last night thinking about kissing.

He took a sip of his coffee and figured he should head to his office, but before he could take a step, she interrupted.

"Jax? If you know that your feelings are your own and not your parents', why not go spend a few days with them? It sounds like you're all busy people. If this is truly a weekend where they're free, why not stay an extra night? Hang out?"

He shrugged, annoyed that she wouldn't let this go. "Why is this so important to you, anyway?"

She looked down into her mug of tea, then lifted her chin and met his gaze. "It just seems to me you're taking your family for granted, which is surprising considering Matt's death." He winced as she continued. "Some people would love to have a family who wanted them to visit. To laugh with and share memories and favorite recipes and, I don't know. I guess I just don't understand turning away from a perfectly good family who loves you."

"Because you don't have one?"

"Yes."

She answered him quickly and firmly and he instantly felt like an ass for snapping at her with something so hurtful.

He put down his cup on the counter and sighed. "I'm sorry, Summer. That was uncalled for. It's a touchy subject for me. You're right. Just because it's difficult for me doesn't mean I shouldn't put in an effort."

Summer nodded. "I can change your flight to Friday if you like. You can fly down late afternoon, have some extra time. The crew here can manage for a few days and you know it."

She was right again. In fact, leaving for a bit might send the message that he trusted the people he'd hired. Which he did, even though he had a hard time letting go of control. Of the constant urge to prove he was... worthy.

Jax thought Summer might already understand that, without him actually saying it. But more than that, his mind kept slipping back to her answer about not having a family. He went back and sat at the table with her again, watching as she typed on the laptop and brought up flight schedules. "You could leave around four," she said. "You'd have to be at the airport before three."

"Summer?"

"Yeah?" She paused her hands over the keyboard and turned her head to look at him.

"Will you tell me what happened to your family?"

A moment of consternation crossed her face, a fleeting glimpse of pain but of something else, too. Embarrassment, or perhaps shame that pinkened her cheeks and had her looking away. "I'd rather not."

And he couldn't push. Even if she'd pried into his. Even if he was unbearably curious.

"Okay. But... I'm here if you want to talk about it."

She gave a short laugh. "I won't."

"Hmm. Maybe someone else needs some time up the lighthouse," he mused, only half teasing.

She finished rebooking the flight and closed the lid on the laptop. "There's nothing to sort out," she replied, getting up from her chair and taking her mug to the sink. "Everyone in my family is dead."

Summer's hand shook as she put the mug in the sink, and tears stung the back of her eyes. She blinked quickly, trying to shove them away, as well as the emptiness that always swallowed her when she thought about her family. When she thought about how not a single one of them had wanted her or ever made her feel loved or a priority. She was always a mistake, a burden, a reminder. She was smart enough to know that she stayed in Jewell Cove because she'd made friends here. She had people who actually did care about her. But she also held those people at arms' length. Never let them too close. That way, if they left—as everyone did eventually—it wouldn't hurt so much.

She also knew it wasn't perhaps the best way to heal, but coping wasn't a competition. It was just... coping. Finding a way to keep going, searching for some happiness like rays of sun peeking through the clouds.

Jax hadn't answered, so she sighed and turned back. He hadn't deserved her blunt delivery of the truth. He was trying to be kind. There was no reason why he shouldn't speak plainly, as she had. Besides, she'd hate it just as much if he tap-danced around it instead of saying what was on his mind.

"I'm sorry," she said quietly, turning and resting her hips along the edge of the counter. "That was blunt, even for me. I don't want to make you feel bad for asking. For caring."

He got up from the table and went to her, and with each step that brought him closer, her heart rate quickened. There was something so intense about him, something that snuck by her usual defenses. As he stopped only a few inches away, she wondered if it was chemistry, or if it was something deeper. A shared knowing. Grief recognizing grief, perhaps.

He surprised her by taking her hands in his, and she hoped hers weren't still shaking.

"You've listened to me. If I can return the favor, or ask the right questions, or help somehow, I'd like to. I don't like to feel beholden to anyone."

She smiled a little, feeling shy. Shyness was not something people generally associated with her, but she was feeling it now. "I get that. I do. Perhaps more than you know."

"When you say things like that, I know there's a story behind Summer Arnold. I'm a good listener, by the way. Heck, I'm a historian. Listening to stories is what I do."

The stupid thing of it all was that he made her want to share, and that was a first. With his gaze so open and unwavering, the urge to say some of the things that crowded in and around her heart was strong. For a long moment she stood on the precipice, with one side keeping her feelings close, remaining strong and contained, while the other side wanted to tell him, to have someone understand. It was how she'd lived her entire life—keeping the painful bits inside. She'd lived life on the surface for years.

Instead, she joked her way through her relationships, tried being the fun and quirky one, keeping things light. She knew a lot of people didn't necessarily take her seriously. It was on purpose. She was serious enough on the inside, but if no one saw it they couldn't use it against her.

Would Jax? If he knew? And would it matter? He was leaving in a matter of weeks. It was doubtful they'd even see each other again.

"What is it?" he asked, and she was shocked to find a tear had gathered in the corner of her right eye. Oh, she wasn't accustomed to this kind of tenderness. It was only made worse when he let go of her hand and tenderly reached up and dotted the tear away with the tip of a finger.

He had depths, this man. And she couldn't stop herself from responding to them.

"I just..." She hesitated, inhaled, bracing herself. "I was actually born in South Carolina. My mom was..." She stopped again, deciding that Jax didn't need to know every tiny detail. "Mom was visiting here one summer and met my dad. I spent my first years back in Charleston, then Baltimore for a while... but when I was nine I—"

Her throat closed over, preventing her from saying the words until she swallowed the grief away. She cleared her throat and lifted her chin the tiniest bit. "My mom overdosed and died. I was put into foster care."

Jax's mouth dropped open. Of course he was shocked; who wouldn't be?

"Oh, Summer. I'm so very sorry. What about your dad?"

Summer turned her head and scoffed, a sound of disgust rolling out of her throat. "He was in prison. When he got out, he was only out for six months when the people he'd pissed off caught up with him."

What an auspicious beginning to her life. Daughter of a junkie and a felon. And neither of her parents had cared about her enough to... to what? Put her first? Try to give her a good life? *Mistake. Burden. Reminder.* That was all she'd ever been to the people who should have loved her most.

"And so you lived with your grandparents. That's what you said, right?"

She nodded, oddly relieved that she'd actually told someone the truth. Not a single soul in Jewell Cove knew the sordid details. Her grandparents had been ashamed of their son and certainly didn't want anyone in town to know he'd been in prison. She had a picture of him tucked away in a box somewhere that she'd taken from her grandparents' house. Not out of any affection for him, but as a reminder of where she came from.

She had nothing from her mother.

When she looked up at him, his eyes were tender and serious, waiting for her to go on, absent of judgment or even shock. His acceptance gave her the courage to continue.

"Social services got in touch with them. My dad was incarcerated and I was in foster care, but my grandparents agreed to let me live there." She looked up at him again, a defiance filling her chest. "On some level I think they did the best they could. But they were also in their fifties, taking in a kid and all the responsibilities of raising her. My grandfather wasn't well, either. He had heart disease, and my grandmother was just...tired. I was in the way a lot. And I know I reminded them of their son, and not in a good way. I don't think they ever got over losing him."

"You don't, when you lose someone you truly love," Jax replied, his voice quiet.

"So there," she said, injecting her voice with a false lightness. "You now know the dark, sordid history of Summer Arnold.

More than a single soul in Jewell Cove knows, actually. In the eyes of this town, my grandparents did an admirable thing, and we were a happy-ish family. No mention of my mother, and the only thing they said about my dad was that he'd been killed in Detroit. What he was doing there, we'll never know."

She'd let out the entire story in a torrent of words, and now silence enveloped the kitchen as she turned her head away, feeling a shame she knew wasn't hers but that followed her anyway. Jax would probably back away now and be sorry he asked.

So why wasn't he moving away?

She swept her gaze upward to meet his, and she saw none of the disgust or plain shock she expected. Instead, his eyes shone at her, his lips unsmiling but approval somehow stamped on every feature.

"You are incredible, you know that?"

Heat rose to her face in a quick flush. "No, I—"

She didn't get a chance to say whatever had been on the tip of her tongue. Instead, she found herself enveloped in his arms, her face nestled against the soft fabric of his shirt that smelled like laundry soap and some sort of cologne or body wash. His arms were warm and firm around her, and she instinctively wrapped her arms around his waist, not just letting him hold her, but holding onto him in return.

This. This closeness. How long had it been? And never in such an honest and open way. Jax was embracing the real Summer, not the fun, easy-going woman everyone thought they knew.

He was holding her close and not running in the other direction.

It wasn't often that Summer was surprised, but this had her completely off balance.

"You are remarkable," he murmured close to her ear, the warm feeling of his breath on her hair sending delicious shivers up her spine. "I have always liked to think I'm resilient. I lost my best friend, my brother, when I was so young. But to lose everyone... to not have..." He pulled back a little, cupped her face in his hands. "I always knew who I was and where I belonged. I knew I was loved. Sometimes I wished they didn't love me quite so much, but Summer..."

"I don't want your pity. That's not why I told you."

"I don't pity you. My heart breaks for the little girl you were, but I'm nothing short of amazed at the woman you've become."

She snorted, starting to get those uncomfortable feelings again, feeling the need to distance herself. "Oh right. I barely passed high school, I've been working minimum wage jobs for years, no relationship to speak of, and I live in a tiny apartment with no air conditioning. I'm a real superstar."

He lifted her chin a little so she couldn't avoid looking in his eyes. "Don't say that. You made it through high school. And when you found yourself alone, you became totally self-supporting as well as an integral part of this town. Don't you think I've heard about you? Is there a part of this town you haven't touched or helped? So don't downplay your accomplishments, all right?"

"But look at you. You and your fancy degrees and business and money and your folks and—"

"Summer, that is solely the result of privilege. Not any extra-special tough moral fiber. I hate seeing you talk like this about yourself."

She knew he was right, and the worst part of it was, accepting her strength made her feel particularly vulnerable. As if those accomplishments, paltry as they were, could be ripped away. It was easier to downplay everything. Then she didn't feel deserving. And there was odd comfort in that, because then no one could let her down.

"You don't have to be so kind," she murmured, shifting her face out of his hands.

"Kind?" He made a sound of disbelief, then put his hands on her arms, gave her one searing glance, and pressed his mouth to hers.

Chapter Eight

Jax's lips were warm and soft on hers, and the kiss itself was compelling, just shy of demanding. It didn't push for more, but it wasn't cautious, either. It just was, and Summer twined her arms around his neck and kissed him back.

She had the fleeting thought that they shouldn't be doing this. She shouldn't have shared so much. She barely knew him. He was her boss, this would make things awkward and inappropriate. The list ran through her head like lightning, but in an instant it was gone and all she heard was the thunder of her heart as his arm came around her and held her close against his body. He was a wicked good kisser, with just the right amount of pressure and a taste like coffee and honey. He lifted his free hand and touched her hair, cupping her head, and she wished she'd worn it down so he could run his fingers through it.

Then the kiss eased, and with a soft parting of lips he drew back. She opened her eyes first, her heart giving an extra thump as she saw his lashes swept down on the crests of his cheeks. They were a slightly darker brown than his hair, and unusually long. Then, when he slowly opened his eyes, she realized the thick lashes really framed a stunning set of blue eyes. Or maybe they were stunning simply because they were still dazed from the kiss.

"I'm sorry," he whispered. "That wasn't being kind. That was being complicated. I mean, I'm not sorry, because that was a fantastic kiss. But I'm sorry if it was the wrong thing to do, sorry if you need me to be. And wow, I'm really messing up what I'm trying to say."

She took pity on him, mostly because she had kissed him back and agreed about the complicated though she wasn't sorry it had happened. "Do you regret doing it?"

His lips pursed as his eyebrows puckered. "I'm your boss. I should regret it. I crossed a line."

"That doesn't exactly answer my question. Jax, you being my boss makes it complicated, you're right. But I kissed you back. It was at least a fifty-fifty effort."

A touch of a smile flitted across his lips. "You're letting me off the hook."

She ran her tongue over her lips; she could still taste him there and tried to put it out of her mind. "If I let you off the hook, I can let myself off the hook too, you see."

It should have eased the tension between them, but it failed utterly. Because all it really meant was that they'd both been unerringly attracted to each other and had acted on it—no matter who had made the first move.

She wanted to kiss him again. Forget about everything else in the world and just lose herself in sensation. And then she thought of what she'd told him, what her plans were for her future, and knew she had to step back.

Summer needed this job. Maybe they could navigate their way through it and still... what, have a fling? But if it got awkward, she was under no illusions. She'd be out of a job and still have tuition and bills in September for her program. And she needed that program. Working part time hours and just getting by was not how she wanted to live the rest of her life. At thirty-two, it was time for more. And maybe, for the first time ever, she believed she deserved it. Nothing could jeopardize her plans for the future—not even delicious kisses from her boss.

Especially not that, come to think of it.

"I don't regret it," she forced herself to say, "but it shouldn't happen again." She stepped away from him, putting some much-needed space between their bodies.

"I see," he replied, and gave her a nod. He wasn't angry, but she sensed he was disappointed. As she was. She'd even used the word "shouldn't" instead of "can't," as if that somehow left the door open.

"It's just... like you said, it complicates everything. Jax, we barely know each other, and we've already gotten far too personal for a work relationship. Even if that weren't the case, in September I'm going to school and you're going home. It would be foolish to start something, don't you think?"

He nodded. "Yes, of course. You're right. You're absolutely right. Being my friend isn't in your job description, and yet..." He sighed. "And yet it feels as if you are my friend. Like if we'd met in town under other circumstances, we would have been drawn to each other anyway."

"I know," she whispered.

"But that's not the case," he added. "I did hire you, and you have done nothing to make me wish I hadn't. Just having your help the last few days has been a game changer for me. I don't want to lose that."

Relief flooded through her, and she relaxed the tension that had taken up residence in between her shoulder blades. Her job was safe, then. Jax moved away, grabbing his nearly empty coffee cup and heading toward the hall and his office beyond. But then, just as he reached the hall, he turned and faced her. "But for the record, I don't regret it either."

He disappeared, and she let out a massive breath. Her lips still tingled where he'd kissed her, and her stomach was a tangle of knots. This was ridiculous. She wasn't fifteen anymore and getting kissed for the first time.

She went back to the table and her laptop, needing to get on with her work and focus on something other than Jax and the sweet taste of his kisses. The whole morning, from the bike ride in the rain to the heart-to-heart talk to the kiss had thrown her off completely. This was her job. She had no business involving herself in Jax's personal life, no matter how much she liked him.

As she opened the dreaded spreadsheet program, she found herself wishing she'd never told him anything about herself.

Her hand paused on the mouse. And yet... he'd called her remarkable. No one had ever done that before. Not once in her whole life.

Remarkable.

She shook off the feeling and tried very hard to focus on her list of tasks. At one point she heard the muffled sound of Jax's voice as he spoke on the phone, then silence again. Perhaps he was as keen to give her space as she was to take it. Or perhaps he was just resetting the work boundary.

School. Bills. Security. All the things she wanted most in her life. And yet they seemed to fade into the background because what she wanted right now, in the present, was Jax. And that was a huge red flag for her.

All her life she'd never been impulsive. At first, she'd simply tried to get by, not make her mom angry, look after things so maybe there'd be food in the house. Then there'd been the months of foster care until guardianship had been finalized. She'd been so careful, not wanting to cause any trouble and get kicked out or moved again. With her grandparents it was much the same. She hadn't been perfect, but she never wanted to give them a reason to give up on her. It wasn't ideal, living there, but it was the most security she'd ever had. And since then, being on her own, she'd never taken a single risk. She'd stayed in Jewell Cove. Kept the same friends. Worked the same jobs. Never stirred the pot. And all because she never wanted to be labeled like her mother: trouble. Uncontrollable. A mess. It was bad enough being a mistake.

She was not her mother. Good Lord, the odd glass of wine or margarita was as daring as she got. She'd never smoked, never so much as taken a toke or a Xanax. She didn't sleep around. She did girls' nights and craft classes and scooped ice cream and went to family picnics...

Family picnics.

The Collins' Fourth of July picnic was coming up and Summer was supposed to have invited Jax. Instead, she'd forgotten all about it.

If she didn't invite him, and Abby and Jess asked her, she'd have to admit she forgot. If she did invite him, she'd end up spending a major holiday at a social occasion with her boss, a man with whom she needed to enforce platonic boundaries. Of course, there was the off chance that he would decline. She could always hope.

While she was waiting for an email reply, she got up and went to the laundry room to put on her own clothes again. She folded Jax's sweats and put them on top of the dryer, along with the socks, and slid into her own trousers. There had been something nice about being in the cozy sweatpants, knowing they were his.

Cripes, she couldn't even set boundaries in her own mind. How was she supposed to do it when Jax was actually around?

It was almost noon when she gathered up the gumption to go to his office and remind him it was lunch... as well as issue the belated invitation. Her stomach was in knots as she tapped lightly on the doorframe, and he looked up from his laptop.

Their eyes met. Hers dropped to the curve of his mouth before she could help herself. When she looked back up again, his cheeks were pink. Heavens, had she made him blush?

"Um... I wondered if you wanted me to get you some lunch. It's noon."

"It is?" He made a show of checking his watch, which seemed a little disingenuous but the whole morning had been awkward, so why not? "I guess it is. But I can come out and grab a sandwich. You don't have to make it for me."

"I forgot to ask you earlier, too..." She cleared her throat. "I am supposed to ask you to join the Collins family for their picnic on the fourth at Jess and Rick's. Abby and Tom will be there, and Rick and Jess, and the rest of the Collins family. There's also Josh and Lizzie, who are both doctors, and Sarah and Mark, too. And their mom, Meggie. It's big but not huge, but they always invite a few extras."

"Like you."

She smiled. "Yeah, like me. And Charlie and Dave Ricker, because Charlie is Lizzie's best friend. It's family and friends who are like family."

"That's not me." He pushed away from his desk and stood.

"Maybe not, but they also are the kind of family who likes to include others who are at loose ends during holidays." She had a sudden idea and squinted one eye while looking at him. "Say, you didn't play high school baseball or anything, did you?"

He burst out laughing. "Me? Do I look like a jock to you?"

It was a trick question for sure. If she said no, she'd be lying. And if she said yes, well, that'd be telling, wouldn't it? Because he did have a nice physique—tall and lean, broad shoulders, decent muscles. "Just saying," she replied, "that there's always a baseball game of the Old Dogs versus the Young Pups in the afternoon after the parade."

"Let me think about it? I mean, at least I know Abby, Tom, and Rick."

"Sure. I just said I'd pass along the invitation." She didn't want it to seem as if she was asking him as a date. It was totally on behalf of the Collins family. "It's on the fourth, of course. Whatever you decide, there's a parade along Main Street, then a bunch of activities in town. I'm assuming you're giving the crew the day off, so they can take part in that stuff too. And fireworks at dusk."

"Okay." He came around the side of his desk and offered a smile. "I'll think about it."

He passed through the doorway, not touching her, and neither of them said a word about the kiss. It was as if it had never happened.

⁕ ⁕ ⁕

The next morning, instead of biking to work, Summer got a text at seven a.m. from Jax telling her he'd pick her up as they had an errand to run in Brunswick. Summer didn't question it; half the crew was staying in Brunswick considering accommodation in Jewell Cove was limited and it was high season. The drive was a pleasant one, as Jax kept the conversation light and about work. It wasn't until they pulled into the rental car place that Summer got an inkling of what he was up to.

"Are you looking to swap vehicles?" she asked, though this didn't quite look like the kind of place that would rent out luxury cars.

"No, we're here to get you a car for the summer."

Summer's mouth dropped open. "But—" She clamped her lips shut again and frowned. "Jax. I don't need a car."

"And I disagree. It's ridiculous that you have to ride your bike from town each morning, no matter what the weather, and then back home again. Yesterday you were soaked."

"I'm not made of sugar. I'm used to it. This is an unnecessary expense."

"You've seen the budget. I think we can manage a small rental for you. Seriously, Summer, it's nothing fancy. A little compact, good on gas, gets you back and forth and running whatever errands you need to run. I know you could use my car, but sometimes I'm going to be away or using it, and this makes things far more flexible."

Summer knew it probably wasn't, but it felt like an apology. A consolation prize for... what? Making things totally platonic again? Which was stupid. Platonic and businesslike was exactly what their relationship should be. She should not be feeling let down.

"It feels extravagant." And it did, but mostly it felt like he was trying to make up for something. "Truly, Jax. All I need is my paycheck on time and I'm good."

He turned in his seat. "Why do you make it so hard for others to do something for you?"

What a question. Summer stared at him for a few seconds, surprised, and scrambled to come up with an answer. She thought about everything she'd told him yesterday. And she thought about what she hadn't. This morning he'd been saying that he wished there was more information on Edward Jewell, but that the man had no living descendants, unlike the other two town founders. She hadn't offered up any information to the contrary. Or the fact that a living descendant was sitting right next to him. A detail that weighed heavier the more she got to know him.

The answer was clear and sad. "Well, I suppose because I don't want to feel as if I owe someone something. Or that if I let myself take, someone will rip it away and leave me worse off than before."

"And yet you are hungry for friendship and love. It's so easy to see when you talk to people, Summer." He turned in his seat. "You want to be loved but you're scared of it."

It was so bang on that she bit down on her lip to keep it from trembling. "Isn't everyone?" she asked weakly, faking a wobbly smile. "Besides, I didn't come here for a call out."

"Yeah," he agreed, his hands clenching the steering wheel. "I get that. But I think maybe it's something only someone who has lost a lot can understand. Like me, with Matt, and you with... well, everything. But Summer, this is a no-strings thing. This is so you can do your job, it's part of the business, and no one is going to rip it away. You're just going to return it when your contract is up." He smiled again, a little easier, and she smiled back.

"Sorry. I'm used to having to fight for every little thing."

"It's all right. But they're going to think we're crazy, sitting out here, so let's go inside and get you straightened away."

They went inside and within ten minutes they were back outside headed toward a little white compact. It was cute, Summer decided, and honestly something she'd buy for herself if she had the means. Economical but fun, no major bells and whistles but a way to get from point a to point b safely. She unlocked the door with the fob and heard the click of the locks disengaging.

She looked back at Jax. "Thank you," she said, and a genuine smile bloomed on her face. "I'm just going to have to remind myself to not get too used to it."

"You're welcome. I'll see you back at the house? I want to run some scheduling by you and then leave you to make some arrangements this morning."

"Sounds perfect."

They seemed, surprisingly, back on equal footing.

The drive back to the cove was delightful. Summer reveled in the freedom of driving the little car, picking a radio station, and setting the air conditioning. She tapped her fingers on the steering wheel, enjoying the summer day during the short but fun drive. Before long she was turning up the hill toward the lighthouse and Refuge Point. It welcomed her in, and she wondered for the first time about its name. The point marked a danger to ships, which was why there was a lighthouse to begin with—to warn vessels to stay away from the rocky, unforgiving coastline. It certainly didn't provide an actual refuge or sanctuary. And yet, the point itself had a serenity to it, a reprieve where it seemed like whatever was "out there" could be left behind for as long as one was on the bit of land jutting out into the Atlantic, with the crashing waves below and the soaring birds above. Nothing else mattered up here.

She parked the car and sat for a moment, wondering about her recent thoughts. Didn't it seem foolish to feel this way about a place? But then, wasn't that why she stayed in Jewell Cove? She'd put down roots here. Oh, they might be shallow—that earlier hesitation she'd mentioned to Jax—but they were roots just the same. The only ones she had.

It was nice to think about, though. That she'd made a home here for herself, with friends and coworkers and neighbors. It touched her more than she'd admit when Jax told her how she was loved by the town. And she loved them in return, in her own way.

But right now she had a job to do, rather than sitting here contemplating life's mysteries.

Once inside, she was surprised to find Jax had started to boil water for tea and turned on the coffee maker. Then she took her laptop into his office and together they worked through his agenda for the morning, with Summer making notes for follow up tasks to work on during the afternoon. They ate lunch and chatted about the project, and while Summer still felt that twinge of guilt at not being totally upfront with him, she listened intently and even learned things that she didn't know about the town's history. After lunch, Jax disappeared to his office again and she set up at the kitchen table after taking an hour to complete some household chores that needed attention. The day went by quickly, and it left Summer feeling slightly off balance. Since the rental car place, Jax had kept the entire day friendly but businesslike. He'd re-established the tone to their relationship, and she knew it was a good thing—even if it felt horribly odd.

At five, with a salad made in the fridge and a steak ready to grill for his dinner, she said her goodbyes and got into the little car to drive home.

It still felt extravagant, but she was going to accept it and not feel guilty. Once home, she made her own dinner of crispy tofu and stir fried vegetables, then sat on her colorful sofa with a pair of chopsticks and a sparkling water.

And thought of Jax, eating alone in that great big house looking over the water. To her surprise, she preferred the coziness of her poky little apartment to the fancy décor and sprawling rooms of the house at the point. Sure, she didn't have air conditioning, her bathroom was tiny, and there was next to no storage space. But it had warmth, and it was hers. What he'd said about her making her own life had stuck with her. She was a survivor. Even if she still had trouble letting people too close, she had finished school and supported herself all these years. Maybe it was time she was proud of that.

Chapter Nine

Later that week, Summer went for an after-dinner walk along the boardwalk, past the colorful little shops across from the wharf and the grouping of picnic tables that held a smattering of people eating fish and chips from Battered Up, the scent of frying oil and vinegar hanging in the air. It seemed odd to not see tourists and locals alike slurping Sally's ice cream from melting cones, and the little square building looked lonely and barren now that it had been gutted and was being renovated. Lamenting the change, she ambled along in the mellow light of early evening to Memorial Square and paused to look up at the statue of Edward Jewell. The monument had been installed years ago to celebrate the man who'd founded the town along with his pals Charles Arseneault and Jedediah Foster in the mid-1800s.

The fabled treasure on Aquteg Island had come from the trio. There was money that had been found, and there were historically important papers documenting the people who had come through the area as part of the Underground Railroad that had been rescued from the caves. Charles Arseneault had been called a pirate; he'd really been a profiteer who ran the blockades and risked himself to bring slaves to freedom—while making a fortune. Foster had been into shipbuilding, a legitimate business that served both the town and his associates well. And Edward Jewell... he'd come from old money. Before the war he had financed a smuggling operation, making his fortune even bigger long before the south was blockaded. He'd been married and fathered two boys, the oldest of whom died at Gettyburg at the age of nineteen, and the youngest who found himself at the business end of a gun in a transaction gone wrong in 1871, taking after his father's proclivity for shady deals.

And he'd had a daughter in 1859, with his mistress in Charleston. A daughter he provided for but never claimed, at a time when he was happy to make money off the backs of enslaved people. He'd never wanted to use precious cargo space to transport runaway slaves, or so the story went. It was leaving money on the table. Somehow, though, the Foster and Arseneault had changed his mind.

The sound of children playing echoed from a nearby playground as Summer looked up at the distinguished man carved in stone, cold and hard. Then she thought of Jax, doing his documentary, lamenting that there were no living descendants from Edward Jewell. But Summer was. She was descended from that long-ago mistress. She'd begun her life in South Carolina, and while good ol' Ed might have supported his daughter, none of the family fortune was shared past that first generation.

There were all sorts of people in her family tree, including some dirt poor relatives during the depression and a few that had made the ultimate sacrifice during the second world war. Her grandparents had done all right for themselves, and Summer vaguely remembered their middle-class house in the 'burbs, but her mother...

Her mother had told her once that the family had disowned her and didn't love her, and it was just the two of them. She'd married Scotty Arnold when she'd become pregnant, but before Summer had been born, he'd been thrown in jail. Summer had loved that idea of the two of them, her and her mother against the world—as much as a child of five or six could. Then, when she started school, she'd quickly come to see that she wasn't like the other kids. She didn't always have clean socks, and her hair wasn't brushed and done up in cute little braids and ponytails. They had moms who packed lunches, and Summer got up in the mornings and slapped jam between two pieces of bread on a good day. Girls in her class had afterschool playdates; Summer went home to find her mom passed out on the sofa from whatever she'd got high on that day.

Edward Jewell had taken a mistress and begun a legacy of... well. He certainly wasn't the hero he'd been made out to be. And every day that Summer worked for Jax, she thought about what she knew and what she was keeping from him, wondering if she really had a good reason. But anytime she considered telling him, something held her back.

"I thought that was you."

Summer turned to find Abby Arseneault coming toward her with a smile, pushing a stroller. Summer shook off her dark memories. "Oh, hi, Abby. I was just out for a walk. It's too nice an evening to spend indoors."

"Tom is dropping some stuff off at Jess and Rick's. She's still at work, so I thought I'd stretch my legs a bit too, and see if a walk would soothe a cranky, teething kid."

Summer peeked into the stroller. So far the tactic had worked. The baby's eyelashes rested on pink cheeks, little lips moving in and out as she slept.

Abby looked up at the statue. "Good ol' Ed. Sometimes I think we should have statues to Charles and Jed too. Seems the three of them were in all this together, but only Ed is the namesake to the town."

"History's a funny thing," Summer said weakly, unsure of how to reply.

"Speaking of history, how's work going? What's the sexy producer up to these days?"

Summer's face heated. The sexy producer had been kissing her just yesterday, but she'd never say as much. She wasn't the kind to kiss and tell, for one. "Oh, he's working away."

"Rick says he hasn't gone out to the site lately."

"Well, he's got a good crew. He trusts them to do their jobs. He doesn't have to be on set all the time." She would never gossip about her boss. Not even to Abby.

"Or maybe he likes hanging around his office at the house?" Abby nudged her arm and gave a little laugh. "It's awful isolated up there. Man could get lonely. But if he had a pretty assistant, that might help take away the monotony of the days."

Abby was teasing, and Summer knew it, so she put on a little smile. "What an imagination you have, Mrs. Arseneault." And then she laughed, because Abby was grinning at her like a fool.

"Do I?" Abby asked, and then motioned toward a bench at the edge of the square. "Come on, let's sit and you can tell Aunt Abby all about it. I need some excitement in my life!"

Summer followed her to the bench and sat, leaning back for a moment and closing her eyes, listening to the sounds around her. The kids playing, but also the sound of birds, traffic on the nearby streets, the barely-there hush of the water, and then the muted drone of someone starting up their lawn mower.

"I love this town," she murmured, and her heart warmed at the truth of it. She opened her eyes and looked at Abby. "I've lived here most of my life. It's where I've felt safe and secure... as much as I could, anyway. It's beautiful, and friendly, and not perfect, by any stretch, but it's home. It's where my friends are. Where my... my heart is."

"You sound as if things are going to change." Abby's brow puckered. "Are you planning to leave? What happened to school in the fall?" "Oh, no, nothing like that," Summer reassured her, putting her hand on Abby's knee. "I just got feeling nostalgic today."

"Jax has been good for you. It's like you... hmmm. Like your edges have softened in one way, but you've somehow also gained more confidence."

Was that really from a few weeks of working with Jax? Maybe it was. After all, she'd told him a lot about her background, usually a no-go area. She'd enjoyed doing her job. And yes, she'd enjoyed being with him, too.

"It's a good job," she admitted. "But honestly, I think I've really started to put my past in perspective. He said something about me supporting myself all alone, putting a roof over my head and what great friends I have and..." She looked at Abby again. "Well, I think I've started to feel less like a loser."

Abby's eyes widened. "A loser? Summer. Why would you think that?"

Summer shrugged. "High school education, minimum wage jobs, living in a tiny apartment that is sweltering in the summer and freezing in the winter? I'm thirty-two, Abby. I was feeling like I didn't have much to show for it."

"He's changed your mind?"

A flash of heat went to her cheeks again. "He's made me challenge some of that thinking, that's all. And he's a good boss. Maybe I'm just starting to see that it is okay for me to want more and that I'm capable of doing it."

"Hallelujah!" Abby threw up her hands and then laughed. "Girl, you have no idea how much people care about you or how you are such a big part of our community. You know everyone. You volunteer for every community event. You've worked for half the businesses in town at one point or another. And when you come to our craft nights and the wine gets flowing? No one makes us all laugh easier than you. If I'd known you felt this way, I would have been kicking your ass with kindness a lot sooner."

Tears stung the backs of Summer's eyes. "But I feel like such a fraud."

"For the love of heaven, why?" Confusion darkened Abby's eyes, as if she truly couldn't imagine such a thing. Summer didn't deserve the faith this woman seemed to have in her.

She'd told Jax about her parents. Maybe it would be okay to share with Abby, the closest thing she had to a best friend. The alternative was hiding for the rest of her life, and did she really want to do that?

"My grandparents... they were my dad's parents," Summer began, looking down at her hands. "I don't remember my dad. He was in jail most of my life. And when he got out, he only lived a few months before his past caught up with him."

Abby nodded. "I didn't know them, since I wasn't brought up here. But Tom told me once that Scotty Arnold had been killed in an accident."

"No accident. He pissed off the wrong people."

"I'm sorry."

"My grandparents told the other story to save face, and I can't say as I blame them. I came to live with them when my mom died. She overdosed in our apartment. I just… I'm not this great person you seem to think I am."

Abby turned on the bench so she was nearly facing Summer. "So? Honey, you are not your parents' sins. Why would you think that?"

Summer shrugged. "Well, I come from a long line of… not so great people, it turns out. And because—"

She stopped. Swallowed around a lump in her throat, and told her friend what she hadn't been able to tell Jax.

"Because my mom told me I was a mistake. When things were good, it was the two of us against the world. But when they weren't, and she was using a lot, she'd tell me it was my fault. That I made her do it. If I'd been better, quieter, cost less money… whatever she wanted to lash out with. And so I just kept trying harder."

Abby sat in stunned silence for a minute. Her phone buzzed and she looked down. "Damn. Tom's done. But I don't want to leave this here. I'll see if he can come back to get me later, because this is important, Summer."

Summer could just tell her to go. That it was fine and she wouldn't share any more. But now that she'd opened the door to this part of her life with someone she trusted, she needed to get it out, and at least if they stayed here, on a bench in Memorial Square, she would maintain her composure. "I can take you both home later, actually. I have a company rental."

"Let me text him back."

Her thumbs tapped the phone rapidly and then she tucked it away in her purse, peeked in the stroller to check on the baby, and gave Summer her full attention again.

"Okay. So, first of all, your mother made her own choice to start using. I know addiction is a horrible thing, and I don't want to make her a total villain, but I know for sure that it was not your fault."

"I know that in my head. It's harder to tell the little girl inside, you know?"

"I do, actually. But surely it was better once you came to live with your grandparents? And what about your mom's folks?"

Summer sighed. "Well, funny thing, really. Bear in mind that I was only nine when Mom died and I went into foster care, but apparently my grandparents on my mom's side wanted to care for me but my grandmother had been diagnosed with MS and they didn't think they could take on raising a child. Gram and Gramp Arnold offered, thinking, I suppose, that when my dad was released he'd take responsibility. And then he died, and I was just... in the way. After a few years I stopped getting cards and presents from my other grandparents."

"So you felt abandoned, unwanted, and a burden. Gosh, Summer, I'm so sorry. I never knew. You always seemed so happy. So... I don't know, carefree."

"I worked really hard on that." Summer smiled. "The last thing I wanted was to be 'trouble.' I was terrified my grandparents would put me back in the system. Maybe it was a labor of duty rather than love, but I had a good, clean roof over my head and enough food to eat and clothes on my back. A lot to be thankful for, really."

"I was raised by my grandmother, too," Abby revealed. "In Nova Scotia. But our relationship was totally one of love. I'm so sorry yours wasn't."

"It's all right. I've never told anyone this, Abby. Not until Jax the other day."

"So it is more than employer and employee."

"We're friends. He's a very nice man, actually. And has his own battle scars. We all do, I guess."

Abby nodded. "Yeah. Even though my gram and I were really close, I didn't know about my Aunt Marian or anything to do with the Foster family until long after she'd died. When people keep secrets, it's usually out of pain or shame. Or both. Thank you for sharing with me, though, Summer. It means a lot that you trusted me."

"I'm trying to do that more. Trusting people."

The evening was waning, and a chill was on the ocean breeze. Abby tucked the blanket more securely around the sleeping baby.

"Come on," Summer said, "I'll give you a lift home. I'm still basking in the glow of having transportation." She grinned at Abby. "Apparently showing up looking like a drowned rat yesterday morning after biking to work was not a good look."

It didn't seem to stop him from kissing her though, she reminded herself.

"So do you think something will happen there?" Abby asked, as they rose from the bench and headed back in the direction of Summer's street.

Remorse filled her heart as she was honest yet again. "I don't think so, Abby. He's my boss and he's only here until September. I think there's some attraction there, but nothing we'll act on." *Again,* she added silently.

"That's too bad," Abby replied, giving her arm a nudge. "Because he called Jess this afternoon and accepted the invitation to the picnic on the fourth. And there's a lot of summer left. You deserve to have a fling. Or maybe even give him a chance."

"Good Lord, woman. Baby steps. I'm a long way from trusting someone to, oh, I don't know, not bail on me? Since pretty much everyone I've cared about always has."

Abby linked her arm through Summer's and gave her a sisterly jostle. "That was before," she said. "Adult Summer has tons of friends, none of whom would ever abandon you if you needed us. That love counts, too."

It did, and the words made Summer long to curl into a ball and have a good cry; the good kind that cleansed a person and washed away their troubles. "Oh, Abby," was all she managed, and she swallowed against a thick knot of tears.

"You're lovable, Summer. I don't think you know how much. But it's never going to work if you don't let someone in. Maybe give him a chance."

Maybe. Or maybe not.

She was such a chicken.

The morning of the fourth, Summer stretched and blinked against the sunlight coming in her bedroom. She'd turned her alarm off last night and had slept a full hour past her usual wake-up time. Now, as she took extra luxurious moments to lie in bed, she thought about what the day had in store for her.

Today was the parade, and the ball game, and the picnic at Jess and Rick's. Jax would be there, and Abby's parting words last week still echoed in her head. That she should try letting someone in. And she'd nearly considered it, but when she'd gone back to work the next morning, Jax was back to being a hundred percent businesslike. It was actually as if the kiss had never happened, or she had imagined it. They worked on files, shared a few laughs, and Summer had taken Friday afternoon, when Jax was off doing a rare site visit, to give the house a good cleaning before the weekend. And then last night, when she'd gone to the door to leave, he'd simply called out a "See you at the picnic tomorrow!"

Summer might have been offended or hurt by the boundary he'd established, except for one thing: she'd asked him to put it there. He was respecting her wishes, so how could she be annoyed with him for that?

She couldn't. But she was anyway, because each time their arms brushed unintentionally, or their gazes met and he smiled, butterflies went winging through her tummy, making her feel like a girl with a crush on the cute boy in math class.

And wasn't she lying here, staring at the ceiling, remembering that she'd see him today and getting excited about it?

She threw off the covers and headed for the shower. This was stupid. She was going to shower, make her hummus and pita to take to the picnic, and then go down to Main Street to watch the parade. Normally, she'd be busy scooping ice cream on a day like today, but not this year. This year she got to enjoy the holiday like everyone else, and she was going to soak in every star-spangled minute.

Despite it being a holiday, the weather decided to be a tiny bit uncooperative. It wasn't supposed to rain, but it was overcast and cooler than usual, so Summer dressed in jeans, knock-off Vans, and a red T-shirt with a V-neck. Goosebumps rose up on her arms as she began to walk the few blocks to Jess's store, Treasures. While the purple building was technically on Lilac Lane and one street up from Main, the sloped lawn in front of the store was perfect for looking down the hill at the parade route while avoiding the crush of people that were already lining the street. She had a beach towel with her to sit on, and a hoodie in case she got cold. It was still a half hour until the parade was supposed to begin, but she wasn't the first to arrive at the shop. Mark and Sarah were already there, their two kids running around with a few friends. Jess was spreading out a beach blanket for herself and Rick and their daughter, and Jess's mom, Meggie, was sitting in a folding lawn chair next to Luke

Pratt, the former mayor. The two of them had been stepping out together, as Meggie put it, for a year or so now, ever since Luke had his heart attack.

"Morning, Summer!" Jess called her name and Summer looked up and waved. The next few minutes were taken up with greeting everyone, then greeting more as Tom showed up with his brother Bryce and his family, and then Josh and Lizzie. The whole front lawn was now dotted with towels, blankets, and chairs, waiting for the festivities to begin. And it would be soon. The sounds of a marching band carried on the faint breeze. The parade would start at the Episcopalian church and end at the high school, where there would be a hot dog barbecue and games for the kids until the annual baseball game began.

"Good morning."

The smooth sound of Jax's voice surprised her and sent her nerve endings humming with pleasure. "Oh! Hello. I didn't realize you'd be here!"

Drat. That made it sound as if she didn't want him to be, didn't it? Why was she so often awkward around Jax Brodie?

He simply laughed, though. "Rick invited me on Friday, when we were coming back on the boat. He said if I wanted to see the parade and not have to be swamped with people or hit in the head with flying candy, I should bring something to sit on and join everyone here."

He was holding a chair in his hands, but other than Meggie and Luke, everyone else was on the grass.

She took pity on him. "Hang on. I'll turn my towel around and we can share."

The towel was big enough for two, but it was cozy. Their arms brushed as they settled on the brightly colored terry, and Summer felt her cheeks heat despite the cool breeze. "Not very festive weather," she commented. The bit of sunshine she'd seen upon awakening looked to be the only clear sky they'd have today.

Jax chuckled. "Well, you're not soaking wet from biking up my lane, so that's something."

"What's the crew up to today?"

He shrugged. "They all have the day off, so they're doing whatever they like. Some might be here in town, or they might be sleeping all day, or... whatever."

The sounds of drums and piccolos grew louder; the parade was on the move. The kids banded together and made a beeline for the street below, wanting to be close to the floats and within catching distance of any candy being tossed. Summer laughed at the sight of them ducking beneath elbows to get right up front.

"Did you ever do that?" he asked.

"Sure. You?"

He shook his head. "Naw. A lot of the time Mom was on call at the hospital, and our neighborhood wasn't near anything. We usually watched stuff on TV. Though one year Dad got us some backyard fireworks." He smiled in remembrance. "We thought he was the coolest dad ever, even though they were nothing overly special."

Todd Smith led the parade with lights flashing on his cruiser, clearing the route for the groups coming along. "Here we go," Summer said, crossing her legs and resting her elbows on her knees.

There were floats from local businesses, marching bands, clowns, horses. A float passed by with some local talent contest thing and a girl was singing a recent hit slightly off key. Jax winced and looked over at Summer, who laughed at his pained expression. The local scout troupe walked by and waved, followed by the ladies of a nearby DAR chapter. Jewell Cove was small, and the parade wasn't that big either, but when the last float had passed by, and the kids raced back up the hill with their pockets bulging with lollipops and wrapped hard candies, it was as if they'd been given a million bucks.

"You ever miss being that age?" she asked, grinning at the group who were now sorting out their candy and making trades for favorites.

Jax was quiet for so long that she looked over at him. His face was tight, his lips unsmiling, and she immediately realized her gaffe.

"I'm so sorry," she murmured, putting her hand over his on the blanket. "I didn't think."

"It's all right. Look, I had a good childhood for the most part. But seeing those two" —he pointed at Mark and Sarah's kids— "running and laughing brings it back. He was my only sibling, and I was horribly lonely after he died. That age... I had friends, of course I did. But everything had changed."

"I know that feeling. I was younger than they are now, but moving here was both exciting and scary for me. I moved in with people I didn't know, in a strange town with a new school."

"How did you cope?" he asked.

She laughed. "I pretended. Pretended to be smart, pretended I was happy, that I could have fun, be good. I basically faked my way through life until one day I realized I was happy, and I had friends, and I knew how to have fun."

"Ah, the old 'fake it until you make it' strategy."

"You bet. And you?"

He shrugged. "I put my nose in a book."

She tried to imagine him as a kid, with that honey-blond hair and blue eyes and serious look on his face, with his books for company. Books would allow him to escape the world he was in rather than pretending everything was all right. "We all handle things in different ways, don't we? And yet here we are."

"Here we are," he agreed, and their gazes clung.

In that electrifying moment, Summer realized that the platonic treatment she'd received the week or so at work had only been an act. That had been him pretending. He looked away now, but it was too late. She'd seen the spark light in his eyes, felt the pull to him as surely as if he'd reached for her. All of it was made worse by the fact that since she'd talked to Abby in the park, she hadn't been able to stop thinking about him. About their kiss. About wanting to do it again despite all the reasons not to.

"Well," she said, hopping to her feet. "I'm going to head back to my place to finish putting together what I'm taking to the picnic later. I'm guessing I'll see you there?"

He stood too, and faced her. "I, um, could help you if you like. I don't have anything on my agenda, and the streets are going to be too congested to try to leave for a while. The parade won't be over until it reaches the high school."

He was inviting himself over. To her house. Anticipation fizzed in her veins, even though she knew nothing could—or at least should—happen between them. Which was why she surprised herself by saying, "Sure. I could use a hand."

That was a lie, because she'd made the hummus earlier and all she needed to do was put her platter, sliced pita, and dish into a bag to take over to Jess's house at four. Not in a million years had she thought he'd want to tag along. But wasn't the food a convenient excuse? At first to escape, but now... Now it was to sneak time together. She could argue against it all she wanted, but the energy between them had changed. They weren't looking at each other now as she folded the towel and tucked it under her arm, and he picked up his chair and hooked the strap over his shoulder. Even so, the air hummed around them.

Her discomfort grew as they walked the few blocks to her apartment without speaking. Making small talk was impossible; talking about what was really happening unthinkable. She climbed the steps to her door, listening to his heavier footfalls behind her, her breath cramping in her chest. Then they were inside and she turned around to close the door, only to be met with his tall, strong body. He finally looked at her. Put down his chair. Blindly shut the door and turned the deadbolt, all while holding her gaze.

And then they were kissing, full, open-mouthed, hands-gripping-fabric kissing. The towel under her arm dropped to the floor along with her keys. He lifted her T-shirt and pulled it over her head, and she did the same with his as their breaths raged and clashed with urgency. Oh God, it wasn't just her, then. He'd been going just as crazy. It was both a glorious revelation and scary as hell.

His teeth nipped her neck and she gasped. "Jax, what are we doing?" she breathed, but instead of pulling away, she wrapped herself around him even closer, craving the feel of him.

He backed her against a counter—how had they made it to the kitchen?—and his hardness pressed against her, answering her question clear as day. She slid her hands over his warm chest and a smattering of soft hair. They were skin to skin as his arms came around her.

This was escalating quickly, and a tiny voice—very, very tiny—whispered to Summer that this was probably a mistake. A much louder voice, one that sounded remarkably like Abby's, told her to go for it. See what happened. Take him to bed if that's what he wanted. She did deserve a fling, didn't she? When had she last had sex? Long enough that it was hard to remember exactly. And Jax was here. They got along well. It didn't have to jeopardize anything if they didn't let it.

And she should just stop thinking.

Jax's hands traced up her back, unfastening her bra and then peeling it down her arms. He filled a hand with her breast, and she sighed against his mouth, the feeling so wonderful she wanted to drown in it. In return, she pressed her palm against the zipper of his jeans, against the hard heat of him.

He pressed his forehead to hers. "Summer, I—" He blew out a slow breath. "We should probably stop."

"Should we?" she asked.

"Shouldn't we?" He leaned back a little so his eyes—pupils blown with desire—met hers.

This was the moment, then. The moment when they could back away and avoid the damage. Carry on as they had been. Or the moment they could throw caution to the wind.

"I'm not interested in forever. And neither are you," she added as he opened his mouth to speak. "But we're sure as hell interested in each other." His gaze burned into hers. "Jax, I'm so tired of playing it safe. Aren't you tired of overthinking?"

His tongue slipped out of his mouth and over his lower lip, and her body kicked into overdrive. Tentatively, she reached out and touched her fingers to his chest, the glorious expanse of it, warm and surprisingly soft. It only took that small touch for him to reach for her again, pulling her against his hard body, while his mouth plundered hers and his hands possessed her.

She gasped as he swept her up in his arms—no man had ever done that to her before—and wrapped her arms around his neck, holding tight as her breasts bounced with each step toward her bedroom. Thank God she'd made her bed this morning; the room looked neat and tidy as he placed her down on the deep red bedspread, her head nestled in the soft orange and golden throw pillows.

Jax got on the bed next to her, leaning over, kissing her lips and then sliding his mouth down over her collarbone and finally to her breasts. She arched as a dart of desire shot straight to her core at the feel of his tongue.

But he moved back up and kissed her again, then pressed his forehead to hers. "I don't have a condom," he murmured. "I didn't expect—"

"I'm on the patch," she whispered back. "And if you're worried about anything else, don't be. I've never had anything, and it's been..." She felt her cheeks heat. "Well, it's been a while."

A slow smile creased his mouth. "Me too. Everything except the patch." And she laughed lightly, loving that in the midst of this moment they were able to talk and be honest without it being... weird.

Her response was to reach down and unbutton her jeans; then he slid them and her panties down her legs. Jax helped her get them from around her ankles, dropping them on the floor, and instead of taking his time as she expected, he crawled back onto the bed, sliding his hand between her legs at the same time and making her cry out.

She hadn't expected... this.

Now that there was no need to hesitate, he made the most of each moment, using his hands and mouth to send her teetering toward the edge of an orgasm and back again. When she surely thought she'd burst into flames, he stood back, removed his own jeans, and positioned himself over her. Summer wasn't sure how it was possible, but more heat blossomed, reaching every part of her body as she reached for him and guided him inside.

He paused for two, maybe three glorious seconds, just enough time for the sensation to sink in, and then he began to move.

It had been a while—that much was true—but Summer was certain her eyes rolled back in her head just a little as she reached up and clasped one of the rungs of her iron bedframe. Maybe it was a vanilla position, or at least Jax's brand of vanilla, but hell, she liked it well enough. But there was more... so much more. He slowed, hooked a leg over hers, and rolled them so she was on top.

A brief wave of shyness overtook her. There was no hiding here. It was the middle of the morning, and she was astride her boss, for God's sake. Except right now he wasn't her boss. He was... he was...

He twitched, and her brain quieted. And then she forgot everything except the sensations of him inside her, and how he made her feel, and she finally, finally let go.

Chapter Ten

J ax opened his eyes and took in the muted light in the room. The walls were a rich cream color, and the décor the same vibrant shades as the living room. For some reason he'd imagined Summer surrounded by cool pastel shades, but the warm tones suited the woman who now lay slumbering beside him, dressed in absolutely nothing.

As he watched, the fine hairs on her arms rose in the subtle chill. As gently as he could, he reached down for a soft throw that was half hanging off the bed and pulled it up, covering the two of them. Her bedroom window was open a few inches, he realized, and he wondered if anyone had heard them. Embarrassment heated his face at the thought, but he wasn't sorry. He'd been attracted to Summer from the moment she'd stepped into his office that first day. They'd had a few will-we-or-won't-we moments, but after their first kiss he'd known they'd be incendiary together if they ever took the risk.

Incendiary indeed.

He frowned, though. Watching her sleep, her face relaxed and her lashes fluttering onto the crests of her cheeks, he felt… proprietary. Not in an ownership kind of way, but wanting to keep her close, to breathe in her scent and hear her voice and to make her sigh for only him. Having her close made him feel *alive*.

The old guilt niggled at him as it always did when he found himself happy. It was hard to embrace joy when he always re-membered his brother would never have these moments. That Matt deserved these moments. And that Jax hadn't been able to save Matt when it counted.

Summer let out a soft sigh and he gazed down at her face, a tenderness stealing over him. She deserved happiness for sure. He knew enough of her story—and could guess a lot of the parts she might have left out—to know that her childhood had been fraught with complications and short on softness. Neither of them were looking for a long-term relationship; she'd stated that as clear as day and she wasn't wrong. But for the time they had, Jax would make sure she never felt in the way or like an inconvenience. A mistake. She was too special for that. And the way she'd looked into his eyes as he'd held her in his arms… it had sent an electric current through him, a pulsing jolt that was foreign and exciting.

The cool, humid air from the open window smelled like summer rain, and Jax closed his eyes, letting out a contented, replete sigh. This morning's exertions had been sorely needed and exceeded all his imaginings.

It was some time later before he opened his eyes again, and found Summer watching him, a small smile playing on her lips. "You covered us up."

He drank in her face, loving the little smile and the twinkle in her eyes. "The breeze is chilly today."

"Normally it's hot as balls in here."

He couldn't help it; he burst out laughing. She was always coming up with little phrases that threw him off guard, and it was delightful, as she was. "It's the rain," he murmured, sliding closer, looping a leg over hers under the blanket. "I, for one, am grateful, because if it were hot as balls, I wouldn't feel like snuggling close to you. I mean, I would, but sweaty and sticky isn't super comfortable."

She winked at him and answered, "Sweaty and sticky has its moments."

"You're not wrong." He shifted so he was on top of her, looking down into her face, her breasts squashed against his chest. "Also, the picnic isn't for several more hours. However shall we pass the time?"

"Hmm, let me think," she said, trailing a finger down his jaw and neck. "We could go for a walk."

"Exercise is important."

"Or visit the activities on the waterfront."

"Very civic-minded."

"There is the Young Pups and Old Dogs ball game this afternoon."

He couldn't stop smiling. "Who would want to miss that?"

"Or..." She leaned up and touched her lips to his, sending off a burst of fireworks in his veins. "We could stay in bed a while longer and see what... pops up."

Jax groaned at the bad joke as she started to laugh, the rise and fall of her chest pressing against his. He circled her wrists with his hands and braced them on the pillow on either side of her head, and then kissed the hollow of her throat where her pulse beat like butterfly wings.

And without saying a word, they made their choice.

Three hours later Summer found herself sitting on the bleachers alongside Jax at the high school ball diamond, cheering on the boy's team and giving the Old Dogs—former JCHS teammates—a good ribbing. The boys looked super intense, not wanting to lose face to the old guys, which Summer found adorable. The trash talk from the stands was inventive and humorous, and she grinned every time Jax chuckled warmly beside her. Truthfully, she couldn't remember when she'd last been this relaxed, and her cheeks heated as she recalled exactly how she'd relieved all her stress. Three times, to be exact.

Jax was a very thorough lover. He was still her boss, too. That niggling thought wouldn't let her alone, but she kept pushing it aside as something for Tomorrow Summer to worry about. After all, he was only here until the first of September. Maybe eight more weeks. It wasn't like it was a long-term job or he'd be her boss forever. He'd be going back to Pennsylvania and she'd be starting her program.

Someone hit a line drive past the third baseman and Jax cheered, clapping his hands and giving a whoop. Summer looked over at his profile and felt a wave of tenderness overtake her. His leaving presented a different problem, however, and one that was possibly harder to navigate than the boss/employee dynamic. If they continued on, she was in big danger of developing real feelings for him and being hurt when he left. People rarely left affairs without some sort of emotional consequences, and she had to prepare herself for that—if this continued past today.

Wrong or right, she wanted it to. How could she not?

The runner stole from first to second base, and another cheer went up from the crowd as the runner slid, leaving a smear of reddish dirt up the side of his white ball pants, the damp earth courtesy of the late morning showers.

"What a play," Jax said beside her, nudging her elbow. "This is fun. I'm glad you convinced me to come. I haven't gone to a ball game since..." His voice drifted off and he sighed. "I don't remember the last time. How sad is that?"

"All work and no play," she chided lightly, her heart softening. She liked Smart, Historian Jax and definitely liked Intense Lover Jax, but she also liked this new side of him. The light and fun side. For a fleeting moment, she once again wondered if this morning had been a mistake. She liked him perhaps too much, and they would have to say goodbye. There really was no other option.

But she shook off the feeling. She'd be all right. She didn't do love. Besides, she'd never allow herself to be that vulnerable. Not ever. This was a temporary job and a temporary fling, an enjoyable interlude before embarking on the journey to a new stage of her life.

When the game was done around five thirty, everyone packed up for whatever plans came next. Some would go back to town for late-afternoon activities. The restaurants and takeout spots would be busy, The Rusty Fern wouldn't have a free chair available, and the beer would be flowing freely. Fireworks would happen somewhere close to ten o'clock, and those who didn't venture to the waterfront generally had friends-and-family plans. Summer and Jax drove back to her apartment to retrieve her hummus and pita, as well as a bottle of wine and a four-pack of beer from a local craft brewery for Jax. Then they walked over to Rick and Jess's, where flags hung from the front porch and little paper ones lined the walkway to the back yard.

A crowd had already assembled. Rick and Jess, of course, and the baby, as well as Josh and Lizzie and Meggie Collins and Luke Pratt, the former mayor. Summer grinned as she watched Meggie hand Luke a soda and he kissed her cheek; the two had been on their own a long time, both widowed, and the quiet romance that had blossomed between them was lovely.

"Summer! You made it. Perfect. And you brought your hummus," Jess gushed. "Not so secret secret, by the way—the baby loves hummus." She put her hand on her slightly rounded belly. "I hope you made lots."

"There's extra in another container," Summer said with a smile. "You've met Jax, right?"

"Of course. Welcome to our picnic, Jax. Where you'll eat until you hate yourself, laugh more than you can remember, and..." She glanced at the back door. "Oh, heck. Hang on. Looks like Rick has got himself into a diaper emergency. Remind me again why we decided to have them close together?"

She scurried off while Summer started laughing. "Jess is a force of nature. Even more so since marrying Rick." Looking around, she realized Tom and Abby hadn't yet arrived and neither had Sarah and Mark and the kids. Along with the diaper emergency, Summer was reminded that it took a lot to get kids ready for an event and they required constant supervision. She was just starting to figure out what she wanted her life to look like. Adding kids to the mix? No thank you. She liked them well enough, but...

Dave and Charlie Ricker came through the gate, carrying their little one, and Summer's heart gave a lurch. The truth of the matter was, having a kid wasn't something she wanted to do alone, and the idea of the whole two-parents-with-a-house-and-a-picket-fence thing made her stomach give a strange lurch. She supposed it happened... for someone, somewhere. But she'd never seen it, never had it. And was pretty sure she wouldn't know what to do with it if she did.

"You okay?" Jax's voice came from beside her, and she realized she'd been staring at Charlie and Dave for a long time. "Where'd you go?"

"Oh, sorry!" She pasted on a bright smile and turned away from the picture-perfect sight of the little family. "I got caught up in my thoughts for a minute. Let me set this out on the table and then we can get a drink."

The yard began to fill as more people arrived, including the Arseneault brothers and their families, and the rest of the Collins clan. Laughter increased, kids started playing tag, and a set of bocce balls was produced. Music came from a speaker somewhere and the scent of burgers on the grill wafted through the air. Jax had excellent social skills, and Summer watched as he smiled and chatted, accepted beer and soda, and basically mingled like a champ. She, on the other hand, found herself on the outside, which was in itself unusual. Usually, she was at the center of these things, socializing, having a few glasses of wine and loving being part of Jewell Cove. These were her people. Her friends.

But today she was still sipping on her first glass, and she found herself dissatisfied. As if she didn't belong. Jewell Cove was her home, not his. And he'd slid into the community and into her life without even meaning to, she was sure. That's what was so odd. She'd lived here for years. She'd stayed here because it was the first place that had ever felt like an actual home.

But tonight she felt like an outsider, and that made her a little uncertain, and even a little bit jealous that it seemed so easy for him.

Jax came over carrying two plates and put one in her hands. "Veggie burger for you. You need to eat something. You haven't even nibbled since we got here."

She looked up, surprised. "You noticed?"

"Of course I did." He shrugged. "I've been watching you, standing over here, wondering why you're so alone. I kind of expected you to be the life of the party."

She swallowed against a strange tightness in her throat. "I usually am. I don't know what's come over me."

"Me," he said, his voice cocky and sure, and it got a snort out of her. Then he sobered and looked into her eyes. "Summer, are we good?"

"Yeah," she said, letting out a breath. "We are. But I'll admit it's possible I've been standing over here overthinking. Which isn't like me at all."

"Right, because you're a do-er." He smiled. "That's the first thing I noticed about you, actually. You had this energy about you that is magnetic. You knuckle down and do stuff, make the best of situations. But that kind of pretending wears thin eventually." He took a bite of his burger, chewed, and swallowed while she stared at him. "Ask me how I know," he added, then took a sip of his soda.

The only thing Summer wanted to do less than eat was to dig deeper into her emotional baggage, so she lifted the burger and took a bite. It wasn't her favorite kind of meatless patty but it wasn't bad, and he'd added ketchup, mustard, and pickles, her favorite toppings. That he knew that after such a short time together meant he paid attention, and she wasn't quite sure what to do with that, either. This whole situation was a novelty.

He was right about one thing, though. Once she started eating, she realized how hungry she was, and she finished her burger and the assortment of veggie sticks he'd put on the side. "Okay," she admitted, "I needed that. Thanks."

"No problem." He'd finished his burger too and piled her empty plate on his. "Now come on. I can tell you don't want to talk, so let's go dance." Tom Arseneault had put together a wooden dance floor and some of the couples were already making use of it in the twilight, dancing to some July 4th, Top 40 Countdown Jess had tuned to. It turned out Jax wasn't a half bad dancer, for an academic. When he did a bit of a bump and grind, her mouth dropped open and he grinned at her, his eyes twinkling. "What?" he said, loud enough she could hear him over the music and laughter. "Did you think I spent my university days in the library and home for curfew *every* night?"

Clearly he hadn't. He had a natural rhythm that, considering their earlier activities, she should have guessed at. He took her hand and pulled her in, then turned her in a circle, never losing the beat. "Apparently not," she replied, laughing.

But Rick and Jess Sullivan's back yard wasn't a dark club, so they kept the flirting light and easy until the music changed to something slower. The kids that had been bopping along beside the dance floor scattered, and a few couples remained, drifting into each other's arms. Jax sent her a questioning look, then drew her close.

Summer looked around her as a knot formed in her stomach. It was one thing to chat while eating burgers and dance a few fast songs, but being held in his arms—in full view of everyone—made her uneasy, and she withdrew a little, putting some distance between them.

Jax felt Summer stiffen in his embrace. Something was off with her tonight. It had been off since they'd arrived, really. Jess had gone off to help Rick with their kid and he'd felt Summer retreat into herself.

He'd wondered if maybe she was uneasy, them being there together, so he'd made a point of mingling, though she hadn't seemed to mind being seen with him at the parade or again at the ball game. And when she put herself at the perimeter of the gathering, her ready smile elusive, he'd changed tactics. The food had seemed like a good idea, and she'd loosened up a little, even enjoyed dancing. But now that she was in his arms, the distance was between them again, and he couldn't figure it out.

"Relax," he whispered, leaning in closer to her ear. "I won't bite."

"I know that," she replied, but her hand was still stiff in his. He tried guiding her around the floor, and she loosened slightly, but something was off.

Was she regretting the afternoon, now that she'd had time to think about it? It wasn't necessarily uncomplicated. He was her boss, after all. And his time in Jewell Cove was short. And yet, they'd gone into it with their eyes open. There'd been no false promises, no declarations made. Maybe she'd changed her mind.

Since slow dancing seemed uncomfortable for her, he stepped back. "Hey, how about I get you a glass of wine. The fireworks will be starting soon." Indeed, the bocce games had turned to tag in the semi-dark, the kids wearing glow-in-the-dark bracelets as they darted around people, picnic tables, and trees. Patio lights were turned on at the back of the house and the red, white, and blue decorated cake was half gone. They hadn't indulged, so he took her hand and led her from the plywood floor to the long table.

Her hand relaxed in his, so he figured not dancing was the right move. "You want some cake?" he asked, after pouring four "glugs" worth of white wine into a small solo cup and handing it to her.

"I'm sorry, Jax. I know I got weird just now." She met his gaze, to his relief. In her eyes he spied what looked like discomfort and a little bit of guilt, which wasn't like her at all. Even when they'd been talking about difficult things, she'd always been so... open. Maybe she'd chosen her words, but she'd never been really guarded. But she was now, and he wondered why. What had changed.

The answer was obvious, wasn't it? They'd slept together. And now she was regretting it.

"It's all right. It's been a weird day." He smiled at her, wanting to regain the old comfortable vibe between them. "A good weird," he added. He would concede that having sex complicated things, but that wasn't the same as having regrets. Which he didn't.

Summer took a sip of her wine, then put it down and grabbed the knife for the cake. "Here. Let's get sugar high and forget about it."

Her voice was light, but Jax frowned anyway. She wanted to forget about it? About the weirdness, or about what happened? Was he that forgettable? His ego took a hit as she handed him a small paper plate with a huge piece of cake on it. Now he was getting grumpy, and he grabbed a bottle of beer from a cooler before they found an empty spot at a picnic table in the shadows.

He stabbed at the frosting with his plastic fork.

"You all right?" Summer asked, picking at her cake.

He put down his fork and faced her. "Listen, are we okay? Tonight's just been weird all the way around, and I'm not sure why, unless it has to do with what happened earlier." He kept his voice soft to avoid anyone overhearing. "If you've changed your mind about it, just say so. I'd rather know than dance around it for the next two months."

She stared at her plate and made similar picking motions with her fork, sending crumbs over the bottom of the plate. "It's not that I've changed my mind," she said quietly. "I just realized that being here together, dancing like that... it's not exactly discreet."

Relief sluiced through him and he sat back, his shoulders relaxing. "Oh. Because you work for me, and you don't want people getting the wrong idea... or rather, the right one."

"Not just that." She still didn't look at him, instead stared out at the group laughing and enjoying themselves in the Sullivan's backyard. "It's not that I regret it, Jax. I'm just unsure how to navigate it." She gave up on the cake and put it on the table behind her.

He hesitated, on totally unfamiliar ground, feeling let down at her words and yet somehow feeling the same. What did they do next? He wasn't a big talker about his feelings, but they were going to have to talk to sort this out, and not here at a busy July 4th party.

"Let's go for a walk," he suggested, putting his uneaten cake aside as well.

"But the fireworks are starting soon." She finally turned her head and looked at him, and his heart did this strange thump against his ribs. She was so damned beautiful. In the time he'd known her, rarely had she ever looked sad. She came across as the eternal optimist. But something had changed today. No matter where they went from here, what he really wanted was to put that smile on her face again.

"So we'll go watch them from the wharf, or Memorial Park or something. Let's just get out of here." The party was still going strong, kids were darting around jacked up on sugar and soda, and they could make a quiet exit unseen.

"I guess I can pick up my dish later," she admitted, and blew out a breath. "Okay, let's go."

They skirted around groups of people who were chatting and sipping on drinks, then exited to the quiet front yard. Cars and trucks lined the curb, both from the party they'd just left and other backyard gatherings, and Jax let out a breath and a good amount of tension with it.

"You too?" Summer asked, looking up at him.

"Me too what?" he asked.

"I'm okay with crowds most of the time, but I'm always relieved when I leave. It surprises people when I say that. Because I'm social, you know? And I generally have a good time. But there's a limit."

"Me too." They headed away from the house and toward the main part of town by tacit agreement. "There's a reason I like history and academia. We're mostly all closet introverts, who pretend to be extroverted when we're together. But we're just as happy with our nose in a research book or studying maps and artifacts as we are... I don't know. Eating canapes and drinking twelve-year Scotch. Though that is more the scene at home. A Brodie Biotech cocktail party. In the history department we might have Scotch or wine or mead and—" He broke off when she started to chuckle. "Sorry. I started babbling. I do that when I'm nervous."

She nudged his arm. "You didn't say a lot this morning. You weren't nervous?"

Something warm coiled within him at the reminder of how they spent their morning. "Actually, no. I didn't take time to overthink it."

Summer blew out a breath. The earlier cloud and light fog had cleared, a few stars started to peek through the dark curtain of the sky, and the air around them eased. "I think maybe *you* started overthinking, though, when we arrived at the party," he added. "I'm just not sure why."

They reached Main Street and began the journey along the sidewalk. Music and laughter came from the pub and the green spaces nearing the harbor; people waiting for the fireworks that would be set off from a barge out in the bay. They passed a group setting up lawn chairs just below the Three Fishermen Art Gallery, a soft-sided cooler in the middle of the group. Somewhere he heard a fiddle tuning up, a laugh, and then a jig start. "I've never been anywhere so very East Coast," he admitted. "It's fun. Comfortable."

"It's community," Summer replied. "I can't imagine living anywhere else."

He considered her words as they strolled toward Memorial Square. The area wasn't large, but it was back a street from the harbor and less likely to be as congested as the waterfront while still providing a decent view. "You've lived her a long time," he mused, reaching down and taking her hand. No one they knew would see them now, in the dark, would they? And why did they have to hide away a simple hand clasp? She didn't pull away, but her last words reminded him that in a matter of weeks their paths would be diverging. She'd stay here, he'd go back to his life at the college.

He would miss her.

They reached the small park. A handful of people sat, waiting for fireworks, but there was a free bench facing Edward Jewell's statue. He led her there and they took their places on the bench. Summer pulled out her phone and checked the time. "It shouldn't be long."

"This is nicer than a crowd," Jax said, crossing an ankle over his knee, trying to relax while deciding where to take the conversation, as it seemed Summer wasn't interested in initiating discussion about the two of them. "Summer, I understand the need you feel for discretion. But you know we didn't do anything wrong, right?"

She nodded, letting out a sigh. "I know. When I first went up to Refuge Point, all I wanted was a job to help me get through until I started school in the fall. I didn't expect to find a friend—"

"Just a friend?" he interrupted.

"—and to find myself attracted to him. I'm no saint, Jax, but I keep work and my personal life separate. Or I did, until now."

"I'm guessing this is leading to you saying that this can't happen again." He was utterly deflated, even though he understood completely.

"I don't know. I mean..." She paused, sighed again. "I need this job and I don't want to screw it up. But truthfully, I like you. A lot. And you're leaving again in September. I just—"

"Don't want to get hurt."

She frowned. "Don't put words in my mouth, or interrupt me."

Heat rushed up his cheeks. "Sorry." The apology was sincere. Interrupting wasn't his style, but he was nervous. And that, too, was a new sensation.

"It's not about getting hurt, not really." She turned on the bench to face him. "I'm not looking for something serious. Or a commitment of any sort. I have a plan for my life, you see. So it's more about..." She stopped, furrowed her brows. "Managing expectations. Being clear, I suppose about what this is and what it isn't."

"It isn't love," he clarified, knowing he should be relieved and somehow feeling a tiny bit resentful. He knew he shouldn't. They'd known each other a short time. Slept together once. Of course it wasn't love. But it might feel nice to *be* loved. Or think it possible.

There must have been something in his voice that gave him away, though, because she softened and leaned against his arm. "Oh Jax, I'm sorry. I've been so uptight tonight. There's been a ton going on in my head, and it mostly has to do with me, and not you."

"Ouch."

She laughed a little. "Not in that way. You haven't done a single thing wrong. In fact, you've done everything maybe a little too right. And..." She bit down on her lip, stared out at the darkness. "I'll confess that scares me a little. It makes me question things about myself, is all. And I hate having to dig too deeply into my own motivations and, well, foibles, I guess."

Jax lifted his arm and put it around her, pulling her closer to ward off the evening chill and to perhaps comfort them both. The first of the fireworks began, sparkling and trailing in bright colors through the sky. "Me too," he murmured, close to her hair. "You've been right about a lot of things about me so far. It's disconcerting how you can read me so well. And I've told you things. Summer, I've let you get close to me and I haven't done that with anyone in years. So you're not the only one feeling off balance here."

"Is it wrong to be glad?" Another pop and then a beautiful array of red and blue sparkles, like a chrysanthemum rained through the darkness. "Jax, I don't love you. But I do care about you. I don't want what happened today to be the only time, if I'm being honest. But you need to know that in September, I'm staying here, I'm going back to school, and whatever is between us this summer will be just that. A summer thing. I don't want you to either have false hopes or worry that I'll get too attached. I won't. And for that reason, I think it might be best if we keep things discreet here in town. I'm not really into PDAs. I also don't want to give rise to gossip."

There was a tone in that last sentence that got his attention. "You've been the subject of it before." It was a statement, not a question.

"Yeah. I had a thing for Josh Collins once. It got around. I got teased a bit, but Josh? I know he did, too. We're not kids."

Summer was so determined to be taken seriously, and why shouldn't she? She was smart, a hard worker, kind. He didn't want to do anything to make her the subject of gossip or ridicule. "I understand totally," he replied. "And no, we're not kids. We're adults who like each other. Who are attracted to each other. It's no one's business but ours."

The fireworks were forgotten as they stared into each other's eyes. Jax's gaze dropped to her full, pink lips and he felt a terrible urge to kiss her, but after her recent comment he would not. Not here in Memorial Square with a handful of other people around. When he lifted his gaze, she was also staring at his lips, and desire flashed through him, as bright as the explosions going off over the harbor.

"Summer," he whispered.

She lifted her eyes, caught his heated stare, and flushed. "Let's watch the show," she said, turning her face to the sky.

But he knew he'd rather watch her, and the way the light flickered over her skin with each colorful burst. Setting ground rules was all well and good, but things could change in eight weeks.

He'd just have to make sure they didn't.

Chapter Eleven

Summer's heart wouldn't stop pounding, and it had nothing to do with the fireworks display high in the sky over Jewell Cove.

It had everything to do with the man sitting beside her. Somehow setting parameters to their relationship had eased the tension in one way and ratcheted it up in another. She was far too aware of him. He'd looked at her lips and she'd felt so drawn to him, craved his kiss and nearly leaned in to claim it. Then he'd said her name and she'd looked up and it was like they were back in her apartment this morning, in that fragment of time before he'd taken her in his arms. Electric. She was sorely tempted to slide over onto his lap and kiss away the serious expression on his face, but they were in the park, there were other people present, and she'd just finished saying she wasn't into making out in public. So she sat back, resting against the back of the bench, and forced herself to look at the fireworks.

They were splendid, but she didn't really enjoy them. She was distracted, far too aware of the man beside her. The shadowed figure of her ancestor was before her, staring down with a formidable expression, and guilt slid over her skin. Just a few days ago, Jax had lamented that the documentary was missing balance because there was no modern-day take on Edward Jewell. And here she was, sitting on that family secret that could help his project, and she refused to say anything.

Did she even have a good reason? She was smart enough to know that she wasn't "tainted" by a man's actions a hundred and fifty years ago. At the same time, bringing any attention to herself meant revealing her own past. Putting her in even a small spotlight was uncomfortable. No one, other than Abby and Jax, knew about her mother and father. She was that poor orphan who had lived with her grandparents, but the people of Jewell Cove didn't see her as the daughter of a junkie and criminal. But they would. It would come out somehow, wouldn't it?

She could help him but wouldn't to protect herself, and she didn't like that, not one bit. Not when her whole life she'd consistently tried to be kind, generous. To be the antithesis of her parents. To help where she could; no job too small or menial. Pride wasn't really her thing... or was it? Was it pride, or its counterpart, shame, that drove her to "be a good person?"

She turned her head, feeling guilty about keeping the secret, wondering if she could find a way to tell him, when she caught him watching not the fireworks but her. The pull between them was so strong; Summer didn't give a damn about the show and simply wanted to be with him again. To feel so incredibly alive and wanted and cherished. She hungered for it, for him. And so she said nothing, but stood and held out her hand.

He took it, and they left the park, heading in the direction of her apartment.

The next morning dawned bright and clear, the sun beaming in through Summer's windows. She rolled to her side and found the other side of the bed empty, the sheets rumpled and the pillow with a dent the precise shape of Jax's head.

They'd come back here while the fireworks were still going on; heard the pop and sizzle of them as they struggled out of their clothes and fell onto the bed. The celebration ended before they did, the quiet of the town enveloping them in a private silence as they explored each other. Even then, they weren't sated. They'd awakened in the middle of the night, too, and indulged their desires.

Summer didn't remember the last time she'd had this much sex or when she'd enjoyed it so much. Jax seemed to instinctively know what she liked, leaving her satisfied and her senses reeling. She'd slept like the dead after, but now she was disappointed he was gone. She hadn't taken him for the kind of guy to slip out in the morning like a dirty secret.

Then there was a sound at the front door, an opening and closing, and moments later he appeared in the bedroom doorway carrying two takeaway cups and a paper bag from the bakery.

"Good morning," he said softly, a sweet smile on his lips, and the world righted again. This was the kind of man she'd expected him to be. Not one to run out, and not one to make false grand gestures, but one to bring a simple cup of tea and what she hoped was a delicious pastry, because she was starving.

"Good morning," she answered shyly, sitting up and pulling the light sheet up to her armpits. "I didn't hear you get up."

"I tried to be quiet. You, uh, needed your rest." His cheeks turned ruddy, and a smile crept up her face. It was sweet, seeing him be a little bashful.

She wiggled her fingers toward the cup. "That smells amazing. Hand it over. I need to get my head on straight before we go to work today."

"Right," he said, coming forward and handing her one of the beverages. She realized he was wearing the same clothes as yesterday; he was the one doing the "walk of shame" through Jewell Cove, and she rather liked the reversal. A sip from the cup revealed a slightly sweet raspberry herbal. Jax took a napkin from the bag and placed a lemon blueberry scone on it, the glaze still soft and warm. "You are hitting me in all the right places," she said, taking a nibble.

"Hmm," he replied, sending her a heated look. "You said that last night, too."

She bit on her lip. "Believe it or not, I'm not used to morning after banter."

"I'm glad. To be honest, I'm not either." He sat on the edge of the bed and took a sip of his own coffee. "Listen, we're good, right? I mean, this thing between us is pretty intense. But we agree: this is just between us, and at the end of the summer, we both know what's going to happen. I don't want to hurt you in any way, Summer. If you don't think we can do this knowing how it's going to end, I'd rather stop it now."

The smile slipped from her lips, and she nodded. "Yeah. I don't want either of us to get hurt. If we're both okay with this being a summer fling, would it be so bad to just enjoy each other?"

"No." He sent her a secretive smile, one that she was starting to realize was just for her.

"Good." She took a big drink of the tea and let the idea of the two of them settle. "So let me get up and shower, and we'll head to your place. There are details to put together in your editing schedule that I want to confirm before next week."

It was important, she realized, to move forward and establish a new dynamic between them. This was the first job she'd had that wasn't retail or food service; even the job at the school was lunchroom supervision and a little academic support. The last thing she wanted was to put her credibility into the toilet because she'd slept with her boss. She was good at this job, even the spreadsheets.

"I'll go ahead of you," he suggested. "Shower at the house."

"That sounds perfect." And a good start for establishing boundaries.

It didn't take long for her to clean up and dress. She braided her damp hair and grabbed her purse, then remembered her phone and shoved it in a pouch in her bag. The drive to the lighthouse seemed different somehow. Like she wasn't just going to work, but that she was going to see him, and she'd just seen him less than an hour before.

Jax was true to his word though, and she was glad of it. When she arrived his hair was still wet and the scent of his fresh aftershave followed in his wake, but he shifted into professional mode and they launched into the day's tasks. And while Summer was filled with a new, different sort of awareness of him, it was far more comfortable than she expected. It was a massive load off her mind. She heard Jax start a virtual meeting and continued on with managing his calendar and working on the production schedule.

She took him a cup of coffee at ten-thirty, then made a list of the housekeeping chores that needed doing. Honestly, her job was not difficult, and if not for the combined roles, there wouldn't be enough to keep her busy. Jax's spreadsheets might have been a bit sloppy when she started, but he was incredibly adept at keeping balls in the air and not dropping any when it came to work. Moreover, he was even more efficient since he'd stopped trying to micromanage everything and delegated better, leaving her with less to do.

Once a load of laundry was started, she made them sandwiches for lunch: turkey and provolone for him, and a stack of vegetables and cheese for her with a delicious aioli from the fridge. They ate at the outside patio, listening to the waves crash on the shore and the gulls circling overhead.

"Productive morning?"

"Very." He smiled at her. "You?"

"Your calendar filled up for next week, but I made sure nothing was booked past Friday at noon. Your flight's scheduled and I wanted to make sure you had time to pack and drive to Portland."

"Right." His smile faded.

"Is seeing your family so bad?"

Jax shook his head. "No. But I hate these society things. I always feel like I'm on display. I agree the causes are important, but the fanfare seems..." He frowned, sighed. "Pretentious."

Summer put down her sandwich. "Jax, you are perhaps the least pretentious rich person I have ever met."

That made him laugh. "I like how you added 'rich' to that. You're not wrong, but I'll tell you a secret." He leaned forward. "Other than funding for the documentaries, I haven't touched my trust fund. Not for my personal use. My house, my car... I make a good salary at the college."

She lifted an eyebrow. "Maybe, but you grew up rich. And I bet you don't have any student debt."

He nodded. "Yeah, you've got me there. I've been incredibly privileged. I guess I just... I don't want you to think I'm careless.

Honestly, I'm saving most of my trust fund for my own kids. Presuming I ever have any."

Summer had finished most of her sandwich and pushed the plate away. "I wouldn't have anything to pass on to my kids even if I did want them." Since they weren't going to see each other after this summer, there was no harm in being blunt. "I can't see me being the mom type, or you know, that cliché American dream of two parents and a couple of kids and a house in the 'burbs. I have enough of a problem providing for myself."

He didn't seem offended or turned off by her admission. "I don't think it's unusual for people raised in difficult circumstances to wonder if they want to venture down that path themselves. I'm not sure I do, to be honest. Watching what my parents went through with Matt's illness, his death... They invested so much of their hearts and time into him and were utterly devastated. Losing a child... It's an unbearable loss."

"I think of my maternal grandparents sometimes," Summer admitted, her heart unusually heavy. "Until I was twelve, I visited occasionally, and when I got back my grandparents here were always tense. They'd ask me for all kinds of details and made me feel like if I said anything nice, I was betraying them. But at the same time, it was the only way I felt connected to my mom at all. My grandmother...she said I looked like her. Then they stopped visiting, and that was that."

"God. I'm sorry. It sucks when kids are caught in the middle. What about now? Have you made contact again?"

She shook her head. "No. What's the point?"

"The point is they're your family."

But Summer wasn't sure she agreed. When her mother died, they'd decided she was too much bother. Perhaps her paternal grandparents hadn't been as kind or nurturing as she might have liked, but at least they hadn't turned her away, even when their son died and wouldn't be coming to get her. They had, as they reminded her frequently, put a roof over her head and food on the table.

"All the family I need is here in Jewell Cove. The only consistency I've ever had in my life has been here. I don't need anything more than that."

Jax picked up his water glass and took a drink rather than replying. Summer toyed with the crust of her sandwich, and wondered if she truly meant those last words. Because if she didn't, it meant her life was not as full as she pretended.

To Jax's astonishment, he and Summer fell into a routine that was perfect.

They spent the weekend together, spending Friday night at the house and waking on Saturday morning to sunlight streaming through the windows and a bright blue sky beckoning them outside. After a lazy breakfast in bed, they rose and Summer took him to see bits of Jewell Cove—a morning walk on Fiddler's Beach, delicious scallops and fish at lunch time from Battered Up on the waterfront, an easy hike to the top of Blackberry Hill, past Abby and Tom's mansion to the summit where the panoramic view of the town and the cove spread out before them, sparkling and fresh. They spent Saturday night at Summer's, not quite as comfortable without the air conditioning, but then Sunday they drove out of Jewell Cove to Pemaquid Beach, where they spent the late morning and early afternoon in and out of the water, lazing on the sand, and grabbing a late lunch at the nearby restaurant. Summer couldn't remember being so relaxed and comfortable with anyone, or when she'd laughed so much. Over Jax's lobster roll and her red pepper hummus wrap, they talked about documentaries he'd already done, shared stories of their students—hers in elementary school and his in college, and the surprising similarities between them.

They drove down to the point and took pictures of the Pemaquid lighthouse, then indulged Jax's historian streak and stopped at Fort William Henry, wandering through the museum until it closed at five and then strolling through the grounds. When the air started to cool and the sun grew hazy, Jax drove her home, where she threw together a simple pasta dish for a light dinner. Tonight Jax would go home to Refuge Point, and she'd stay at her apartment, and they'd go back to business tomorrow morning.

But as Summer sat next to him, sipping a glass of cool white wine, she realized she hadn't had such a lovely weekend in a very long time—if ever.

"Jax, this weekend… it was perfect. Thank you. The hikes yesterday, and the beach and fort today… More than that, too. I laughed a lot. I just want to say thank you."

There were other things that had been great, too. Like the sex. Like waking up next to him three mornings in a row now, curling up to his warmth and the scent of his skin, sleepy and soft. Her body hummed from the physicality of their days together; the touch of his hands and press of his body against hers, the cool slide of the ocean as they swam and dipped in the waves, the sweet sheen of sweat when they reached the top of Blackberry Hill. Tonight she knew she would sleep like the dead, because her body and her heart were so relaxed.

"It was for me, too," he answered, putting down his ice water. He reached for her hand. "Tomorrow is back to work for both of us. But this was nice." He grinned. "More than nice. Nice is such a bland word. I had a great time with you."

"Maybe next weekend we can do something else. There are tons of museums, or we could hike Mount Battie, or do a sailing tour—"

"I'm home next weekend, remember?"

Her smile faded. "Oh, right. Never mind. I got carried away." She smiled sheepishly.

Jax looked like he was about to say something, but he halted, then put his hands on his knees and got up from the sofa. "I should go. But I'll see you bright and early tomorrow?"

"Absolutely."

"I have a scheduled trip out to the site tomorrow. Would you like to come? See what filming this is all about? It's one of the more challenging shoots. We're doing some stuff in the caves."

She loved that he'd invited her, and after days of dealing with calendars and administrative details, it would be fun to see things in action. "I'd love to."

"Meet me at the waterfront parking lot at nine, then. Rick will take the crew out, but we'll be on a different boat. I'm not planning to stay the entire morning, but this is probably the trickiest day of shooting and the weather's supposed to be fine."

"I'll be there."

"Meanwhile, I should go. Or else I won't, and that wasn't what we agreed."

It wasn't. He'd already parked his car outside her house two of the last three nights. It was wishful thinking someone wouldn't notice.

"Don't get up," he murmured, as she moved to put her glass on the table. "I'll see you tomorrow." And then he leaned over and dropped a light kiss on her lips before heading to her door.

"See you tomorrow," she murmured back, though she doubted he heard her. It didn't matter, though. She took another mouthful of wine and basked in the glow of the wonderful weekend. It couldn't last; she knew that. But damn, she could get used to these sorts of moments of perfection.

Chapter Twelve

Jax shifted from foot to foot waiting for Summer. When he finally spied her, walking through the parking lot wearing a windbreaker and sunglasses, he let out a breath of relief. He was anxious to get this show on the road. Today was an exciting day. They were filming in the caves, the site of the biggest part of the treasure. And not the jewels and gold. The logs of names and dates that had been kept hidden for over a hundred years—of those who traveled this way on the Underground Railroad and those who helped them. Including the founders of Jewell Cove.

"Sorry if I kept you waiting!" Summer jogged along the paved lot, consternation showing on her face. "My water died this morning and I was dealing with my landlord, and then I lost track of time."

"Everything okay?"

She nodded. "I hope so." She gave her shoulders and arms a shake, as if shedding the stress of the morning. "Are we ready?"

A woman of maybe thirty-five was at the wheel of the boat that Jax had chartered. "Good morning," she said cheerfully. "There's a little more chop than we expected this morning, so I hope you don't have light stomachs. Beautiful day, though. Keep an eye out for whales. There've been a number of seals on the east side of Aquteg, too, so you never know. Shark sightings have become a lot more frequent."

Jax's eyes widened with alarm and Summer grinned. "They're after the seals, not you, silly," she said, jostling his arm and settling herself at the rail. The boat gave a small jolt as they began to move, then smoothed out as they exited the harbor. The smoothness didn't last long, though. As the boat moved toward open water, the twenty-four footer crested the waves, jolting in a rhythmic motion. Summer held onto the rail, then, as the dips became more pronounced, she sat on one of the leather seats, the wind whipping her blue nylon jacket and blowing her hair around her face.

He'd never met a woman so game for anything.

It was impossible to carry on a conversation over the sound of the engine, the water, and the wind, so he sat in the opposite seat and thought about the past few days. It hadn't mattered what he'd suggested, she'd been there with a "yeah, let's do it!" answer. He'd never imagined her an outdoor girl, either, but hiking the hills and frolicking at the beach had been simple and fun. She'd been equally happy to listen to him prattle on about lighthouses and then explore the fort with him, even though he'd become nerdy historian for a while. Now she was bouncing along in a boat on the way to a documentary shoot. He'd never met anyone with such a thirst for life before—and yet with such a hesitancy for getting close to people.

Because as much fun as they'd had, and as mind-blowing as the sex had been, there was something about herself that she held back. They'd agreed this was a summer affair, and he was fine with that, but he got the sense that she was desperate to have it so. That she was afraid of caring too much.

Considering her background, he got it. Hell, he was much the same way. But while he wasn't interested in falling in love, he wasn't desperate to avoid it.

"We're heading into rougher water now," the woman said, turning her head toward them. "Sorry!"

It wasn't horrible; the ride was bumpy but facing into the waves kept Jax from feeling ill and Summer looked all right, too. The island came into view, and they passed the dock where Rick normally dropped the crew, heading southeast around the island, along the rocky shoreline. The boat slowed a little as they approached, and Jax spied several seals sunning themselves on gray boulders. He pointed, and Summer got up from her seat, going to the rail and hanging on as she took in the shoreline.

He joined her. It wasn't quite as rough here, and he always liked the feel of the wind in his hair and standing on a boat deck rather than sitting. "Aren't they cute?" she asked, turning to him and smiling. It was hard to see her eyes behind her sunglasses, but her lips were turned up with pleasure.

He went to the woman at the wheel. "When we get close, skirt us around the rest of the crew and the other two boats, as quietly as you can. I don't want to interrupt a shot. It's going to be challenging enough without me wrecking anything."

"You got it."

She did exactly as he asked, heading a bit north as the crew came into view, and then bringing them in slowly and quietly. Jax directed her to pull alongside Bryan's boat, where he was watching from a monitor. The film crew was in a zodiac with the host, Sam, inside the cave, with handheld cameras. Rick's boat, *Mary's Delight*, was anchored a few hundred yards away, the rest of the tech crew on board.

Bryan was watching a monitor intently, so Jax held his tongue until the other man relaxed. "How's it going?" he called across, when Bryan gave him a thumbs up.

Bryan came to the side. "It could be better. The tide is higher than I anticipated, and it's worse because of how rough it is. Sam's struggling a bit, and the rocks are slippery so it's just slow going. But we knew it was going to be a challenge. The light and sound in there is shit."

Summer joined him at the rail. "Hi, Bryan." Her smile seemed slightly more forced, and Jax wondered why.

"Good morning, Ms. Arnold."

"Summer's never seen any of the filming," Jax explained. "I figured this was as good a day as any to bring her along. Show her what it's all about."

"Weatherwise maybe. She won't see much, though, with the crew in the cave." He looked over at Summer. "Sorry."

"Oh, don't be!" Her face brightened. "I've been working on the project for a while, is all, and I've been curious about how this all works. Don't mind me."

Bryan relaxed and for a few minutes Jax talked to him about the challenges of the day. But when Bryan mentioned a few of his ideas for smoothing out the process, Jax took a mental step back. "Whatever you think is best, Bryan. It's worth a try."

Bryan paused for a moment, looking a bit stunned, before he recovered and nodded, relief on his features. "Good, right. We'll try that, then. Do you want to come aboard and watch the monitors?"

With some finagling, Summer and Jax managed to move from their boat to Bryan's, and joined him in the wheelhouse where they could see the filming. He lifted a radio to his mouth and gave some instructions, and Jax stood back and let him do his job. The next take was better, the angle lending extra clarity and an improvement in lighting. "That looks good," Jax said, clapping Bryan on the shoulder.

"I trust my camera people," Bryan said, satisfied.

"And I trust you." Jax held out his hand for Bryan to shake. "I know I have a tendency to micromanage, but truly, you got this job because you're damned good, and I trust that. Honestly, Bryan, I think it's me I don't trust. Not fair to put that on you and the crew."

"No worries, boss. We know what your vision is for this thing. Let us give it to you."

They chatted a few more moments about the cave shoot, and then Bryan spoke up. "We thought we'd take tomorrow doing some B-roll in town. Maybe the statue of Jewell in the square, that sort of thing. Some landmark footage we can use for voice-over. It's just a damn shame there's not more for Edward Jewell, since he's the town's namesake. This is slanted so much toward Arseneault and Collins."

"I know. The trail just dried up after the war. Lines died out. That's going to have to be our angle. Perhaps that money and legacy don't guarantee a man's longevity."

They returned their attention to the monitors and setting up the next take and had been chatting so long that Jax didn't notice Summer retreat to the back of the boat. He turned his head and saw her now, leaning over the side. When she lifted her head, she was white as a ghost.

He slipped out of the wheelhouse and went to her. "Hey, you all right?"

She swallowed, pursed her lips, and blew out a breath. "Not really. I don't usually get seasick, but I think it's because we're stopped and just rocking." At the word she looked a little green, gulped in some breaths, and clenched the rail.

"Focus on the horizon, not the water," he suggested. "Hang on. I'll see if we can transfer back over and head back to Jewell Cove."

"No, don't! I don't want to cut your day short. I'll be okay." She smiled weakly. "Promise."

"Summer." He put his hand on her arm, the stiff nylon of the windbreaker crackling beneath his fingers. "I talked to Bryan, I saw some shots, and I trust them. I don't have to be here. I'll do a run-down with him tonight and review the day's footage. Then we can decide if we need another day or have what we need."

"I'm just jealous you're not sick," she muttered, a grumpy note to her voice.

"I'm surprised I'm not," he responded. "And it's probably because I was focused on what was going on. Give me a few minutes and we'll get on the move, if you can hold tight until the crew takes a quick break again."

It was nearly twenty minutes before another break. Summer was looking quite a bit worse for wear by the time they were back on their own boat and the engine was fired up to make an exit. The pilot handed over a bottle of sport drink and told Summer to sip at it and that once they got moving she'd feel better. Summer sat in the seat and dutifully sipped as they began cresting waves again. The change from the slow, lateral rocking helped put spots of color back in her cheeks, and Jax hoped she was feeling better. Truth be told, he'd gotten a bit queasy himself.

They hadn't been traveling long when the boat slowed and the woman at the wheel turned it in a wide, slow circle. They weren't far from the island and Jax was about to go forward to see if something was the matter when she lifted her left hand and pointed.

Summer had been sick on this trip, but maybe it could be salvaged by a whale sighting. He squinted and scanned the water.

The pilot pulled back on the throttle even more, which made Jax wonder if Summer would feel sick again, but just as he turned to check on her, he saw a dorsal fin cut the surface maybe a hundred yards away.

Summer appeared at his elbow, still holding the sport drink but her eyebrows perked up in interest. "What is it? What do you see?"

The engines were quiet enough now that they could hear the pilot. "Shark. Could be a mako, could be a great white. I'll be able to tell better if it gets any closer."

Jax realized he was holding his breath, waiting for that dorsal fin to break the surface again. Summer, too, clutched his forearm. "A shark. Oh my God, this is so cool."

"I take it you're feeling better?" he asked, glancing over at her.

"Much. My head's a little weird and my stomach is touchy, but once we got moving and I had some Gatorade, I felt a lot better."

"Except we're stopped again."

"It's worth it." Her voice held a note of excitement. "Hey, do you suppose if I get sick again it'll be like chum in the water?"

He started laughing. "Gross."

"I couldn't help it. I've already lost all my dignity." But she was smiling.

"There," called the pilot sharply, pointing behind them. "Keep watching." She kept her hand on the wheel, ready to shift position. But the shark was curious, and Jax watched with utter fascination as it came within ten feet of the boat, gliding stealthily through the water with such grace he was awed.

"It's half the length of the boat, at least," Summer whispered beside him. "Holy shit." The sun glinted off a flash of white belly. "Jax, that's a great white!"

The pilot was grinning widely. She'd pulled out her phone and started videotaping a few seconds earlier, trying to get a decent shot. To her delight, the shark turned and crossed the bow, giving her a clear few seconds of footage. "This is awesome," she exclaimed. "First sighting I've had this year. I'll report it once we're back in Jewell Cove."

"I've never seen one before." Summer was nearly dancing in her excitement. "I've seen whales. I once saw a humpback breach and that was amazing. But this... so freaking cool."

Jax laughed. "I think the shark sighting is cooler than the documentary shoot."

A funny look enveloped her face, as if she'd committed a horrible faux pas. "I didn't mean that," she explained, but he waved her awkwardness away.

"It's all good, Summer. I was just teasing."

The pilot started them up again now that the shark had disappeared below the surface, and pointed them toward home.

When they arrived back in the harbor, Jax helped Summer off the boat and then suggested they stop at the café for something light since she now had an empty stomach. Breezes was doing a brisk business even though the lunch rush was still a half hour or so away. When Summer suggested they get iced drinks and cinnamon buns, he didn't object. They got their food to go and sat outside on a bench overlooking the wharf, watching boats come and go, sailboats sliding across the neck of the cove and heading out into more open water. This town was growing on him; he understood why Summer loved it so much. Right now, breathing deeply of the salt air, watching the sails and birds, and sipping on iced coffee with a beautiful woman... Life didn't get much better than this.

The old guilt started to slide in again, but he pushed it away, tamped it down. Matt wasn't here and he never would be. And for the first time Jax could actually remember, he wanted to feel happy without the albatross of his grief and guilt around his neck.

Was it so wrong to want things for himself?

Summer had some sort of iced tea in her cup, a pinkish-red liquid that looked sweet and refreshing. He watched as she peeled off a section of cinnamon bun and popped it in her mouth, closing her eyes and smiling a little at the taste. Summer knew how to enjoy things. She knew how to live in the moment. Maybe that was the biggest lesson she was teaching him this summer. To let go and live a little.

At times it scared the hell out of him. But not enough to make him run. And that was perhaps because the time for them to be together was finite. It took a lot of pressure off, if he were being honest with himself.

Summer licked some sticky cinnamon and sugar from her thumb and looked over at Jax. He had his sunglasses on, and he was relaxed, looking out over the water. She was starting to feel much better now that she was on land, though the dull feeling in her head persisted. Eating a full lunch was out of the question, but she was hungry—losing her breakfast over the side had made sure of that.

She was horribly embarrassed about it, though Jax seemed to take it in his stride. And while the shark sighting had been amazing, she'd been extremely relieved when they had got underway again, at a decent speed so that they skimmed the waves rather than undulated on them.

Her stomach flip-flopped just thinking about it, so she took a sip of her raspberry hibiscus iced tea and then broke off another piece of her cinnamon bun.

What she was really thinking about now was how he'd handled things with his director this morning, and how pleased she was.

"Hey, Jax?"

"Hmm?"

They were getting lazy in the sunshine, a warm, languid feeling that was perhaps her favorite feeling of summer. "What you said to Bryan this morning... is it weird for me to say 'good job?'"

He turned to her and frowned. "Good job for what?"

"Your conflict from a few weeks ago, you know? He nearly quit because you were too hands on. Today, one of the hardest days of filming, according to you, anyway, you backed off and trusted him to do his job. You showed you trusted his judgment and didn't try to take over, even though I'm guessing you wanted to."

"Yeah. I was tempted for a minute, wanting to be the one in the cave, and then I realized that it's not my job to get in the way or slow things down, especially on a day where every moment matters."

"Progress," she said simply, smiling, and popping another bit of pastry in her mouth.

"Doesn't mean I liked it, though," he replied, a bit grumbly. "I do wish I could be more hands on with it."

"Then why don't you do something different with your next project? You own the production company, right? But why don't you narrate it and hire a producer to do what you do? You've got a good voice."

"A good voice doesn't mean I can host a show," he replied. "I'd probably need to do some voice training."

There was a hint of enthusiasm in his tone, though, and Summer wondered if she'd planted a seed. "Look, you told me you're passionate about telling these unknown stories. You've never said you were passionate about financing and management. So perhaps the best thing is to be the storyteller. I'm just sayin'."

"I'll take that under advisement," he stated, a bit dryly, and she chuckled. Then he nudged her elbow. "You're feeling better?"

"Much. So much for having sea legs. Thank you for taking me though. It really was super interesting. We didn't get to see any actual filming though—or at least I didn't because I was busy at the back of the boat." She made a wry face. "Could I look at... what do you call them, the dailies? The footage from today. See how it turned out?"

"Sure. I won't get anything until after dinner, probably. If you want to stay."

"I have a roasted cauliflower dish I wanted to try." She laughed when he made a face.

"I'll eat it, but only because you actually seem to know what you're doing with this vegetarian thing. I'll be a tough sell, though. Cauliflower smells like farts and doesn't taste much better."

She laughed again, delighted at his sense of humor. "Challenge accepted. Should we head to the house? There's a ton of stuff on my to-do list that I want to cross off before the end of the day."

"Sure." He gathered up their garbage and found a wastebasket while she waited for him. The temptation was there to reach for his hand as they walked to his car, but she reminded herself that they were keeping things professional during work hours, and those boundaries had to be maintained.

She wanted to, though. And the thought both pleased and annoyed her. Being attracted to someone was one thing, but genuinely liking them? That had the potential to lead her into dangerous territory.

Chapter Thirteen

The next few days only made Summer like Jax even more. Not once did he challenge the boundaries they'd set for work. It was almost like their dynamic before, but with an added layer of familiarity between them. It was as if they both carried the knowledge that they weren't just coworkers, but instead of getting in the way, it made their work relationship even smoother. She wondered if it was because they'd got to know each other so much better during the previous weekend's downtime.

Whatever the cause, they quickly seemed to settle into a routine. She made coffee or tea in the morning and they worked in their respective spaces, only chatting if they needed to consult with one another. Around noon she saved all her work and put together a light lunch for them both, and they ate either in the kitchen or out on the patio if the day was clear. The afternoons she dedicated to household chores, meal planning, and errands, unless there was something clerical that needed her attention; those tasks always came first. And they ate dinner together at the end of the day, talking not only about work but about Jewell Cove and life in general.

The part Summer didn't like? Going home. She hated leaving in the evenings, especially since on Monday she'd stayed late to watch the day's footage and then they'd shared a few too many kisses by the front door before she actually managed to go. But keeping it professional during the week was what they'd agreed and sticking to their plans was paramount. Kissing by the door was one thing. Staying over was something totally different.

Until Thursday afternoon, when she was in the laundry room folding a load of towels and she heard Jax shutting cupboard doors rather loudly and muttering to himself. Summer placed a soft towel in the laundry basket and then made her way to the kitchen, only to find Jax standing by the kitchen window with a glass of water. His stiff posture suggested he was agitated, and she wondered what had happened to wind him up.

"Hey," she said, entering the room. "You okay?"

He turned and she saw his jaw was tight. Clearly something had happened.

"Yeah, I'm just tense, I guess. I'm not looking forward to this thing tomorrow. I just got off the phone with my mom. She means well, but—" He shook his head. "She does mean well. I know that."

"But there are demands being placed on you for Saturday?" She'd nearly forgotten he was headed to Philadelphia tomorrow. "It's just a reception, isn't it? And brunch."

"She wondered if I'd say a few words at the dedication."

"Well, you teach for a living, so I'm guessing you're not shy about speaking. So it must be about Matt, and your feelings about him that have you tied up in knots."

He let out a breath. "And the fact that each time I speak to my folks, another layer of involvement in the weekend gets added. First it's come to the reception. Then it's brunch on Sunday. Now it's say a few words."

Summer's heart ached for him. He found this so difficult, and she understood, because what if someone asked her to speak to a bunch of people about, well, parents with drug addiction or being orphaned? She would rather do just about anything else. Jax had so much survivor's guilt that for him, speaking to a bunch of rich people and medical professionals about childhood cancer was like a hundred little cuts to his heart.

"I gather it didn't go well."

"We argued," he admitted. "And it got a little..." He sighed, ran his hand through his hair. "She hit me where it hurts the most. Do this for your brother. Your father will be so disappointed."

"Ouch."

"Yeah, ouch. But she's not wrong. I said I'd do it. Look, I've done a lot to disappoint my dad, so I'd rather not add to the list."

"Are you sure? About your dad, I mean. I can't imagine anyone being disappointed in how you turned out." She offered a smile and moved forward, placing a hand on his arm in reassurance.

"Yeah, I'm sure. It doesn't matter. Mom was right. I can do this for my brother."

Summer heard the pain in his voice, and she slid her hand down to his hand and squeezed. "You idolized Matt, didn't you?"

He nodded. "He was my best friend when we were little. We did everything together, though he was a few years older so he had to show me a lot. And he was patient when I needed time to catch up or couldn't do something. He was my hero, Summer."

"Then say that. Tell everyone he was your hero. Celebrate the legacy he's leaving behind—this amazing cancer wing so that other kids might have a fighting chance. It doesn't have to be long."

"I'm just... I'm the odd one out though, you see? Dad's company, Mom's expertise... all science and health care. And then me, and what do I do? Go chasing treasure in the summers and stand in front of a group of students the rest of the year. What I do doesn't change the world. It doesn't save anyone's life or... aw, fuck it."

Summer lifted her hand to his face, cradling his jaw in her palm, reminding herself to tread carefully. "Why do you have to change the world?"

"Because he would have."

Summer considered that. "And if you don't, then what? You're a failure?"

He stared at her. "Relatively speaking, yes. Do you know what I heard my dad say a few weeks after Matt died?" Anguish colored his words, made them heavy and dark. "He asked why. Why it had to be Matt. Right. Why was it Matt and not me?"

"I'm sure he didn't mean that." The words hit her like a punch to the gut, but she also wondered if Jax had misheard, or heard out of context. "Don't you think any parent would question why a child was taken?"

He pulled away from her arm, took a few steps away. "Sure. Except he didn't ask why Matt had to die but why it had to be him. You see the difference? It's just begging for the words 'instead of.' I'm the only other kid. I always knew Matt was the shining star of the family. Hell, even I could see he was perfect. Which I, clearly, am not. My dad... we aren't close. My mom tries to smooth it over a lot, but it's strained. So all this family togetherness? It just puts me on edge. Will I do it? Yeah. Because I'll look like a jerk if I don't. But I'm dreading it so very much, Summer. You've no idea."

"I'm sorry," she murmured. She didn't want to offer platitudes, nor did she want to insert herself into his problems by reminding him that at least he had two parents and wasn't all alone in the world. It wasn't a competition. Even if she did feel like he was lucky to have a family.

"Have you ever told them all of this?" she said softly, going to him again.

"Ha. Of course not. Dad would tell me I'm being ridiculous, and Mom would sit and worry, bracing for the time when she needs to smooth things over. My family... we're very good at faking harmony."

"Maybe it's time to stop faking."

"Or maybe I just need to get through it." He sighed. "I'm sorry I dumped all this on you."

"Don't be silly. I don't mind at all." And she didn't, really. Truthfully, this was the closest she'd felt to another human in a very long time, and it felt good. Scary, but good. It was a damned hard thing, craving intimacy with someone but not wanting to go to deep. The deeper she got, the more she risked being left behind, picking up the pieces over and over again. It was no way to live, but she didn't really know how to do anything else. Not one single person in her life had ever stuck around. Jax wouldn't either, but at least she knew it well in advance.

"Maybe..." Jax started, but then he shook his head. "No, never mind."

"Maybe what?" There'd been a note of hope in his voice just now. If talking it through helped, she didn't mind, even if it was still technically their workday.

Jax met her gaze. "Maybe you could come with me. You know, for moral support."

The invitation took her by surprise, and she pulled her brows together. "You mean act as a buffer between you and your parents?"

"Not exactly. That sounds... hmm." He made a sound in his throat. "Maybe it is a little like running interference. I mean, everyone will be on their best behavior if there's an outsider around."

"Wow, you're really selling me on it," she remarked. "I mean, you make it so hard for a girl to refuse."

He smiled a little at her blatant sarcasm. "Point taken. And I don't blame you for not wanting to go. I just had the thought that a wingman might be nice."

That she understood. Even as awkward as last weekend had been, going to the ball game and party had been much nicer with Jax by her side, rather than being the odd person out in a gathering of couples. As much as she thought Jax should just talk to his parents or, better yet, talk to a professional about the effects of his brother's death, she knew she couldn't judge. Not when she had so many unresolved issues of her own surrounding her childhood. What he was really asking for here was a friend. That was hard to refuse, because friends were really important to her. Friends, after all, were her only connections in the world, and she didn't want to take any of them for granted.

"I, uh... I could try to change your plans. See if there's another seat available on the flight. And..." She paused, unsure of how to handle accommodations. "Also check to see if there's another room at the hotel."

Jax came forward and pulled her into his arms. "I can't believe you're thinking of coming. It's like I can breathe again."

"Okay, but Jax, if you're this relieved, I'm wondering what I'm possibly getting myself into." He'd spoken well of his parents even though this particular issue troubled him, but was there more to it?

"No, no. I know I probably made it sound horrible. At worst, Summer, it's strained. I just hate going into these things alone, all trussed up in a suit, smiling and shaking hands and feeling out of my element. Having a friend with me changes everything. Besides, I can show you around, and it'll give me something other than the dedication to think about."

He dropped a kiss on her forehead, then stepped back. "Oh, sorry. It's still our workday. I totally disregarded our rules, didn't I?"

"It's all right." She went to the fridge, took out two beers, and popped the top. "Come on outside and relax for a few minutes. I'll bring the laptop and check to see what I can arrange."

They went outside and Summer opened the laptop as Jax cranked up the patio umbrella, cutting down on the glare so she could see her screen. As she did a search for his flight, she took a sip of the cold beer, letting it slide down her throat. It was hot today, and what she'd really like to do was slap on some sunscreen and soak up some vitamin D. This would do, though. Jax sat and tipped back his bottle, then let out a gusty sigh. "I don't know why I get so wound up over this," he mused.

She looked up from the screen. "Have you thought about talking to someone about it?"

"You mean a therapist?"

"Sure. You've got a lot of feelings about your brother and your place in the family, the burden of expectations... It might be helpful. Just think about it. You deserve to be happy. You've said that you were determined to do what you love, which is history. And that's awesome. Everyone should be able to choose their own path in life and good for you for sticking to it. But it's also cost you in other ways, know what I mean?"

He nodded, turning his bottle on the glass tabletop. "You make a lot of sense, Summer. I guess that's why I hired you."

"And here I thought it was for my cauliflower." The flight information came up and she saw there were still two seats available. She quickly picked one in economy and tried not to blink at the price. "Last minute flights aren't cheap, by the way."

"If there's a seat available, book it." He sent her a crooked smile. "We can always economize by sharing my hotel room."

She clicked the booking button and then met his gaze steadily. "Is that what you want?""Do you? I mean, let's be realistic. If we had two rooms, we'd spend the night in one or the other. But I also understand if you want your own space. Let's just say, the invitation is open."

He wasn't wrong. Maybe she should insist on separate rooms, but why? They'd been super professional all week, and at least for her, the idea that the no-work weekend was approaching was a tantalizing prospect.

"Then I accept," she replied, butterflies fluttering in her stomach at the idea of spending a weekend in a hotel with him. "In the spirit of economy, of course."

"Of course."

They sat back and drank a little more of their beers, until Jax spoke, his voice soft and warm. "Summer? Thank you."

"You're welcome," she answered.

"Oh, and P.S.? The reception is formal. Get out your best dress and shoes."

The moment dinner was over and the kitchen tidied, Summer headed straight to Jess's after sending an SOS text. She'd been so caught up in the idea of the weekend with Jax—and the possibility of family drama—that she hadn't considered her wardrobe. She didn't have a single thing that would suit for a formal event. At the very least, she'd need a fantastic cocktail dress. Something more than most people wore in Jewell Cove.

Jess was in her kitchen when Summer arrived just before eight, and Abby was there too. "I called in reinforcements," Jess explained. "You're closer to Abby's size, and I'm a whiz with a needle and thread if anything needs a quick alteration."

Abby reached for a garment bag that was hanging over a chair. "Okay, Summer, strip."

Summer gaped. "Good gravy, girls. Don't you think you should buy me dinner first?"

Jess giggled. "Cute. But seriously. Off with this." She waved her finger, encompassing Summer's outfit with the motion.

"The boys are over at The Rusty Fern until nine playing darts, Abby got a sitter, and my little one's in bed. That gives us an hour to find you two amazing dresses."

"Two?"

"One for the event, one for brunch. We've got you covered, sister."

She knew the sister was just a solidarity thing, but it warmed her heart just the same. She'd never had sisters, and what she'd thought about the importance of friends earlier was true. The past month or so she'd been a little less social, and she realized that it was because Jax had arrived and stirred up a lot of emotions. It wasn't necessarily a bad thing, but as Abby started to pull out the first dress, Summer realized how much she'd missed easy evenings like this, hanging with the girls. Other than the impromptu breakfast at the café, and the party the other night, she hadn't seen them at all since school let out.

So right there in the kitchen she pulled off her top and skirt and stood in her underwear. Abby held up an empire-waisted floor-length dress in a subdued purply-gray. The high waist sported a jeweled band about two inches tall, giving the plain but pretty gown some necessary sparkle. When she put it on, however, the spaghetti straps and bust didn't fit right.

Jess stepped in and made some tucks, playing with pins to see if she could adjust the fit. "If I take it in here on either side, and then shorten the straps a pinch, it'll fit much better."

Summer liked it, but wasn't sold. "Okay, let's put it in a maybe pile," she replied, turning her back for Abby to unzip her again.

Next up was a pretty floral print in a comfortable and flattering jersey fabric. "This would be lovely for brunch. The V-neck is super flattering, the floral print feminine, and if you pair it with a good pair of heels it's both elegant and not overdone." Abby made the sales pitch while Summer pulled it over her head. The material fell beautifully over her shoulders and hips, and while the wrap-style V gaped a little, Jess merely waved a hand and said, "oh, that's a super easy fix. Two stitches is all it'll take. What do you think?"

Truthfully, Summer loved it. The deep pink in one of the flowers even almost matched the pink stripe in her hair, which was beginning to fade from its original magenta tone to something more like a deep rose. She did a little swish with her hips and the skirt fluttered just above her knees. "Do you have a mirror?"

"Of course I do. Here." She led Summer down the hall and opened a closet door. There was a full-length mirror on the back.

It *was* flattering. It made her bust look a little bigger than usual, her hips slightly curved but not too much. The creamy hue set off her skin and the floral pattern added a gorgeous palette of color. It was the perfect brunch dress.

"Do you have shoes?" Abby asked. "What size are you?"

"Seven and a half," she answered. "And I have some neutral pumps I could wear."

"For a fancy brunch? Perish the thought. Hang on. I'm an eight, but I have a pair of shoes that runs on the small side that might work." Jess's eyes lit up as she went to the stairs and up to her room.

Summer looked at Abby. "I don't know how to thank you guys. My wardrobe is pretty limited. And I'm stupid nervous about brunch. I said I didn't have to go, but Jax said he'd feel awful, leaving me in the hotel room."

Abby smiled and put the previous dress back on the hanger. "Never turn down an opportunity for fancy brunch, especially when someone else is paying," she joked, winking at Summer. "And I know what you mean about limited wardrobes. Jess is the one with the fashion sense. I'm lucky because I inherited so many vintage things—that's in again. And if I need something else, Jess takes me shopping. I wore this to a christening last year."

"You don't think the brunch thing is too...couple-y?"

Abby tilted her head and stared at Summer for a moment. "Well, not if you don't want it to be. What does Jax say?"

"I'm going as a friend. His assistant."

"There you go, then."

Jess came back, a pair of pink pumps in her hand. "Check these out," she said, wiggling them. "I only wore them once and then said not again because they pinched."

Summer slid her left foot into the first shoe—a perfect fit. The right was a little big, and her heel slipped a bit when she tried walking across the kitchen. Jess frowned. "You know, if you put one of those little inserts in, it might be perfect."

"I don't know if I have time to find them... the flight is tomorrow."

Abby bit her lip, thinking. "Maybe you could have some sent to your hotel."

"I have a better idea," said Jess. "Hang on."

She disappeared again and then came back from the downstairs bath holding a small, wrapped square in her hand.

"Is that a... pantyliner?" Summer's mouth was agape, then she closed it and started to giggle.

"I promise, it works." She grabbed a pair of scissors and cut the liner, then stuck it in the shoe to make a heel liner, trimming the excess from the top. "Try it again."

It was a perfect fit.

"You're a genius," Abby declared, shaking her head. "I never would have thought of that."

"Desperate times..." Jess began, and grinned.

"That's one outfit down," Abby said. "We still need a killer dress for Saturday's reception. Summer, you said you have something fine for the hospital dedication, right?"

"I do. Jax said it's not as formal, so I have a great pair of pants and a sleeveless blouse I thought I'd wear, and put my hair up. More of a professional look."

"Perfect. Evening though, you'll want something to knock his eyeballs out." Abby reached into the garment bag again. "I have a cocktail dress in royal blue that will bring out your eyes and give you bangin' curves." She shook the hanger, and Summer looked longingly at the dress, which was deceptively simple with a straight line across the bust and spaghetti straps, and a hemline that would presumably come a good three inches above her knees. "Or I have this."

Both Summer and Jess let out a gasp as Abby pulled out a waterfall of peach silk. "Oh my God, Abby, I couldn't possibly."

"Sure you can. It's no fun if these never get worn again. What good does it do to have all these vintage dresses if they just rot away in an attic? Try this on. With your peaches-and-cream coloring and light hair, this will look amazing on you, I can tell."

Summer took off the dress she was wearing, and then carefully stepped into the panel of silk. It whispered over her thighs and then she slid her arms through the openings and the dress took shape, skimming over her breasts and belly before falling to the floor in effortless folds. The neckline draped dramatically in a cowl shape. Summer knew without even looking in the mirror that it was stunning and perfect.

"Oh, my God," Abby breathed, once the buttons on the back were secure. "Summer. It's... I can't even. Go look. No, wait." She grabbed a nearby hairclip and gathered Summer's hair into a quick twist. "There."

Summer looked into the mirror and hardly recognized herself. She looked taller and impossibly elegant, especially with her hair gathered up. "Jax won't know what hit him," Jess remarked, a note of reverence in her voice.

"Oh, that's not—" Summer began, but heat crept up her cheeks and she broke off. Because knocking the man's socks off was indeed part of the plan, even if it shouldn't be.

"I've seen how you look at each other," Jess said, coming forward and touching Summer's arm. I know things were a little tense at the picnic, but at the ball game? Summer, I've never seen you laugh like that. He's good for you."

"He's also leaving in September, so don't get your hopes up," Summer quipped, though inside the thought sat like a stone. "I work for him, you guys. And in September when he returns to his life, I'm starting school. Honestly, I'm really looking forward to this. To starting something new." She hoped she sounded more enthusiastic than she felt. The thought of doing anything without Jax being part of her day was like taking all the color out of her life, leaving it monochrome and gray. "I just have to enjoy it while I can. Though I had hoped we weren't so transparent. It's weird because he's my boss."

Abby smiled. "And Tom was my contractor, and Rick is Jess's brother's best friend... there's always something that makes it awkward. Doesn't mean it's wrong." She nudged Summer's elbow. "Friend and assistant my eye."

Summer dared to meet their gazes. "I like him. A lot."

"Then you need to blow his mind. This dress. I have another set of shoes for you, and I recommend taking your neutral pumps just in case. I also recommend going with an understated eye but bright lip, especially if this is in the evening."

"It is."

"You'll need accessories. Good ones." Abby snapped her fingers. "I have the perfect necklace. When do you fly out?"

"In the afternoon."

"Can you stop by the house in the morning?"

Summer knew Jax wouldn't mind if she was late. Besides, she still had to pack for the weekend, and her brain was trying to inventory her makeup, wondering if she had something for a dramatic lip. This was all a bit overwhelming, but she'd never felt more like Cinderella getting ready for the ball. Not even her prom had felt so exciting, but that might have been because she went with Dale Dorcas and he was more interested in what was under her dress than having a good time.

"If you don't mind me coming early. Around eight thirty?"

"Perfect."

"I just..." Guilt took over again. "What if I get something on it?"

"That's what professional cleaners are for." Abby brushed off her concern. "Jess, you're going to loan her your gold sandals, right?" "Right!" Jess disappeared again while Abby helped Summer out of the dress and put it back on the hanger and in the garment bag.

"Summer, why don't I take these home, and I'll put everything together for you in a different bag? That way you can carry it on the plane."

"I don't know how to thank you," Summer whispered, slipping back into her regular clothes, which suddenly seemed dowdy and plain rather than cute. "I'll be honest, I'm already a little terrified. Jax is down-to-earth, but he was brought up very differently. A lot of money and privilege. I don't want to embarrass him. Or myself," she admitted.

"You won't. And you know why? Because no matter what you wear, you're the kindest person I've ever met. You put people at ease. You meet them where they are. You have a warm smile and a welcoming demeanor. This dress? It just matches what's already inside."

Summer blinked away hot tears. Never had anyone said anything so lovely to her before. "Oh, Abby."

"I didn't mean to make you cry." Abby sniffed, and then muttered, "Damn it. Now I'm crying."

Jess came back with the shoes. "What the hell happened?" she asked, stopping short in the doorway.

Then Abby and Summer started laughing, and everything was right again.

Chapter Fourteen

J ax was nervous as hell as he sat next to Summer at the gate, waiting for boarding to be called. He and Summer would have tonight all to themselves. Once they arrived, he'd rent their car for the weekend and they'd go to their hotel. He'd decided to wait until the morning to make the trip to his house for his black tie wear.

He'd made reservations for dinner and then they'd be staying in his room, with a big king-sized bed and a soaker tub. Imagining Summer in the bath, surrounded by bubbles, made his pulse jackhammer.

He was glad she'd agreed to come with him, because he truly didn't want to go through the events of the weekend alone. On the other hand, he was quickly getting in too deep with her. This week had shown him that. It wasn't just the great sex from last weekend. It was how much he liked her, cared for her, wanted to be the one to put the smile on her face. He loved how honest she was with him, never letting him get away with his crap. She sat next to him, nonchalantly reading a book while they waited, and all he could think of was that they'd agreed this was a summer fling and instead he was possibly falling in love with her.

It scared him to freaking death.

"Jax. Hey, Jax? That's us."

"What?""Where did you go?" Summer laughed. "They just called boarding. Well, boarding for you. I'm in a different zone."

He actually hoped not. He'd tried to get her an upgrade to business class when they reached the gate, but there were no promises made.

"I can wait for you," he said. "They're not going to give my seat away."

But she shook her head. "No, go. I'm fine. Go get settled."

He shouldered his carry-on just as one of the agents called her name, requesting that she come to the desk. When she returned, she was wearing a big smile. "I got upgraded. We're not sitting together, but I'm up front. I've never flown first class before."

It was business, not first class, but it was still a step above. And he remembered her saying at one point that the last time she flew she had been as a child.

Was it wrong that he wanted to give her these types of experiences? To make her world a little bit bigger?

When they got settled in their seats, Summer turned around and caught his eye, smiling widely.

The flight wasn't a long one, and as they disembarked, he carried Summer's overnight bag while she grabbed her garment bag. He'd asked what was inside, but she'd simply said clothes for the weekend. Tomorrow night was formal. What kind of dress did she have in there? There was another forty minutes of torture where they walked through the airport, found the rental car desk, and got their vehicle. It wasn't until they were inside the Cadillac that they both let out a breath, turned their heads and looked at each other, and laughed.

"Alone at last," he said, trying to crack a joke.

"Not quite alone," she replied, her eyes lighting with what looked like anticipation as a group passed by the car window, rolling luggage behind them. "But soon. How long to the hotel?"

So she was counting the minutes, too. "Not long." He pulled out of the parkade and into Friday afternoon traffic.

"Jax?"

"Hmm?" She'd fiddled with the stereo system and found a radio station she liked, but now turned it down in favor of chatter.

"Did you have to pay for me to fly first class?"

She was really hung up on the money thing, wasn't she? "No, Summer. If there's a seat open, there's usually not a charge if they upgrade."

"Okay, good."

"Would it have been a problem if I had?"

She frowned. "I don't know. I mean... I guess... It's just at work our financial differences don't matter. I work, and I'm paid for my effort. But this isn't work, and it feels really lopsided to me."

"And you don't like to feel indebted to anyone, do you?" He chanced a glance over at her before putting his eyes back on the road again.

"I don't," she admitted. "I guess I generally end up feeling like there's something asked of me in return, or else I'm getting pity or charity. Both make me feel pretty powerless, if I'm honest."

His heart ached at her admission. "You mean like your grandparents?"

She was quiet for a moment, then she nodded. "Yeah. I never escaped the knowledge that I was an obligation, or an inconvenience. And when it came to friends, or people at church when I was little, I was always 'poor Summer Arnold' who had no parents and who wore a lot of thrift store clothes and took peanut butter sandwiches in her lunchbag."

He thought about that for a moment. Gosh, their lives had been so very different. He'd never worn a hand-me-down in his life. And his parents had never made him feel like an obligation or inconvenient. If anything, he was smothered with both love and expectation as their only child. Maybe that was their meet-in-the-middle point. He'd had an incredibly privileged life when it came right down to it.

"I get the 'something asked in return' thing," he said quietly, slowing for an exit. "In a different way, of course. But when someone loves you and it comes with strings, whether it's obligation or expectation, it sets you up for trouble and a lot of self-guilt."

"How do you mean?"

He felt her gaze on his profile, and he made himself focus on the road. He didn't dare look over and get lost in her eyes. "I mean that you feeling like an inconvenience set you up for a lot of guilt. With me it was the weight of expectation. I had to be the super son for two of us, not just one. I could always feel the way my parents seemed to pin their hopes and dreams on me, and I never wanted to disappoint them."

"Aw, Jax."

"Intellectually we both know what's true and what's not, you know? But that doesn't stop the feelings, or the little voice that crops up from time to time reminding us of where we fall short."

It was hard to admit that; that he'd fallen short and been a disappointment. He was successful, he supposed, and he knew he was good at what he did. What bothered him was knowing his family wished he'd done something else.

"I'm surprised that you stood your ground and went into history," she commented, tucking her hair behind her ear before reaching for and adjusting the air conditioning. "That took guts, you know. A lot of kids don't know how to stand up to their parents. I sure didn't."

"I got my acceptance letter and threw up before going to tell them, I was so scared," he admitted. "The fact I wasn't going into sciences or even business was an issue. Thankfully, I didn't have a big aptitude for math or chemistry. I probably would have flunked out of calculus. They knew it, too, and so off I went."

They'd reached the hotel now, and Jax wasn't sure if he was relieved or disappointed the drive was over. He wanted to ask her what she meant about disappointing her parents, but instead he busied himself with finding a parking spot and then getting their bags from the car. They took an elevator to the lobby, and he caught Summer looking around herself at the sumptuous décor. Thankfully his parents weren't arriving until tomorrow, so there was no chance of running into them. When Summer turned back to him with shining eyes, all he wanted to do was get her to their room and pull her into his arms.

Keys were put into their hands. They made their way to the elevator and the seventh floor, down the hall, to the room tucked into the corner. A quick beep and click and he was opening the door, ushering them inside.

"Oh, Jax. This is gorgeous."

It was. Summer had made the travel arrangements, but this morning when she was running her errands, he'd called and managed to change his standard king room to an executive suite. In addition to the huge bed, there was a beautiful sitting area with a sofa and chairs and a glass-topped table, a desk and chair, and a spacious bathroom with a glass-walled shower and tub.

On the table sat a huge bouquet of flowers and a bottle of champagne in a bucket, the scent of the lilies filling the air.

She stared at him, and he smiled. "Welcome to Philly."

"You did this? The flowers and champagne and…" She put her garment bag over a chair and walked around, stepping inside the bathroom. "Holy cannoli. This is huge." She came back out and said, "I feel like Vivian in Pretty Woman when she says the bathroom is bigger than the Blue Banana."

"You know that movie?"

"It's a classic."

It was also one of his mom's favorites.

"Yeah," he said softly, "I did this. I do know how to dial a phone, you know." But the words came out teasing, rather than a criticism, and he loved it when she smiled back at him.

"Next thing you'll be after my job."

"Not likely. I'm starting to realize you're irreplaceable."

And with those words, something in the air changed. It softened, grew heavy with emotion and want and the weight of the veiled revelation that he was falling for her.

"Jax…"

"Let's pop that cork, Summer. We have two hours before our dinner reservation, and I don't want to waste a moment."

Summer had never seen Jax in such a state.

She'd seen him angry, frustrated, quiet, happy, and a myriad of other emotions, but never nervous. Not like this. His jaw was tight and his fingers tense in hers as she gave them a quick squeeze and released his hand. They'd agreed that today they would abstain from outward expressions of affection, so all she could really do was stand beside him as they hung back from the assembling crowd in the new Matthew Brodie Pediatric Oncology Center.

There was to be a short dedication—where Jax would speak—and then a tour of the facility. Tonight's event was billed as a celebration, with major donors and key players from city and state offices in attendance. The wing had been nearly a decade in the making, and Jax had said his father wanted to throw the gala to show his appreciation for the community. They had yet to see his parents, and Summer wondered if that was the source of his agitation.

"Jax?"

A woman's voice came from behind them and Jax and Summer turned. Summer felt a jolt of recognition as a couple in their late fifties approached, smiles on their faces. Jax looked so much like his mother—the thick, wheat-hued hair, clear blue eyes, and the shape of his nose. He got his height from his dad, clearly. Mr. Brodie had completely different coloring, though, with darker hair and deep set eyes. Summer wondered if Matthew had favored his father.

The couple reached them and his mother—Dr. Brodie—reached up for a hug. "You look marvelous. You've been getting some sun and fresh air on this project, haven't you?"

"A bit," he admitted, then kissed her cheek. "Dad," he said, and held out his hand.

They shook, the moment slightly awkward, but Summer rather thought it was a "not quite sure what to say" moment rather than anything truly negative. These were two very successful men, but it appeared they were not great at communicating with each other.

Then Jax turned to her, and his smile relaxed a tiny bit. "Mom, Dad, this is Summer Arnold. She's my assistant on the Jewell Cove project."

Of course he wouldn't introduce her in any other way, not this early and perhaps not at all because their relationship was temporary. It shouldn't have stung, being referred to only as his employee, but it did just the same.

But she wouldn't mention it, because she knew Jax was already tied in knots about the day's events.

"Nice to meet you," she said, holding out her hand and shaking first his mother's hand, then his father's. "I've heard a lot about you."

It occurred to her that they likely hadn't heard anything about her and her smile faltered, but they politely didn't mention it.

"We'll be getting started soon," Mr. Brodie said. "Are you ready?"

"Of course I am," Jax replied. And the tension was swirling around them again. Summer frowned a little and then met his mother's eyes. To her surprise, they shared a look that said the men were being frustrating again.

"I'm sure Jax knows what he's doing. Let's go, dear. It's nearly two."

"Of course." But then Mr. Brodie's expression turned hopeful. "We'll see you later too, right? You're coming tonight?"

"We wouldn't miss it," Summer said smoothly, not leaving Jax room to have an out. It was easy to see that Jax's parents loved him. Granted, there was thirty years of context she couldn't see, but love? That wasn't the issue. Pain, awkward communication? Certainly. And perhaps a hefty dose of pride. Jax did have a lot of it, and she suspected his parents did, too. It was hard to admit being wrong, or at least share in accountability.

"Perfect. We've put you at our table, so in case we miss each other after the ceremony, with the tour and everything, we'll see you for dinner."

Dr. Brodie put her hand on Summer's arm ever so briefly, a gesture of familiarity and, Summer guessed, solidarity. She liked his parents, who seemed much less stiff and formal than she'd expected. His dad seemed like a tougher nut to crack, but they didn't come across as cold or snooty. It was a relief, because she'd been worried about that—feeling uncomfortable and out of place.

They found their seats as the ceremony began. Mr. and Dr. Brodie welcomed everyone to the event and gave a little background into the genesis of the project and how pleased they were at its completion. Then they invited Jax up to say a few words.

Summer reached over and gave his hand a reassuring squeeze and sent an encouraging smile. "Use your professor voice," she whispered. "I like it. Warm and authoritative."

"You're crazy," he whispered back, rising from his chair, but his lips were quirked in a half smile. He adjusted the button on his suit coat and made his way to the podium, then took a moment and cleared his throat.

"My brother wanted to take care of everyone," he began. He stopped for a second, took a breath, and then lifted his chin as the mic carried his voice to the back row. "He was two years older and ten years wiser than me, I think. If I needed a snack, he'd give me his granola bar. If I was stuck on a spelling word before a test, he'd quiz me." He paused. "If I had a nightmare, I didn't sneak into my parents' room. I went to Matt. We played video games and sometimes he let me win, because he knew otherwise I'd stop playing with him—no one wants to lose all the time.

"But then he got sick, and it wasn't a game anymore. There were no winners. We all were losers, because Matt was the heart of our family. And when he was gone, we were never the same. There will always be a Matt-sized hole in our family."

The room was utterly silent, except for a small, emotional sniff.

"Matt loved helping people. He was a wonderful son, brother, and friend. I know in my heart there is nothing that would make him happier now than knowing there is a place where kids like him can go to get the best cancer treatment in the world, with top physicians and state-of-the-art equipment. Today we dedicate the Matthew Brodie Pediatric Oncology Center, and his memory will live on, in every child who gets to go home to their mothers, fathers, siblings, friends. In every boy or girl who gets to hug their dog one more time, play street hockey, or sneak a book under the covers with their mom's book light that she 'lost' a month ago." He looked down at his parents with a smile. "Sorry, Mom. I promised I wouldn't tell."

Summer reached inside her purse for a tissue. She hadn't quite known what to expect from Jax, but it wasn't this warm, open man. Whatever his issues with his folks, whatever feelings he had about not measuring up—they were nothing compared to the love he had for his brother. How very devastating... and how wonderful that he got to experience that love.

"Thank you all, for your support and your kindness. While my family misses Matt to this day, we're so happy that his memory will live on for years to come. Thank you."

The audience clapped, the sound echoing through the atrium. When he stepped down, his parents rose. His mother touched her hand to his face with a tender smile, but it was his dad's actions that had Summer reaching for her tissue again. He embraced Jax in a hug. And Jax hugged him back, then both stepped back and cleared their throats while Mr. Brodie swiped a finger under his eyes.

Jax came back to his seat. When Summer moved her hand to touch him, he whispered, "Don't."

At first she was hurt at the rebuff. Then she looked at his face. His jaw was tight, his eyes held a film of tears. He was riding a very thin emotional edge. The speech, the hug... it had cost him, and he was trying not to fall apart. She recognized the look; she'd been there herself, many a time. So she turned her attention back to the ceremony, where Mr. Brodie was now thanking VIPs for their contributions.

Jax was called up once more for the ribbon cutting, though he only had to stand with his parents, the hospital chairman, and the mayor while the ribbon was cut and photos taken by the press.

Once that was over, guests were invited to take a tour. Summer put her purse over her arm. "If you want to do the tour, we can. But if you need to get out of here, that's okay, too."

Jax reached for her hand. "I need air. Let's walk."

"Whatever you need, Jax."

And she meant it. Maybe more than she liked. Because right now? The tender-hearted, intelligent, handsome man beside her could ask her anything and she'd agree if it made him happy. She had to be very, very careful. She was falling for Jax Brodie—something she hadn't thought she was even capable of. And their time together was ticking down.

Chapter Fifteen

J ax straightened his tie for the fifth—or was it sixth—time. They were due at the gala in thirty minutes, and Summer was still in the bathroom, getting ready. But he wasn't going to rush her. He didn't give a damn if they were a little late. It had been a rough day so far. The fact that he was even going was a major concession.

The truth was, he could bear disappointing his parents; he was used to it by now. What he couldn't bear was disappointing Summer. And he knew if he backed out now at the eleventh hour, he'd be letting her down.

He still wasn't happy with his tie, but he gave up and decided to pace instead. Something had changed today. It started when he'd introduced Summer to his parents as his assistant and carried on when he'd turned away her gesture of support. Neither had felt right. The first, he'd decided, was because she wasn't just his assistant, and the second was because the last thing in the world he ever wanted to do was hurt her. What made everything ten times more difficult was how those two things were in opposition to each other. If he declared her his girlfriend, partner… it would only hurt her in the end when they parted ways. As they must. He understood now that Summer had plans and wouldn't leave the security of Jewell Cove. And his life was not in Maine.

That didn't stop the feeling, though. In a matter of weeks, he'd gone and fallen in love with her.

Telling her the truth about his feelings would only make things worse when it came time to leave. But Summer was also a woman who had never felt loved in her life. Didn't she deserve to know that she was lovable? He could give her that gift…

And yet to do so would still cause her pain in the end.

"Nearly ready!" she called out from the bathroom, and he stopped his pacing, shoving his hands in his pockets as he mulled over the end of the afternoon. They'd gone for a walk, aimlessly, without any direction or destination in mind. While the others toured the oncology center—and he felt he was horrible for skipping it—she took his hand in hers and made him talk. Really talk, about Matt and all the things they'd done as kids. She'd also reminded him that he'd been lucky to have Matt, as painful as it had been to lose him, and then she'd made a staggering point: Matt's legacy lived on in the oncology center. It didn't have to live on in Jax. He had the right to be himself. The second part he wasn't as sure of. She'd insisted that his parents felt the same way, and that they were proud of him. It was in the way they looked at him, how they tried even though sometimes communicating was hard. He wasn't convinced; she'd known them all of ten minutes. When he'd said as much, she'd replied, "I know love when I see it, Jax. They love you. I don't think it's their forgiveness you need. I think it's your own survivor's guilt you need to deal with."

But not today. Today was for going to a fancy dinner and holding her in his arms as they danced and then making love to her back in their suite. Perhaps tomorrow, at brunch. The thought of having a real heart-to-heart made his stomach churn with nerves, but maybe, just maybe, it was time.

She still wasn't out of the bathroom, and he started pacing again. Tomorrow, brunch. Monday, back to work. He let his mind slip there for a few moments, anxiety tensing his shoulders. It wasn't that the production wasn't going well; it was. But it was missing something. He felt it, Bryan felt it. Could they finish this and release it? Of course. But it wouldn't be his best work, and that didn't sit well. For each of the founders of the town, for each of the men responsible for the treasure and the historical significance of the island, there was a living descendant interviewed. All they had for Edward Jewell was narration about the family dying out after the second world war and a few old photos. If there were other relatives, he hadn't been able to trace them.

The bathroom door opened and Summer stepped out, a hesitant smile on her face. "Well? What do you think?"

He couldn't think. His brain went blank for the space of a few seconds as he simply stared. Then a single word left his lips: "Exquisite."

Her cheeks blossomed with pink as she accepted his praise. "Do you like it? It's vintage. Abby says it's from the thirties."

He couldn't give a damn about the dress's credentials. The peachy silk clung to her ribs and draped over her hips and to the floor in a sexy yet subdued panel. He could see a hint of her collarbones as the silk draped in folds from her shoulders to just below her breasts, and her arms were left bare. At her neck was a necklace formed of three strings of pearls with a cameo in its center. She looked elegant and sexy, timeless and fashionable all at once. Like the Summer he knew and then also like a stranger, exciting and new.

"It's... My God, Summer. You're so beautiful I can hardly breathe."

She bit down on her lip, which held a slick coating of ruby lipstick. "Let's not go crazy, now."

"No, don't downplay it." She'd even put her hair up in some sort of twist, revealing the slender column of her neck and the pearl earrings at her ears. "I mean it. You take my breath away."

She swallowed, then averted her eyes and reached for a small gold clutch. "You look pretty smashing yourself, Jax," she replied. "Black tie looks good on you." She went to stand in front of him, reached up and tweaked his tie with her free hand. "It's not really who we are, but I'll admit, it's fun to play dress up once in a while, isn't it?"

"Mmm hmm."

He lifted his hand and let his fingers trail over her arm. Bumps rippled up under his fingertips and her eyes widened. "I can't believe I'm going to say this," she murmured, "but are you sure we have to go to this thing?"

He laughed then, delighted. "There is nothing more I'd like than to stay in and be with you all night long. But we'd be missed. And…" He let his gaze rove over her before meeting her eyes again. "There is one thing I'd like more. And that's to take you to this gala on my arm, and be the envy of every guy in the place."

"Those are very pretty words."

"They're also honest. Come on, Summer. Before I change your mind and that dress is wasted."

The gala was in one of the ballrooms, so they didn't even have to venture outside. Instead they stepped off the elevator and made their way to the designated room, Summer's hand looped through his arm. "Don't rush me," she whispered to him. "I'm not used to heels like this."

He smothered a smile and adjusted his gait. "Nothing I do tonight is going to be in a hurry." He looked over at her until she looked back. "Nothing," he promised.

"God, this is going to be a long evening," she lamented, and he laughed.

And that was how his parents found him; laughing at something Summer had said.

"Jax! And Summer." His mother came forward and shook her head. "That dress is amazing. Wow. Men are lucky. They get a black tux and they're set. We have to find just the right cut, color... You're absolutely stunning, Summer."

"Thank you, Mrs. Brodie. Honestly, it's a loan from a friend."

"She's actually one of the subjects of the documentary," Jax added. "Her ancestor was one of the town founders, and she has a mansion full of history."

"Including a vintage wardrobe," Summer added. "It's pretty incredible."

"The dress she's wearing is around ninety years old," Jax said.

Summer laughed lightly. "Thanks. Like I wasn't already paranoid about getting something on it."

"That's what professional cleaners are for, dear," Dr. Brodie replied, moving forward and taking her arm. "Come with me. Let's get a glass of wine and leave these two to... oh, something."

Jax stared after them as they departed. His mom had taken to Summer like a duck to water. The two of them had their heads together as they approached the bar, as if they were old friends.

"Assistant my ass," his dad said, arching an eyebrow and prompting Jax to turn his attention away from the duo. "You are in up to your neck, son."

"No, it's not like that," Jax insisted, but he knew he didn't sound convincing.

"Don't kid a kidder. It's written all over your face. I was the same way about your mother." His gaze shifted to the two women, now holding glasses of white wine in their hands, and his face softened. "Still am, really."

Jax tried to contain his surprise. He usually thought of his parents as the CEO and the high profile doctor, not really in terms of their affection for each other. But now that he thought about it, they had always been united. In their love, their grief, anything that came their way. So many couples couldn't withstand high profile and high pressure jobs, kids, hell, life for that matter, let alone losing a child. But his had, and still loved each other.

He was past thirty and finally realizing that his parents were people too. That his relationship with them was only a part of their life. And that maybe Summer was right. Maybe it was his feelings about Matt getting in the way, and not manufactured expectations that he used as a smoke screen.

"You're in love with her," his dad stated, putting his hands in his pockets. "I'm happy for you, Jax."

"I could be," he answered, still feeling unsure, and really off balance confiding in his dad. "It's complicated, and it's been a long time since I really cared about someone."

"It's always complicated. Let's get a Scotch before dinner and the boring speeches."

Boring? "I thought you loved this kind of thing?"

"God, no. I don't know where you got your public speaking gene. I can manage in a boardroom; that's my element. Put me at one of these things and I'd rather eat the microphone than speak into it."

Jax laughed and then went to get a drink and join the ladies. As Jax took Summer's hand and smiled at her, he wondered if he was finally getting to know his parents, and if he hadn't up to now because he'd been the one doing the shutting out. He'd just had a whole conversation with his dad without tension and anxiety. Not once had Jax's career come up as an issue. His father hadn't even mentioned Jax's absence at the tour this afternoon.

"You okay?" Summer asked, nudging his arm a little.

"I am. Better than I expected. Realizing some things. Things I wouldn't have if you hadn't made me come, so thank you."

She beamed up at him, then impulsively rose up and gave him a quick peck on the lips. "I'm glad," she replied, turning away a little shyly. "Your mom is lovely, by the way. She told me she's never seen you so happy."

"You're good for me, Summer."

"And you're good for me. I've spent a lot of time staying in my comfort zone. I'm starting to realize there's a whole world out there that I don't have to be afraid of."

Did that mean there was hope for them? That perhaps, as the summer went on, they'd find a way to be together? Because he liked that idea. He liked it a lot. The thought of going on without her was impossible.

Summer felt like a princess at a ball, which was both wonderful and utterly disconcerting. She lived in fear of saying the wrong thing or breaching some sort of etiquette she didn't know, but at the same time, seeing the way Jax looked at her filled her heart with pride and affection and, honestly, desire.

Something had changed between the two of them today, something that had nothing to do with sex—they'd been doing that for a while now—and was instead a change of heart. It had really happened during the ceremony today, seeing him with his family, hearing his words, witnessing his pain that he tried to keep hidden all the time.

She sat next to him at the banquet table and ate some sort of fancy kale salad, and then an entrée of agnolotti stuffed with roasted eggplant and studded with mushrooms and truffle oil. And just when she thought she couldn't eat another bite... or drink the paired wine for the course... she was served a raspberry rose sorbet with hazelnut wafers.

The conversation had been light and easy, an effort made by both Jax and his parents, who were doing their best to make her feel welcome even if she acknowledged, at least inside, that she was horribly provincial. She had a high school education, came from nothing. But while her world was utterly different, neither of the Brodies made her feel she was anything *less than*.

She didn't quite fit in, but did she need to? By Jax's own admission, he spent very little time in this world. And granted, he came from academia, which was also daunting, but his day-to-day lifestyle wasn't grand. Look at the house at Refuge Point. Beautifully appointed and large, but Summer didn't feel out of place there. Even his house closer to the university was nice but not ostentatious. They'd made a quick trip this morning to pick up his tux and she'd liked the leafy middle-class suburb with old sturdy houses and little back yards.

All she knew was that she had said all the right and sensible things this week about this being a summer affair and how they'd go their separate ways; she'd even convinced herself she wasn't interested in love, wasn't worried about it because she hadn't been truly in love thus far in her life. And despite all that talk here she was, in a hotel ballroom, eating dishes with ingredients she'd never tasted before, in a vintage gown, thinking that when September came, she didn't want this to be the end of their relationship. She didn't want to give him up.

Which meant that at some point she was going to have to be honest with him about her connection to Edward Jewell, and soon. The idea sat so uncomfortably, she put down her sorbet spoon.

Following dessert there were a few more brief speeches, thanking donors and patrons for their continued support of Brodie Biotech's charitable endeavors. Jax didn't have to speak this time, and before long the music started and Jax led her to the dance floor, claiming her for the first dance.

"Just think," she said, happy to be in his arms, "a week ago we were dancing on the plywood floor at Jess and Rick's."

"To be honest, I think I enjoyed that more," he said, his lips close to her ear. "I usually hate formal events. But having you here, and in that dress… suddenly the night is a whole lot better. I'm so glad you came with me." He added a little pressure of his hand at her waist as he said it.

"I'm glad I did, too. And that I sent Jess and Abby the SOS. Confession: I do not own a floor-length dress, let alone anything this gorgeous."

"The dress is beautiful," he said softly. "But not as beautiful as you."

She didn't answer, but instead swallowed around the lump in her throat. Things were moving so quickly, especially on the emotional front. Maybe it was the weekend and things would tone down when they returned home to Jewell Cove and back to business.

"It's hard to imagine being back to work on Monday, isn't it?" She tilted her chin to look up at him. "Two days of hotels—not even two, really—and already the daily grind seems a world away."

"It's not, though. I've been wracking my brains trying to find the missing piece of this story. Something that will fill it out and give it that extra something special. I keep hoping it'll come to me. Problem is, I'm a historian. I follow the facts and the sources. I'm not a storyteller."

"But what is history if not a story? You'll find the pieces, Jax, I'm sure of it." She hesitated. Now was not the time or place, was it? But she could tell him. She could reveal her ancestry and give him a link, a place to start.

Except... A little part of her insisted that if he knew, there was a chance he'd only want her for the story. That what they had would come a distant second to his project. Hadn't he always insisted that he didn't do love, that this was his labor of love and passion? Right now she was Summer the assistant, Summer the... Well, she wasn't really a girlfriend, was she? Summer the temporary lover, she supposed. But if he knew about Edward's mistress, their relationship would change.

Plus, he'd be angry. A lie of omission was still a lie, and she could have chosen to be honest with him from the first. Heck, during her interview she'd told him she could point him toward people and places to look. All the while knowing she had knowledge that could help him.

"Hey, are you okay?" His voice interrupted her thoughts.

"Oh, sorry. I drifted away on my to-do list," she lied. "And my feet are hurting a little. I could use a glass of wine or tonic and lime or something."

"Of course." He stepped back and held out his hand, and she took it.

Their shoes clipped across the glossy parquet as they left the dance floor and looked for a circulating server. Jax ordered her a glass of wine—some kind she'd never heard of—and she took a moment to escape to the ladies' room to freshen up. When she returned, Jax was holding her wine and he was talking to another couple. They were older, perhaps in their sixties or so, though Summer found it hard to tell. The woman was standing, but she had crutches, the kind that looped around the forearm, and her back was slightly stooped.

"Ah, there you are," Jax said, handing Summer the wine. "This is the woman I was telling you two about. Meet Summer Arnold."

Summer smiled and held out her hand, but to her astonishment the woman across from her blanched while her husband gaped, his mouth open. There was a moment of embarrassment as she realized the woman might have trouble shaking hands, and worse, no one was making an attempt to meet her grip. She dropped her hand to her side. The man, at least, recovered quickly and said, "Did you say Summer Arnold?"

Summer frowned, feeling suddenly very off balance. "Yes?" It came out unsure, like a question, even though she was sure of her own name.

"Jax, where did you say you were doing this documentary?"

"Up in Maine. A little town called—"

"Jewell Cove," the woman answered, finding her words again but still looking just as pale.

"I'm sorry, do I know you?" Summer asked, her heart pounding. This woman knew her somehow, but Summer knew no one in Philly. And yet there was something strangely familiar about her, too. Perhaps she'd been to Jewell Cove in the past and Summer had waited on her at one of her jobs. They did get a lot of tourist traffic in the summer.

"I..." The woman swallowed tightly, then looked to her husband, as if floundering for words and needing assistance. Then she turned back as he put his hand on her shoulder. "My dear," she said, her voice slightly hoarse, "I believe you're our granddaughter."

Summer could do nothing but stare. Words failed, hell, thoughts failed. It was as if the word "granddaughter" was on an endless loop in her brain.

"Granddaughter," she parroted dumbly. The shock was abating a little and in its place came anger, shocking in its own right. "You're saying you're the grandparents who haven't made an effort to see me in over fifteen years?"

The man flinched as the woman frowned. "I know," she murmured. "I got sick around the same time as Emily died, and we had no idea how debilitating my MS was going to be. Your grandmother—your father's mother—insisted it was fine if you were to go live with them. Do you remember when we used to visit?"

She did—vaguely. "A couple of times. No wonder you look familiar. But also not. It's been a long time. I couldn't have been more than ten."

The woman nodded again. "Yes, it has. After a few years, your grandmother insisted that it was doing more harm than good, having us around. That any reminder of your mother put you into days of grief. We couldn't bear the thought of causing you pain. Not when you had already suffered so much."

Which was an absolute lie. She'd lived for stories of her mom, especially the good ones. Yeah, there had been some bad shit; stuff no kid should ever see or remember. But there'd been good times, too. At least she might have felt wanted, or part of a family and not just an inconvenience. Why would her grandmother have said such a thing? And why on earth had these grandparents accepted such a thing, unless they hadn't really cared?

She stuffed that down, though, for now. "What are you both doing here? It's a bit of a trip from South Carolina. "

"We've supported this charity for years," her grandfather interjected. "Actually, Jax's mother operated on me several years ago. Saved my life, really. And we're not in Carolina any longer. We're in Harrisburg."

They were strangers, and it was a sick and twisted coincidence that the only family she had living was standing in front of her at some stupid gala. They could be bothered with this and not with their own granddaughter? She stopped caring at that moment. They knew where she was and had done nothing, nothing! All the years of emptiness, thinking they didn't care, thinking they considered her a problem because her mom had been such trouble. She wanted to shout at them, but they were in the middle of a formal event and she would never make a scene and cause trouble for Jax.

"I'm sorry, I can't do this," she muttered, and turned on her heel, gathering up her skirt in one hand to assist her exit. On the way out the ballroom door she brushed by Jax's mom, who called out to her but she didn't stop. She just kept walking until she was in the lobby, then out the doors and standing in the street where she could breathe.

Her grandparents, here. Her mother. Dead. At least her mother had died. That was a reasonable enough reason to not see your kid anymore. But her grandparents clearly had money and could have come to at least visit at any time. Instead they'd turned their backs on her, and now they were meeting at a public party, acting as if this was surprising but not devastating. Maybe it wasn't to them, but it was to her, and that was the worst part of it.

Jax came out the door to stand beside her. "I am so sorry that happened," he murmured, wrapping his arm around her. "I had no idea that Dorothy and Hal were related to you."

"Different last name," she said, staring out into the street. "I took my dad's last name. I know she had just been diagnosed, and I do remember a few visits. That's why she looked so familiar, but I was so young, Jax. Then there were just presents in the mail, the odd card. Then nothing at all."

She sniffed and blinked rapidly, trying not to cry. "My grandmother told me that they didn't care to see me. That they thought I was just like my mother. But now I hear something completely different. I don't know what to believe anymore."

"Summer," came a voice from behind them. Her grandfather, Hal, stood there, his face heavy with sadness, making his wrinkles more pronounced. "We did care. We loved you and we loved your mother, too, and it broke our hearts knowing we couldn't fix the mistakes she made. When your father was out of the picture, we tried to convince her to bring you home, but she wanted the chance to turn her life around on her own, and we thought she deserved that. And she did it, for a while. When she died, we were just devastated. But Dorothy had been showing some odd symptoms and we'd found out the week before that she had MS."

She turned to face him. "I get it. I would have been an inconvenience. In the way. Oddly enough, I felt that same way with my Arnold grandparents. They didn't want me either, and told me that when my dad got out of jail he was coming for me. But he didn't. He was killed and I was an orphan. And where were you? Nowhere, that's where."

"We didn't know."

"You didn't fight for me. No one has ever fought for me."

Tears clouded the older man's eyes. "I am so sorry. Not fighting for you has been our biggest regret. And when your grandmother wrote to say you didn't want any more contact, we wanted to respect your wishes, even though it broke our hearts."

Summer stepped back. "Wait, she said what?"

There was a long moment of stunned silence. The doors to the hotel slid open and Dorothy emerged, her steps slow and measured with the crutches. Something sad twisted Summer's heart. She wasn't immune to the fact that this woman had received a difficult diagnosis and had lost her only child at the same time. It didn't erase her own feelings, but she did have a smidge of compassion just the same.

When Dorothy had joined them, Summer swallowed her fear and said, "Is it true? My Grandmother Arnold told you I didn't want to have any contact with you?"

Dorothy and Hal looked at each other. "It broke our hearts," Dorothy said. "We'd already cut back on our visits, but we wanted to at least write to you. See you now and then, watch you grow up. But we also wanted to respect your wishes. I could understand you having negative feelings about our family, considering how Carol died."

Summer shook her head. "I said no such thing." She clenched her fingers together. "Gram told me you were too busy to bother with me."

"Never!" Dorothy took a halting step forward. "We loved you. We still do. We only wanted to do what was best for you, and we blamed ourselves for a lot of what happened to Carol. Oh, Summer. I'm so sorry."

They were still standing outside the hotel. The whole time, Jax had been by her shoulder, stepping back from the conversation but there to support her just the same. "Maybe you can start again," he suggested, his voice warm and comforting. "Second chances don't come around very often."

Summer looked at the older couple who were watching her with such hope it hurt her heart. They'd made mistakes, but what if the mistakes had been well-intentioned? It didn't erase the harm, but it did mitigate it somewhat. Especially if Grammie Arnold had been influencing things for her own gain. Summer wished she could say she was surprised, but she wasn't. Gram had been a cold, aloof woman, unreachable much of the time and devastated at the loss of her son—and blamed Summer's mother for it. Now Summer could never ask her why. Why, when they didn't really want her, they'd prevented her from seeing her other family.

"This is a lot to take in, but… I think I might like that," she admitted, the idea growing on her. They seemed like nice people, and earnest. Would it hurt to at least talk?

She was treated to broad smiles. "Oh, that's terrific," Dorothy breathed. "Heavens. When we bought our tickets for tonight, we never dreamed something like this could happen. If it weren't for Jax doing his latest project in Jewell Cove… we might never have met. Maybe now we'll have an excuse to visit again. In fact, I wish your parents had told us you were working up there, Jax. We might have been able to help."

"Help?" Jax stepped forward now, his expression neutral as if he were thinking, "what kind of help could these two give me?" Summer recognized the look, like bored interest.

"Of course. Our ties to that town go way back to when it was founded. Hal is descended from Edward Jewell, you know. Didn't Summer tell you?"

The knot in Summer's stomach that had started to ease suddenly tightened, sending a pain through her abdomen and a cold sweat trickling down her back. The snug silk of her bodice was constrictive, making it difficult for her to breathe, and the heat of the summer evening was cloying. Why, why did this have to happen now? So soon after she'd decided to tell him? Before he could open her mouth to say anything, Hal piped up. "Edward Jewell is my ancestor."

"But the last of his line was killed on the battlefield in WW2," Jax insisted. "There are no records of other children." He sounded confused, and unbelieving. Summer wanted to rewind everything to thirty minutes ago. She might never have approached Jax and the couple she now knew were her grandparents. She would have had time to tell him herself.

"That's because Eddie had a mistress, and she had a child. I'm surprised Summer never filled you in. It's quite the family scandal."

Jax's silence said it all. Regret and panic hit Summer all at once, but her grandparents didn't seem to notice her distress. "Eddie gave his mistress an emerald ring and a gold locket for the baby," Hal finished.

"We intended to give it to Carol when she turned twenty-one," Dorothy chimed in. "It's been passed down all this time, and not a soul has ever tried to sell it or pawn it despite what financial straits they've been in. But Carol was already into drugs at that point, and we were terrified she'd try to sell it for money for drugs." To Summer's surprise, she reached out and grasped her hand. "You should have it, Summer. As a direct descendant of Jewell's."

"You knew?" Jax whispered, a harsh accusation beneath the soft words.

"We can talk about it later," she suggested, but now her whole body was taut as a string in a bow. How had such a perfect evening turned into such a disaster? All Summer wanted at this moment was to be back in her cozy little apartment that was always just a little bit too hot, with her cozy little life, and her friends and...

And no worry about being rejected—again. Abandoned, again.

The sultry summer heat cooled considerably as Jax withdrew, both physically and emotionally, creating an icy wall around him. Summer was suddenly aware of the sounds around them. Traffic, honking, voices talking as they passed by. The smell of car exhaust, the weight of the humidity and heat. It all over-whelmed her, made her want to run. But of course she couldn't. Even if she wanted to flee, the logistics of trying to escape in this dress, with the narrow skirt and long hem made it impossible.

"I'm sorry." She forced out the words and tried to paste on a smile and feared it was more of a grimace than anything. "This has all been so much. I don't want to be rude, truly, but I think I need to go inside."

Dorothy's face softened with understanding. "Of course. What a shock for all of us! But Summer... do you think we could come see you sometime soon? After you've had time to think things through. We'd really like to get to know you." She reached out a hand and placed it on Summer's arm, where it was both a comfort and a shackle. "We've missed so much time."

"Of course. I'll be in touch, I promise. I just need some time to absorb all this."

She pulled her hand away, and then she ran. Physically her steps were measured and sure. But emotionally, she was getting the hell out of there. Away from the quiet acceptance of her grandparents and away from Jax's hurt and angry face.

Chapter Sixteen

"Excuse me. I need to make sure Summer is all right."

Jax sent Hal and Dorothy a smile and followed in Summer's direction, long strides eating up the cement walk outside the hotel. Inside he was as angry as he could ever remember being. Angry and hurt. Earlier today, with all they'd shared, how close they were becoming... hell, he had even thought himself in love with her. And all this time she was holding onto this secret? And for what?

A voice inside of him cautioned that Summer was fragile right now. She'd lost her entire family, thought her mother's family had abandoned her, and had suddenly been thrust into this new situation. He wasn't unaware of that fact. Still, he couldn't stop feeling the sting of betrayal in his veins. He'd trusted her. But she hadn't trusted him.

He entered the lobby just in time to see a flash of peach silk at an elevator door. By the time he reached the elevator bank, the door had closed and she had disappeared, so he pushed the button to wait for the next available car. It took forever, and once he was inside he slid his room key over the sensor and pushed the button for their concierge floor.

Outside their room, he hesitated, key card in hand, and took a few deep breaths. He was angry, but he didn't want to fight. He had things to say but he refused to lose his temper. All he could think of was how many times he'd expressed frustration at the production, how he wished he had that missing piece, how Edward Jewell had no living descendants, and she'd known. All this time, she'd known. And she had kept it from him.

He held the card up to the pad and the green light illuminated. He opened the door softly, reining in his anger, wanting to handle this well. He ignored the part of him that acknowledged their affair was over after this. How could he trust her again?

"Summer?"

"I'm in the bathroom," she called, her voice subdued as it echoed behind the bathroom door.

"Can you come out here, please?" Jax realized his hands were shaking, his body quivering. He was a giant ball of emotion, all of it riding just below the surface, waiting for him to crack.

"I'm... I'm trying to change," she replied, and then he caught the sound of a sob.

He was angry and hurt, so why did the sound of a single sob reach in and wrap around his heart?

He waited, then started to pace through the room. She was hiding from him, wasn't she? What did she think was going to happen? That he was going to yell at her? Had she been yelled at before? Or was she ashamed and hiding, avoiding dealing with what had just happened?

It wasn't her style. Summer dealt with things head on. At least... he thought she did. But how did he really know that? He didn't really know her at all, did he?

"Jax?" The bathroom door cracked open a little. "Um... I can't get the buttons undone by myself."

He swallowed around a lump that suddenly formed in his throat. God, touching her was not on his list of ways to get through this situation. "Do you need some help?" he asked.

"Yeah. I think I might."

He went to the door, his heart pounding with each step. She opened it, then stood with her back to him and he spied three buttons right in the middle of her back that she hadn't been able to release from their loops. Fingers trembling, he reached out and slid the buttons free, while the dress gaped open, revealing the soft V of her back and shoulders as the fabric drooped.

"Thanks," she whispered. "I couldn't breathe anymore. I need to—"

Another little sob, and a slight sniff.

"Why?" he whispered hoarsely. "Why didn't you tell me?"

"I don't know!" The words burst out of her lips and she lowered her head. "Please, Jax, just let me get changed. I'll come out and we'll talk, but I... I can't do this standing here holding a dress up and feeling..." She took a gasping breath, barely hanging on to her emotions as her back shook. He stepped away, giving her space, because she was right. She was vulnerable right now, and he wanted to talk about this on equal ground—the way they'd dealt with everything so far.

"I'll wait," he answered, and left, closing the door behind her.

Ten minutes he sat on the sofa, listening to her cry in the bathroom, wanting to go to her and soothe her pain, yet knowing he had a right to his feelings, too. When she finally emerged, he sat up straight, then watched as she came toward the living area of the suite and sat, not on the sofa, but in the club chair opposite it.

"I'm sorry," she whispered. She was looking at her hands but she lifted her head and met his gaze briefly. Her eyes were red and swollen, and he hated that she'd been crying. The backs of his eyes stung, too. Today had been so amazing. He'd been so sure that they were going to find a way to make their relationship work. Now it had all crumbled apart.

"I am, too."

"You didn't do anything wrong."

"I'm sorry that you're hurting," he clarified. "I'm angry, Summer, and very hurt. But I'm also upset that you're hurting. I hate everything about this."

She sniffled again. She'd put on the trousers and blouse she'd worn yesterday, which he understood because to his knowledge, she hadn't brought casual wear and this was not the time for lace-trimmed negligées. He was still in his tux, and he reached up and undid the tie that had given him such trouble earlier in the evening, and then released the collar of his shirt.

"I had no idea that Dorothy and Hal were… I understand that must have been a shock for you."

She nodded. "There's a lot for me to sort through, there. A lot of stuff I grew up knowing that might not be true. A lot of processing what happened tonight, in a social setting, with no warning. And…" She stopped, sniffed, and her lower lip wibbled. "And also knowing that you're angry with me. None of this is what I wanted for tonight."

It was hard to be furious with her when she was so clearly hurting, and it wasn't that he wasn't angry and disappointed and feeling betrayed. It just wasn't the red-hot sparks of indignation from before. Now it was a heavy weight, knowing that because of what happened tonight, nothing would be the same.

He'd had several of those moments over the course of his lifetime; moments where in a flash the path of his life had changed course. Sometimes they were good moments, like when he was accepted for his doctorate, when he'd wrapped from his first documentary. Then there were other times that left scars in their wake. Losing Matt. The moment he'd told his parents he was pursuing a degree in history and seeing their crestfallen faces. Falling for someone and having it go wrong, leaving him alone again. And tonight, when he'd finally thought maybe he deserved to be happy, only to have it come crashing down around him.

"I don't get it," he admitted, resting his elbows on his knees and clenching his fingers together. "You knew you were Edward Jewell's descendant. I told you tons of times how the production seemed to be in a slump and what a difference it would make. How I researched his line and there was no one. I tied myself in knots trying to sort out what I could do to make this documentary outstanding, to fill out the stories of the founders in a balanced trio, and you said nothing. You worked on this project with me from the beginning of the summer. You listened to me, kissed me, made love to me. And not one word. Not one peep about how Edward Jewell had an illegitimate line and that you were actually descended from it."

She lifted her head. "Is that all I am to you? A way for your precious documentary to be a success?"

He sat back at the sharpness in her tone. "When have I ever said that? How is that even possible, since I didn't know of the connection until tonight? You know damn well you are important to me. But you know, maybe I've been the one who made a mistake. Maybe you just wanted the job and a fling and nothing else really mattered to you."

"Don't say that."

"Just tell me why. Why you kept this a secret. Why you weren't honest with me, why you didn't trust me. After everything, Summer... I let you in. It hurts to know you didn't do the same."

"I don't know, okay?" Her voice raised and then she let out a breath and quieted a little. "I mean I do, but I meant to tell you eventually. And then every time I thought of it, I didn't know how, and then I knew that you'd be upset the longer I let it go. But I was going to tell you, Jax. After this weekend...

something changed. When I thought you were going to pack up in September and go back to your life, it didn't seem as important. But then this weekend, I thought maybe we really had something—"

"Something built on a lie. And if not a lie, an omission of the truth."

"I know. God, I *know*. Look, I've thought endlessly about why I found it so hard to tell you this simple thing. The truth is, Edward Jewell had a mistress and they had a child together, all while he pretended he was a devoted husband and father. His legitimate children inherited almost everything; the mistress had been given the house she lived in, a few jewels, and whatever money he'd managed to give to her before his death."

"Sounds like a real great guy."

"Look, I've told myself that it doesn't matter what Edward did generations ago, how does that affect me? But it does. Because the only thing I have in this life is Jewell Cove and the life I've built there. The friends. If I told you about him, then it would become a matter of record. And so would everything else about me that..."

Her voice trailed off again and she turned her head to stare at the window. It was dark outside now, and all that was visible was spots of light from nearby buildings and neon signs. Jax waited, feeling like something important was coming and putting aside his own impatience to give her space to say it. She sighed and turned back. "So would everything else about me that I don't want anyone to know. That my grandparents kept secret, too.

I was 'poor little orphan Summer' for a really long time, and I could just imagine what would happen if everyone knew the truth. Mother a junkie and father a jailbird. One long line of low-lifes. Half would pity me and the other half would gossip about it until it followed me everywhere."

He didn't know what the truth was, but he was hurt that she thought he'd gossip. "You really think I'd do that?"

"No, not intentionally." She met his gaze. "But you'd want the information for your documentary. You'd want to interview me. And then people would ask the same questions you're asking. Why didn't I say something? Who is Summer Arnold?"

She wasn't wrong. He had to acknowledge that part. He would have wanted her to share, and he would have asked to interview her. Knowing this about Edward, knowing it would change the documentary for the better, he would have asked.

"The people of Jewell Cove don't know that my mom died of an overdose. They don't know about the years I spent with her, wondering where we'd be living, how we were going to eat, spending the night by myself when she didn't come home. And I sure as hell wasn't going to tell anyone, because as rotten as it was, she was all I had and if I said anything I'd be taken away. And my dad? She had nothing good to say about my dad and the horrible things she did say were probably accurate, because he was in prison for some pretty bad things. I moved to Jewell Cove and my grandparents made me promise to never talk about my dad being in jail. He was going to come for me. But he didn't. He got himself killed, too. Not in some random accident like they said but gunned down by someone with a grudge. Maybe you believe people wouldn't judge me based on that, but they would. I've heard some of the gossip around the cove and it's not always nice."

"Then maybe it isn't the idyllic spot you say it is. And besides, your parents' shame and mistakes, hell, Edward's shame and mistakes, are not yours. You do not have to carry them."

"Really." She gave a short laugh then. "Just like you don't carry around guilt over Matt?"

The arrow hit its mark. He sat back, quiet for a moment as what she said sank in. "Okay, fair. We both have unresolved issues in our pasts. But Summer, I shared mine with you. I let you in. And you... you didn't do the same. You thought I would use that information to my benefit without any thought of you and your feelings, and I have to say, if you think that, you don't know me very well. When it comes down to it, documentary be damned." He meant the words as he said them. "You didn't trust me, and you didn't really let me in. I might have issues, but I've never hidden them from you. I don't think I can be with anyone who can't be open and honest with me. Who can't trust me with their truth."

She got up then, paced to the window. "Trust you with my truth? When this is nothing more than a summer fling?"

He wondered if she realized how every time she spoke, she hurt him a little more. "It's more than that for me. I thought it was for you, too."

"Everyone has a right to their own secrets, Jax."

He never moved from the sofa. "That doesn't mean keeping them won't have consequences."

Now she refused to look at him. "Maybe we were just fooling ourselves."

Sadness filled the corners of his heart. "Maybe we were."

"I don't think I can make brunch tomorrow." God, now her words were cold and flat. The conversation was over. She'd explained, he'd said more—and less—than he'd intended. But that last sentence said everything. She was distancing herself, not even going to try for appearances.

"You can take the bed," he replied. "I'll sleep on the couch. Tomorrow I'll make your excuses at the brunch and arrange for a late checkout for you. Then we can just meet at the airport for our flight home."

"O-okay."

He got up then, and went into the bathroom to brush his teeth and strip off his tux. There was an extra blanket in the closet, and when he returned to the room he took one of the pillows from the bed and stretched out on the sofa, his feet hanging over the arm. Summer was still standing by the window, but once he was settled she moved, also going to the bathroom, then coming out and crawling into bed, the rustling of the sheets loud in the abnormal silence. There was a click and the light went out.

A few minutes later, she spoke. "Jax, I'm sorry."

He closed his eyes tightly. "I know," he answered, and then laid awake in the dark long after her breaths evened out in sleep.

Jax woke early, before the sun was truly up. The sky was that peachy purple palette that marked the beginning of dawn, and he sighed and looked over at the bed. Summer was asleep, her hair sprawled over the pillow, her eyes still puffy from crying. He'd heard her last night, though she'd tried hard to be quiet. The soft, restrained sniff every few minutes told him she was quietly weeping, and he battled with himself to keep from going to her.

He didn't, though, because he was still hurt she hadn't trusted him enough to be honest.

He hadn't been honest, either. Not with other people in his life. It was funny how he'd shared his hopes and fears with Summer but not with the others who meant the most. Perhaps that was the lesson he was meant to learn in all this. Without waking her, he rose, quietly packed his few things into his bag, dressed in the trousers and dress shirt he'd packed for today's brunch, and then scribbled out a note before leaving.

He took his time. First he stopped at a favorite coffee shop and grabbed a large coffee and a bagel, then sat on a bench in Penn Treaty Park and looked out over the water, taking the time to sit and breathe and figure out what to do about the situation in which he found himself. After an hour or so, he walked back to his car and drove to Laurel Hill Cemetery, where he walked the paths that were so familiar to him now. He came here every April tenth, on Matt's birthday. Sometimes he came just because he missed his brother—still, after all these years. Today he needed to talk to Matt, even though he knew his brother couldn't answer. Maybe he couldn't even hear, but Jax felt the need to say things anyway. So he took his time getting to the marker that said Matthew Adam Brodie, and then stood and looked down at it, trying to form the words.

"Hey, bro," he began, but his voice caught and he cleared his throat, looking around to see if anyone was watching or could hear. Of those walking the grounds, none seemed interested in him, and he turned back to the grave again. "I did it again, Matt. I went and screwed things up and I don't think it can be fixed this time. I fell in love with a girl but she isn't in love with me. And that sucks."

He could almost hear Matt's voice saying, "Boo, hoo, suck it up, bro." Jax gave a little laugh. Matt always made some snarky comment first, and then got to work sorting out whatever was troubling Jax. "What's going on?" he'd say, and Jax would end up spilling his guts.

Matt wasn't there to ask the question, but Jax told him any-way. "We thought we could do this summer fling thing. I know, stupid, right? It's never that easy and there are always strings. But I got in over my head. I really fell for her. I told her about you, and Mom and Dad, and how I struggle with being the one left behind. I've never done that before, Matt. I trusted her. But she didn't trust me back."

He waited. The Sunday morning songbirds were singing their hearts out in the trees, while robins pecked at the ground, looking for tasty worms in the soft soil. The sun was up now, beams of it filtering through the leaves, and Jax wished he had on a pair of old jeans so he could sit next to his brother and really talk. Instead, he was reduced to squatting down and putting his hand on the stone marker.

"I know," he finally said, sighing. "She had her reasons for not telling me. Maybe I don't think they were good ones, but she had a rough childhood. Every single person she ever loved abandoned her, you know? Or didn't care enough to stay. And yeah, she was right. If she'd told me, I totally would have seen it as a way to fix the problem in the documentary. It wouldn't have been the only reason I wanted her around, but I can understand why she'd feel that way. After all, I'm not in any position to judge why someone does what they do after suffering a loss."

He stopped and stared at the etched stone. "Well goddamn, Matt. I did judge her anyway, didn't I? Because my feelings were hurt. And I'm not saying I don't have a reason, because I do. And I want to be angry with her for it, but I'm not. And that scares me, because what does that mean?"

It means you forgive her, numb nuts.

Jax laughed at the answer, closing his eyes and chuckling. "Yeah," he whispered. "I do."

But forgiving her didn't mean it would work out, did it? And maybe it shouldn't.

"Matt, I've blamed you for a lot of stuff in my life. I'm still angry at you for leaving. But the one I should be angry at is me. I spent so much time feeling I needed to be you, and then not wanting to be. Afraid of disappointing Mom and Dad and then terrified of what would happen if I lost myself in the process. I can't do that anymore. I can't use the burden of expectation as my excuse for... for..."

The air carried the sound of sirens from somewhere nearby while Jax tried to figure out what was holding him back.

He finally sighed. "For feeling the need to hold everything so tight and control it. For thinking if I fail at one little thing, I've let you down. Because I'm going to fail at a lot of things over the course of my life, and I need to learn how to do that or I'm never going to move past this moment. I don't want to be alone, Matt. I don't."

His knees were tiring so he stood again and shoved his hands in his pockets. He knew without a doubt that Matt would want him to be happy. Even yesterday, with his parents... they'd looked genuinely glad to see him. There'd been the moment of awkwardness between he and his dad, but then at the gala they'd been warm and welcoming to Summer and asking about his project as if they were truly interested. "Summer would say I was projecting my own feelings on them," he muttered, then laughed despite himself. "Why is it we're so good at understanding someone else but clueless when it comes to ourselves?"

Again Matt's voice echoed in his head. *What do I look like, a therapist?*

Jax sighed. Bingo. Again.

"I blew it with her, Matt. And she blew it with me. I don't know if it can be fixed. I think we need to fix ourselves before we can be with anyone else, and I don't know if she'll ever be willing to do that. She's so afraid, Matt. So afraid. Afraid no one will stay. And I think afraid of what will happen if they do."

And in that moment, he knew what he had to do.

"Thanks, bro," he said, swiping at a couple of tears that had gathered in his eyes. "You always come through."

Soon it would be time for brunch with his folks, and he had some thinking to do before then. About things he wanted to ask, things he wanted to say. But he did know this. He had to stop feeling guilty about being the one left behind, stop putting pressure on himself to be a success for both of them. He had to, at some point, be enough. If he could forgive Summer for not trusting him, why couldn't he forgive himself?

He had to try. He had to do it for both of them.

Chapter Seventeen

Summer blinked awake and squinted against the sunlight flooding the hotel room. She stretched and realized she was in the bed alone, and the memory of last night's argument—if she could call it that—rushed back.

She'd expected him to be angry, and he had been, but she hadn't been prepared for the hurt in his voice and even his body language. Maybe she should have been. He was the kind of man who felt deeply, and she'd betrayed him. It was true and she felt awful about it.

She knew she had reasons. But as he'd pointed out last night, those reasons had consequences. And her lack of trust in him, her desire to protect herself, had driven him away. She was pretty sure there was no coming back from last night. It was over between them.

What he didn't realize was that losing him was actually breaking her heart, because for the first time in her adult life, she'd allowed herself to love someone.

She stretched in the sheets and realized the hotel room was incredibly quiet. A quick check as she sat up showed her to be alone. There was no sound coming from the bathroom; no shower running or electric razor humming. The extra blanket was folded and placed on the sofa, with the pillow on top of it.

He'd gone, then. He hadn't even waited until he needed to leave for brunch with his parents, he'd been that anxious to get away from her.

Tears stung her eyes but she blinked them back. She was so sick of crying. Hot tears had leaked from her eyes as she lay staring at the ceiling last night, after already being swollen and sore from her crying jag in the bathroom in the moments before he'd come to the room and then while they'd talked. Her throat was sore from holding so much in and swallowing it down. But this—Jax leaving before she waked—hurt a lot. As if he couldn't wait to get away from her.

When she thought of Friday night, and the dinner last night, and how the weekend was supposed to go, she wilted.

After twenty minutes or so, she crawled out of bed and went to have a shower. It wasn't until she re-entered the room to dress that she saw the hotel note pad on the coffee table and a pen on top of it.

With the towel still wrapped around her, she went over and lifted the paper.

Summer,

I've gone to run an errand this morning and then off to brunch with my parents. Don't forget to check in three hours before the flight, and I'll reimburse you for the cab to the airport. I'll see you at the gate.

Jax

Nothing personal, just a set of instructions like he'd give her while they were at work. She stared at the paper and his handwriting. Working together now would be impossible, wouldn't it? She couldn't bear the thought of going to the house every morning and having to see his face, hear his voice, take instructions; the household tasks were even more personal. Making his bed, doing his laundry, the scent of his cologne wafting up from the fabric. Cooking for him, doing his dishes, rinsing out the coffee cup where he'd placed his lips. No, she couldn't do that.

She'd have to put in her notice and make the money she'd already made stretch throughout the summer. Once school went in, she could do her classes in the morning, work at the school in the afternoons, and somehow make it all work.

Without him.

God, those two words created such an emptiness within her.

The only clothing she had to wear today was the dress she'd borrowed for the brunch, so she put it on, then did her hair and applied a little makeup so she didn't look like she'd been pulled through a knothole sideways. The poor sleep and crying headache behind her eyes made her feel as if she were hungover, but she pushed through, packing her things, checking into her flight, and then checking out of the hotel and taking an Uber to the airport. If she had to wait for her flight, she'd rather go through security and wait there than sit in the empty hotel room where they'd made love only thirty-six hours earlier.

Right now he was at the restaurant with his parents. What would he tell them had happened? Would he lie or tell the truth? It really wasn't any of her business, not anymore, but she found she cared just the same.

Despite her internal anguish, she found she was hungry and grabbed an egg white and avocado croissant and salad at a restaurant through security. She considered wandering through the terminal to pass the time, but she had flown carry-on only and carting around her overnight bag and the garment bag with the dress and shoes from last night was cumbersome. In the end, she went to the gate, found a seat as far away from everyone as she could find, and pulled out her phone. She could always read on her ebook app until boarding. Or until Jax showed up.

But time ticked on and she looked up occasionally, searching for him. No Jax. She wasn't even absorbing the words she was reading right now; she was preoccupied with where he might be and, as the time to board drew closer, if he was going to show up at all. He wouldn't leave her to fly alone, would he? How would she get from Portland to Jewell Cove? She checked her messages again and there was nothing from him. Her lip quivered as the old feelings crowded inside her. Left alone. Always left alone, or left behind. Worse, not worth coming back for. No one had ever come back for her. Not even Dorothy and Hal. If not for the accidental meeting last night, they would never have taken the steps to find her.

"Get a grip," she whispered to herself. Sitting here and pitying herself wasn't going to help. She was smart enough to know she had reason to feel that way and where those feelings came from, but also that she had to stop letting them drive her life. That fear was what had kept her from getting too close to Jax, what kept her from telling him the truth in the first place.

Preboarding was called, then general boarding zones. Summer rose and, feeling utterly miserable, went to the gate and scanned her boarding pass. There was no upgrading today; she stayed in economy and slid into her seat by the window after stowing her bags.

Five minutes before departure, she saw him. His hair was tousled and he looked flustered but he was here. He scanned the back of the plane briefly but didn't see her, she was sure. Instead he disappeared from view as he took his seat up in business class.

An ache settled just behind her breastbone, a heavy weight of pain and regret that she couldn't dislodge. And as they rushed down the runway and headed into the clouds, she closed her eyes and tried to forget, even for a little while, how she'd messed everything up.

Jax settled into the leather seat and cursed the accident that had slowed traffic on the way to the airport. He'd wanted to talk to Summer, even just briefly, before boarding. It hadn't been an easy few hours. He'd made some decisions, though. That Summer probably wasn't going to be beside him as he implemented the changes to come made him sad, but perhaps this big failure, this dented heart, meant he would move forward better.

They had a half hour drive from Portland to Jewell Cove, however, and he doubted they'd go all that time without saying a word.

Perhaps she wouldn't want to talk to him at all. It was probably foolish to think that he could confide in her about what had happened today. The closeness they'd shared was gone. How stupid was it that he wanted to tell her about it, even knowing that she'd broken his trust? And yet he thought of his "conversation" with his brother, and the hope he'd felt in those moments, and knew that he had to try.

He sat with that uncomfortable thought throughout the flight, while sipping on a ginger ale and nibbling on a tiny bag of pretzels. When they finally landed, he disembarked and walked up the jetway to the exit, and then waited for her so they could go to the car together. His stomach was a mass of knots. The last thing he'd said to her was a curt "good night" as he covered himself with a blanket and she pulled up the covers on the bed. She was probably angry with him, and he didn't blame her. He'd barely made the flight. Had she wondered if he was going to make it at all?

At least thirty people passed him before he saw her approaching, her bag over her shoulder and her garment bag folded over her arm. When she saw him her face crumpled a little, but then she recovered and flattened her expression. This was easily the most awkward, painful moment he'd ever shared with a woman. The knowledge that they were all but over yet had to spend a half hour alone in a car together was, at least for him, a sweet torture.

"Hi," he said softly when she reached him. "Let me carry this to the car."

She didn't say anything when he took the garment bag from her arm and draped it over his own. In a muddle of confused feelings, he walked beside her through the terminal and to the parking garage where he'd left the car. She offered nothing and he didn't know where to start, but the silence grew and grew to be an ungainly presence, the proverbial elephant in the room, until he couldn't form a sentence at all.

Instead, he stowed their bags in the trunk. Then they each got into their side of the car, shut the doors, buckled their seatbelts. The tension was so palpable Jax wondered if his bones would grow brittle and break under the strain.

One of them had to say something, and he figured that since he was the one who'd left this morning, it should be him. A sidelong glance as he backed out of his parking spot showed her lip barely trembling; she had to be feeling as on edge as he was.

"I'm sorry I left as I did. I wasn't mad. I—" He stopped, frowned, then rolled down his window to insert his parking stub. The gate lifted and he rolled through. "I went to see my brother," he explained, his voice tight. It was impossible not to get emotional over Matt, and he hoped that never changed. They'd loved each other and shared a tight bond in their short time together.

Her lips relaxed the slightest bit. "Oh."

"I didn't know how to explain that in the note, and wasn't sure how you even felt about... It's all a mess, Summer."

"I actually wasn't sure you were going to make the flight."

The soft uncertainty in her voice hurt his heart. "No matter what happened between us, I wouldn't leave you stranded. God, I hope you know that much about me."

She nodded, then looked out the window, he suspected to hide any inkling of tears.

"You had brunch with your parents?" she asked, stronger now.

"I did. We talked a lot."

"What did you tell them about me?"

"I just said you'd had some surprising news last night, and you weren't feeling up to it. They were disappointed, because they liked you, Summer. They liked you a lot."

They were on the highway now, and he set the cruise control. The traffic was light as it was a Sunday afternoon, and they'd make good time back home. Huh. Home. Oddly enough, the house up at Refuge Point did feel that way. It was only his until

September, though. Earlier, if he wrapped up the documentary early.

"Don't," she said sharply. "Don't try to be kind or make this more than it is, all right? It's hard enough."

"I'm not trying to make it more difficult for you. Summer, I'm not going to press you about Edward Jewell. Not for me, not for the documentary. Every person I approach has the right to say no to having their story told."

"Well, I'm glad I'm like everyone else."

He took a moment after her sharp retort to think about what to say next. "You're not like everyone else. Not even close. But I absolutely owe you the same courtesy, and not take advantage of our relationship to press you into doing something you don't want to do."

She turned in her seat. "Then why did you say what you did last night? About me knowing how much you were struggling with the project and keeping key information from you?"

"Because I was angry!" It came out louder than he expected, and he blew out a breath. "Because you didn't trust me enough to do the right thing. You assumed I'd pressure you, assumed I would only want you for that. It would have been nice to have had the option to say 'no, Summer, if you're not comfortable I'll find another way.'"

She looked away.

"I can't deny that I think about the documentary and look for new ideas all the time. Or that your connection would have been the answer to a prayer. But if you'd trusted me, told me no,

I could have at least had a starting point to research. Now we're well into July, and the time to complete this isn't unlimited. I could have done this without putting you in the spotlight."

She sighed, leaned back against the seat, and closed her eyes. "My whole life, Jax, no one has ever considered what I wanted. I guess I didn't even consider it would be different this time."

"I figured that out. Which is why I'm not angry at you. I'm just... sad."

"Thank God you didn't say you were disappointed."

"I am, but not in you. Just disappointed that this pointed out that neither of us is ready to really be with someone. I need someone who is going to believe in me, Summer. And you need to have someone you can trust. I'm just not sure you ever will."

That heavy silence of before descended over the car as Jax put on the directional for the Jewell Cove exit.

"Can you take me to my apartment, please?" she said, straightening.

"Of course." He was glad they'd talked, but hated how the weekend was ending. Last night while they were dancing he'd thought he'd tell her he loved her today. How things could change in a moment, never to be the same.

Another right hand turn onto Main. "And Jax, I think it's best if I hand in my notice. I—" Summer took a breath, blew it out. "It would be too hard for me to see you every day, to work through a to-do list and know... after we..."

"I don't like it, but I understand. I just... you need this money for the fall."

"I'll manage. You've paid me well. It'll tide me over for a while."

He considered offering her the balance of her contract but knew pride would keep her from accepting it. "I'll pay you the two week severance agreed on in your contract," he said instead.

"I hate leaving you in the lurch."

"I'll manage."

"But there's so much—"

"I'll manage, Summer. I promise." Then he pulled into her driveway, put the car in park, and reached for her hand. "Your comfort is more important than any to-do list."

She pulled her hand away. "Don't, Jax. God, don't be kind. I don't know what I'm doing right now. Being with you hurts me, I'll admit it. And I'm trying to sort through so much in my head, about my grandparents and what I'm going to do next and what my childhood even means. I'm a hot mess right now, and if you're kind for a moment more I'm going to lose it. I'm trying really hard to hold myself together, so just get me my bag and let me go, okay?"

"All right," he agreed, because the last thing he wanted to do right now was hurt her further.

He left the car running and went to the trunk to take out her bags. "Do you want help carrying them up?"

"No, I've got it." Her gaze strayed to the car next to them, her rental. "I'll take the car back tomorrow."

"Whenever you get to it, Summer. There's no rush."

"It doesn't feel right."

"Whatever you want."

"Stop!" she hissed, then pursed her lips together. "Stop being nice. Stop pretending you understand because you don't!"

What he understood was that she was used to people leaving. To feeling like people never wanted to stay, or that she wasn't worth staying for. Nothing he could say would change that.

"Take care, Summer," he said instead, and though it damned near killed him, he went back to the driver's side and got behind the wheel.

By the time he'd buckled his seatbelt and put the car in reverse, she was up the stairs and opening the door to her apartment.

Chapter Eighteen

On Tuesday, Abby followed Summer to the rental car agency in Brunswick and then drove her home. On the way back, Summer filled Abby in on the basic details of what had happened. Abby understood more than anyone she knew what it was like to feel left out of family. Her grandmother had kept her own secret, never telling Abby about her family in Maine until it was too late. She and Summer were both orphans. Both had found their adopted homes in Jewell Cove. There was just one difference. Summer was terrified that when people found out about her mother and father, they'd look at her differently.

But Abby had a different take.

"Okay, I get what you're saying," she said, "but if this is your home, and the people you care about are here, and people care about you too, they won't give a shit. Honestly, they'll respect you all the more for becoming the awesome person you are." She flashed a grin Summer's way.

"Something Jax said nailed it, though," Summer admitted. "I don't trust that people will care about me, or that it won't matter. Because everyone I've ever cared about has let me down. I spent my whole life trying to be good enough. Worthy of it. Oh Abby, it sounds so stupid when I say it out loud, but believe me when I say the feelings are real."

"I know they are, honey. I've had my own share of demons." She took one hand off the wheel and gave Summer's a squeeze. "And I'm honored that I'm one of the few you trust."

"I should have told him. I know that. But I didn't want anyone pry into my family. And with the feelings I had for him, I knew I'd be devastated if he only wanted me for what I could provide for his research."

"Jax doesn't seem like that kind of guy."

"Deep down, I know he's not. But that's what so hard. He was right about one thing for sure. My inability to trust brought us here. I never once considered that if he knew he'd accept my refusal to participate."

"Because Summer Arnold is a people pleaser."

Summer's head snapped toward Abby's profile. "What?"

Abby glanced at her and then back at the road. "Summer, my love, is there any job in Jewell Cove you haven't done? Someone you haven't helped? You are a wonderful friend and a tremendous member of this community, but is it partly because you think friendship is conditional on your... I don't know, your willingness to say yes to everything?"

Summer stared. People pleasing? And was Abby saying her relationships were purely transactional? She hated that idea. Rejected it.

Unless it was partly true.

"You don't trust anyone will love you just for you. And sweetie, that's going to leave you very lonely unless you do something about it."

Summer sniffed. She was lonely. As much as she filled her days with work or social outings or volunteering for various things around town, she was still horribly lonely. Because she gave of herself, but she never let anyone all the way in.

They were heading back into Jewell Cove. "Hey, do you want to come to the house for a bit? We can hang out. Have lunch. And I thought I'd work in the rose garden a bit. I swear, nothing helps me work through problems like time in the garden. Maybe it'll help you, too." She looked over at Summer. "You don't have to be alone, you know. You can just be you. And hopefully someday you'll realize that you? Well, that person is enough. It doesn't matter how your mother died, or that your father was in jail, or that your grandmother kept you from your mom's side of the family. You can break that toxic pattern right now. It can end with you, and something better can start with you."

"You," Summer said, tears in her throat, "are the best cheerleader a girl ever had."

"Thanks. I try." Abby winked, then turned toward the south part of town and Blackberry Hill, toward the mansion whose secrets had started the discovery of the long-lost treasure on Aquteg.

The treasure. Abby had found pieces of Jed Foster's portion it in her Aunt Marian's attic. Rick Sullivan had found a piece in his mother's safety deposit box. Josh Collins had discovered artifacts on Aquteg—Lovers' Island, pieces of Charles Arsenault's efforts during the Civil War. The piece that was missing was within her grasp, wasn't it?

The question was, was she brave enough to ask for it?

Summer came to the conclusion that Jax was a very patient man.

One week went by, then two. Her bank account grew by the amount of three week's wages—the one that was owed and then two for severance. He even emailed a couple of times with questions about appointments and spreadsheets. They ran into each other at Gino's one Friday night, and while Summer nearly felt sick with nerves about it, he'd merely smiled and asked how she was doing before picking up his pizza box and leaving.

Jess offered her part time hours at the store for the rest of the summer, while she and Rick and their baby went on a family vacation for a week, and then she took additional time off for doctor appointments and repainting the nursery. Since

Summer loved Treasures, it was not a hardship to spend three days a week in the sunny space, selling candles and yarn and items made by local artisans. It wasn't full-time money, but it would help her stay afloat for the rest of the summer until school started up again. She did wonder who was ferrying the film crew out to the island, but it wasn't her worry anymore.

She missed it, though. She missed it and she missed Jax horribly. Sometimes she thought about biking up to the lighthouse and asking him for a second chance, but to what end? He was leaving. Being without him was inevitable. Middle of September he'd be back in the classroom. And she'd be starting her paralegal program so she wouldn't be in retail her whole life.

One thing she did do was reach out to her grandparents. Since Summer didn't have transportation, they came to her on a bright sunny day and she took them to Breezes for coffee. She wasn't quite ready to invite them into her space, and the café was always cheery and welcoming.

Dorothy was the first to reach for her hand. "We were so glad to get your call, Summer. The night of the gala must have been so overwhelming for you."

Hal nodded. "We got thinking afterward that it probably turned what you knew on its head. The last thing we want to do is push in, of course. But we'd love to see you more often."

"Hal," Dorothy chided. "Remember what I said about baby steps?"

Summer smiled. Gram Arnold had called her mother's family hoity toity snobs, but they seemed just as down-to-earth as anyone. "Let's find a table," Summer suggested. "And you're going to want to order pie. It's the best on the midcoast."

They sat at a table overlooking the harbor and placed their order with Linda, who looked on curiously but didn't pry. Summer took a breath and smiled up at the waitress who'd been at Breezes as long as she could remember. "Linda, these are my grandparents, Hal and Dorothy."

"It's good to meet you," Linda said with a smile.

"You as well. Summer recommends the pie. Any particular flavor you'd suggest??"

A brisk nod accompanied her choice. "This morning we have fresh strawberry rhubarb and first-of-the-season blueberry."

They all ordered, as well as coffee and tea, and then Summer took a breath and explained the reason for her invitation.

"You both know that Jax is doing his documentary on the treasure at Aquteg Island. I'd like for you to help him."

Hal leaned forward. "How do you mean?"

Her throat tightened with regret but she pressed on. "I hadn't told him about my connection. The reasons are complicated, but I should have been honest and I wasn't. Jax hasn't pressed me to have anything to do with it, which I appreciate, but I also know how much this means to him. But maybe you could help him. Tell him what you know, that sort of thing. Or even just give him a good place to look."

"You don't want to do that yourself?" Dorothy looked puzzled, and at that moment Linda returned with her tray of pie and beverages.

Summer waited until Linda was gone and out of earshot. "Only two people in Jewell Cove know about my parents, you see. Jax and a good friend of mine. I just... I don't want people digging around in my past. It would be bad enough in a small town, but in a documentary that could be streamed every-where..."

Hal and Dorothy looked at each other for a long moment, then Dorothy took a sip of her coffee. Summer wasn't sure what to say, and her grandparents were taking their sweet time responding.

Hal reached over and took Dorothy's hand, then met Summer's gaze. "Do you feel ashamed, Summer?"

The question surprised her. She'd thought her grandparents would understand her reluctance implicitly. It made her uncomfortable, so she redirected the question. "Do you?" she asked.

"We did," Dorothy said. "We didn't want anyone to know about Carol and what had happened to her. And then we realized that we were looking at everything the wrong way. Addiction is a disease and kicking it was a battle she didn't win. Hiding it under a blanket of shame and secrecy isn't going to make things any better."

"But I—" Her lip wobbled. "I'm sorry. I thought I was ready to talk about this, but it's so hard."

"She loved you, Summer," Dorothy insisted. "She fought to keep you for so long. Honey, if I have any regret, it's that we stepped away when we shouldn't have. If you were unhappy here… that breaks my heart. We should have found a way to manage."

"Not unhappy, exactly," Summer replied. "I love Jewell Cove, and being by the ocean, and I've built a life here with friends. But Gram and Gramp Arnold were not loving influences, I guess. I spent a lot of time trying to be good, to get their approval. I think at first they thought my dad was going to come back to get me. When he didn't, they were stuck with me, and I always knew it. They weren't bad to me. They just weren't…" She hesitated, searching for the right word. "Nurturing."

Regret shone in her grandmother's eyes. "I'm so sorry, Summer. And I'll always regret not fighting harder. We thought we were doing the right thing for you."

"I know," she answered, believing them. "I don't know why Gram wanted to keep you away when it was clear she didn't really want me, either."

Hal spoke up. "I think I might know why. She hated your mother and blamed her for your dad going to jail. Keeping you from us was… well, a way to stick it to us, I suppose." His cheeks reddened. "I'm sorry, Summer. I shouldn't speak of her that way. She brought you up, and you're a lovely woman, so she deserves some credit."

"No, it's all right." She paused to take a drink of her peppermint tea, trying to settle her feelings. "She gave me a roof over my head, clothes on my back, and food on the table. I'm grateful for that."

"But we're so sorry you weren't loved. That you felt you had to beg for affection," Dorothy said softly. "You are loved, Summer. And all you have to do to earn it is exist."

Summer looked down quickly, overcome with emotion, not wanting to show it in a public place. She'd thought Breezes would be a safe spot to avoid getting emotional, but her grandmother's simple declaration hit her right in the heart, right in the spot that had sat empty for most of her life.

Hal cleared his throat. "You were right," he said, perhaps a little too cheerfully. "This is the best pie I've ever had."

Summer looked up. All of them had tears shining in their eyes, and all three of them gave self-conscious laughs to dispel the moment. It eased the emotion and settled Summer into a new one: acceptance.

She cut into her pie with the side of her fork, took a bite, and let the ripe blueberry goodness explode on her tongue. It was the best thing she'd ever tasted, and that was only partly due to Gus's skills in the kitchen. For the first time she could remember, she was sitting with family and feeling unconditional love wash over her.

"In answer to your question, Summer, we'll help Jax. As long as you're okay with it."

"I am. If you want, I can give you directions to Refuge Point."

They spent the rest of the hour chatting about all manner of things, getting to know each other better, filling in the gaps. When it was time to go, Dorothy adjusted her crutches and gave Summer a warm smile. "We're staying at the Evergreen

Inn tonight and driving back tomorrow. Could we take you to dinner somewhere?"

"I'd like that," Summer replied. "Actually, I'd like that a lot."

"Perfect. You pick the place and text me. We'll come to get you if you need a lift."

Then Hal leaned forward and gave her a hug. "Thank you," he murmured in her ear. "You've made me very happy, and my wife is over the moon." When they drew back, his eyes glowed at her with happiness and gratitude. If Summer took anything away from the two encounters she'd had with her grandparents, it was that they loved each other in a way that was beautiful. Even after nearly fifty years. She got the feeling he'd do anything to make his wife happy.

"Oh!" Dorothy said, as they made their way outside to the small parking lot. "I have something for you."

Hal reached inside the car and took out a gift bag. Inside was a velvet box. Summer knew what it was before she even opened it, but she wasn't prepared for how beautiful the ring was. A stunning oval emerald was surrounded by a halo of diamonds, resting solidly on a gold band. "We had it checked and cleaned before bringing it," he said. "The locket, too. Look inside."

He held the box while she took out the gold locket. The oval was over an inch tall, with etchings of flowers and a butterfly in the middle. She stuck a fingernail between the layers and gently pried it open. There were two photographs inside.

"The old one is actually the original with Edward and his mistress. But the other one... that's you and your mother, Summer, shortly after you were born."

The woman in the photo was beaming, holding a tiny baby in her arms. Summer touched a finger to the image, wishing she remembered this version of her mom. "She was beautiful," Summer whispered.

"You look a lot like her, actually," Dorothy added. "They're yours now, sweetheart."

"Thank you, Grammie," Summer said, and then they all had an emotional moment.

"You haven't called me that since you were a little girl." Dorothy's voice was watery with emotion. "It's lovely to hear it again."

Summer carefully put the jewels back in the box and slid it into the bag. "Thank you for this. I'll cherish it, I promise."

"Well, we should get going." Hal stepped in and lightened the mood. "We'll go see Jax and then maybe take a little drive up the coast. But we'll see you for dinner." He leaned forward and kissed her cheek.

When they were gone, Summer walked home and then sat on her sofa, opening the box again. She took out the ring and slid it over her finger, admiring the sparkle and marveling at the weight of it. Then she took out the locket and opened it again, staring at the photos inside.

"Mama," she whispered, staring at the blonde woman smiling so brightly. "I miss you, Mama. And I'm sorry." Not sorry because she'd done anything wrong, but sorry that their lives had turned out the way they had. She thought about her grandmother's words about shame and blame.

Was there any way for her to let go of either of those things?

Chapter Nineteen

Jax stared at the computer screen and couldn't believe his luck. No, not luck. He had Summer to thank. Even though he hadn't spoken to her directly, a week ago he'd been paid a visit by Hal and Dorothy Robinson, who, with Summer's blessing, had offered him what information they had on Edward Jewell and his mistress, who'd been a resident of Baltimore during 1850s and 60s. Edward made frequent trips into port with his shipping business and had set her up in a house of her own. In 1860 she bore a daughter; the war started and blockades made things more challenging. Tom Arseneault was a blockade runner and snuck in and out of ports all along the south, but Edward was far more into playing it safe and let others take the risk. He was more than happy to invest, however, and made a fortune.

Jax had spent the last several days researching the mistress, scouring genealogies and shipping records and anything else he could think of. What was emerging was a picture of a man who was more interested in profit than altruism. Piecing things with what he already knew was forming a fuller picture of the man who'd had a town named for him. It was becoming clearer to Jax, however, that the man most had considered a "pirate" was actually the best of the bunch. Charles Arseneault had enjoyed the finer things, but he'd been the one to press to smuggle slaves out of the South and to use Aquteg as a stop on the way to Canada. He'd made his profits, but he'd also carried precious cargo north, risking his own life in the process while Foster and Jewell played it safe.

Jewell paid off the mistress then forgot all about her and his daughter, instead playing the devoted husband and respected businessman. He'd built himself a mansion, which burned in 1897, and his descendants withered on the family tree thanks to world wars one and two. Most of the family fortune was lost in the 1929 crash. Jewell had shone brightly but then his flame had flickered and gone out.

Until now. Because that mistress had taken her money, left Baltimore for small town life, and opened her own going concern, a general store which her daughter inherited and expanded into three stores, and her daughter into ten. They were all gone now, but it had provided enough of a foundation that generations to come had good starts to life—with the exception of the struggles during the depression. Edward Jewell's descendants had been mostly middle class with access to education, all the way up to Hal Robinson, a lawyer who'd been smart enough to engage top corporate entities as clients and savvy enough to ride the stock market wave of the 80s.

Jax loved this story, one that proved that riches guaranteed nothing, and humble beginnings did not mean a lifetime of poverty.

That money came and went, but what it couldn't buy was integrity and happiness.

The only fly in the ointment, so to speak, was that painting a disparaging picture of Ed Jewell could mean perpetuating that sentiment on future generations. Right now he was gathering information, but then he'd focus on the angle he wanted—the other family tree, with its deep roots and resilience. He even had a crew going to Harrisburg to interview Hal and Dorothy, since she sometimes found travel difficult.

What it didn't solve? His relationship with Summer.

He missed her so much. At least a dozen times in the past weeks he'd considered phoning her, asking if they could meet, but he didn't want to hurt her more than he already had. It was now August; in a few weeks he'd be due back at Penn State for the new term, and he couldn't be less excited for it. He still loved the job—teaching was in his blood. But the thought of leaving Jewell Cove and not seeing her again left an emptiness in his heart he wasn't sure would ever be filled again.

The fact that she'd sent her grandparents his way? It had said a lot. She wanted his project to succeed, even if she didn't want to be on camera herself. He would never have contacted Hal and Dorothy on his own, out of respect for her. That had told him she wasn't still angry at him. And he wasn't angry at her, either. Time away from each other had made him realize that it wasn't really about trust. It went deeper than that. It went all the way down to the pain beneath everything. It was about a little girl who never felt loved. Who never felt first. Who always felt she had to prove something, and boy did he relate to that.

Rick was back from holidays and had mentioned that Summer was working part time up at Treasures to help lighten Jess's load a little. He'd nearly stopped in there, too, but what would he say? How awkward would it be, especially if there were customers around, which there was sure to be as tourist season was in full swing.

He sat back in his desk chair, away from the archive site he was on, and rubbed a hand over his face. He wanted to see her. Needed to. He was patient and he'd decided weeks ago that he wanted to prove to her he wasn't going to run or use her for his own gain. How could he do that if he were too chicken to even talk to her?

In the end, he picked up his phone and sent her a message.

Summer, thank you so much for sending Hal and Dorothy my way. I'm making changes to Jewell's part of the story and I'd like you to vet it before I proceed. Can we meet?

He threw the phone on his desk and sighed. What did he ultimately want out of this, anyway?

There was no immediate reply, so he went out to the lighthouse and climbed the stairs to the top, to the platform where the wind blew his hair from his face and the ocean glittered in the sun, as far as he could see. He remembered her up here, looking so free and pretty, her braid in tatters from the sea breeze and her eyes the same stormy blue as the water that crashed on the rocks below. She'd urged him to stop micromanaging, to let things go, to trust his team. She'd made him laugh. There were times she'd seemed far away and other times it felt she was part of him. The attraction was one thing, after July fourth it was more than that. Sex changed things always, but not always the heart. Yet it had for him. That day, he'd started to live and breathe for her, and the past month he'd merely been going through the motions. The work was fine, but his heart was a mess.

"Penny for your thoughts," came a voice, and he spun around to find her standing there, in a pair of white denim capri pants and a China-blue T-shirt that brought out her eyes. He swallowed, unable to form words, marveling at how he'd thought about her and then suddenly conjured her up out of nowhere.

"You did say you wanted to meet," she said, stepping forward with a smile. "I texted, but I guess you left your phone in the house."

"What if I hadn't been here?"

She shrugged. "I've missed it. I would have gone and sat by the cliffs and listened to the ocean and the birds and filled my well."

Lord, he'd missed her.

"You look good," he offered, downplaying it because he secretly thought he'd never seen a more beautiful woman in his life.

"Thanks." She smiled again. "I've been doing a lot of thinking and taking time for me. Though I'm at Treasures a few days a week."

"I know. Rick told me. Do you like it?"

She lifted an eyebrow. "It's not a career, but yeah, I like it." She moved to stand beside him at the rail. "This is still the best view in Jewell Cove."

"Yes," he said, "it is." But he wasn't looking out past the point. He was looking at her, and when she realized it, her cheeks turned pink.

"So," she said, changing the subject, "you want me to vet this new direction. That's nice of you."

"I don't want to do anything about your family without clearing it with you first. To be honest, what your grandparents told me helped a lot and I've been able to dig into a lot of research. The mistress was named Matilda Jackson, by the way, and she had a daughter, Pauline. It's unfair to simply call her 'the mistress.' She was a person, with a name, and a legacy of her own."

"Really?"

What he really wanted to do was pull her into his arms and say he was sorry and pretend nothing had ever gone wrong. Instead, he told her what he knew about her ancestor—what a strong woman she was, how she'd picked herself up after being abandoned by the father of her child and built her own little empire. He told the story while gulls and terns swooped and called, while the sun shifted and cast her face in shadow, and boats bobbed on the water, chugging their way along the coastline. When he was done, he hoped he'd painted a picture that did Matilda justice, that told the story without opening Summer to any of the speculation and scrutiny she dreaded.

"She sounds amazing," Summer said, looking up at him. "Almost like… well, being left behind doesn't mean being limited."

"Exactly," he said. "You know, she made me think about you a lot."

"Because I've limited myself? I mean, I haven't exactly made something of myself."

He shook his head, shocked at her blunt answer. "No, it's not that at all! Strength and success aren't measured by wealth. Look at Edward Jewell. He had riches but how strong was his morality? He was a man who balked against doing the right thing because it would cut into his profits and endanger his business. You're not like that at all. You have strength and integrity. People love you because you care about them. No matter what you're dealing with on the inside, you're a good person, Summer, independent and stronger than you realize. It's one of the things I love about you."

For the flash of a moment, everything froze. The words had just come out without any forethought. And she'd heard them, her face registering surprise and… not dismay. He wasn't sure what she was feeling, but she wasn't turning away, and a surge of hope rolled through his chest.

"Summer," he said softly, barely audible over the wind, "I'm not leaving you. Not unless you send me away. I want to stay. I honest to God do not know what that's going to look like, but I do love you. I'm not angry about the secret anymore. All it took was putting myself in your shoes to realize that you keeping this to yourself had nothing to do with me and everything to do with what you've kept locked inside for so long. I hope you can see that you have family now in your grandparents, and you have me. You will always have me. You are not alone, Summer. Not anymore."

She nodded, her eyes watering but she didn't cry; instead she lifted her chin and met his gaze. "I realized a lot of things after that weekend. Most of all though, I realized that my fear of loving someone was going to mean I'd be alone my whole life. That while I had reasons for keeping this from you, they were really excuses to keep me from getting in too deep. Oh, Jax. For years I've been getting in my own way, because I've been stuck being that ten-year-old girl who realized her mom was gone, her daddy wasn't coming for her, and the only people she had left weren't happy at being stuck with her. In my head I knew that wasn't true for everyone in the world. In my head I knew love existed and even thought I wanted it for myself. But my heart was still always that little girl. It wasn't until love actually came along that I realized I was scared to death of it. And just when I thought I might be brave enough to tell you how I felt, to tell you what I'd been holding back—"

"You met your grandparents and they beat you to the punch."

"I'm not sorry, though. They're lovely people. We can't go back in time, but I want them in my life now. I believe them when they say they thought they were doing what was best, because I know how Gram Arnold could be. I wish it wasn't true, but it is."

"You mean you… trust them?" He said it with a sly smile, and she smiled in return.

"Go figure," she answered. "I guess I had to start somewhere."

They were quiet for a moment, letting things settle between them.

"I'm sorry, Jax. For not trusting you. I'm sorry for the argument that night of the gala, for the distance since, for all of it." She turned to him and held his gaze. "I don't know what's ahead, but I do know I was in the wrong. I know you felt betrayed."

"It wasn't just that," he admitted. "I was starting to realize I'd fallen in love with you, and that just flattened me. Besides, you're not the only one with a past baggage chip on your shoulder."

"You fell in love with me? You really did?"

"Yes, sweetheart. I really did. And it surprised the hell out of me."

"Then what the hell took you so long? It's been weeks since we got back!"

He gave a low laugh. "I was waiting, sweetheart. Biding my time. And trying to figure some things out before I was ready to come to you."

"Oh, Jax."

She reached out and took his hand, squeezed it in her fingers, and then rose up on tiptoe to kiss his lips.

At one point, Summer had thought she might never taste his lips again, but here they were, standing at the top of the lighthouse, the place they'd come that first day they'd met, and she was kissing him, and nothing had ever felt so good or right in her whole life.

When their lips broke apart, Summer rested her forehead against his chest and let gratitude and hope wash over her. He had forgiven her for holding back the truth and he admitted he'd fallen in love with her. She hoped against hope he didn't mean past tense, but the way he'd tenderly kissed her back suggested he hadn't fallen *out* of love with her.

His broad hand cupped her head in a loving, protective gesture that made her eyes sting. "If you've had to take a long look in the mirror, so have I, Summer. I spent years measuring myself against a yardstick that didn't even exist. Matt wasn't perfect, but he was so close to it that when he died, I felt like I owed it to him to be the best. He told me to live the life he wouldn't get to. I was a kid. Hell, we both were. He didn't mean for me to *be* him; he meant for me to go and live it to the fullest."

She wrapped her arms around his waist, her body fitting against his in a way that felt like home. "Which you've tried to do. But then felt guilty about it, because you felt like you weren't honoring his legacy."

He nodded, resting his chin on her head. Oh, she could stay like this forever. She'd settle for this moment, though, and make it last as long as she could.

"I never told you about brunch." He ran his hand down her arm and back up again. "After our falling out, and going to see Matt at the cemetery, I was pretty worn out. Mom noticed. We were finally all honest with each other and I was wrong, Summer. So wrong. I mean, Dad admitted he was disappointed when I decided to do my history degree. But then, when he saw me excel, when it was clear this was what I loved, he was happy for me. Proud of me. Problem is, my dad doesn't always say these things. Because I never heard the words, I shut him out. The more I shut him out, the more our relationship became one of politeness. And so everything festered."

"I'm sorry." She looked up. Had things soured with his parents? She hoped not. She'd liked them, too, even if Mr. Brodie had seemed a little reticent.

"Don't be. I finally said how I felt, and Mom had pretty much already figured it out. Apparently, when your kids grow up, they 'have to come to things in their own time.' I'm a smart guy, but turns out I was a slow learner about this. I was trying to live up to an ideal that doesn't even exist."

She could relate to that in a weird sort of way. "I guess we're both people pleasers," she said with a shrug. She hadn't let go of him, but she knew she had to in order to say what she needed.

"Speaking of people pleasing... please know that what I'm about to say is because this is what I really want and not because I'm trying to please anyone else, okay?" She stepped away, reached into her back pocket, and took out the little box. She held it out for him to take, which he did, and his lips dropped open when he saw what was inside.

"Is this...?"

She nodded. "It is. The ring that Edward Jewell gave Matilda Jackson, and the locket he gifted his daughter. Antiques and worth quite a bit, according to the last appraisal done a number of years ago."

"Your grandparents?"

"It's my own family heirloom. Something that connects me to generations of the past. Now that you've told me her story, I think that the scandalous beginning doesn't matter near as much as the fortitude that began this lineage. I want you to feature it in the documentary, Jax. And if you want, I'll consent to being interviewed for it."

"You don't have to do that. You—"

"I want to," she reassured him. "I've been doing a lot of thinking about shame and trying so hard for people to like me, not trusting what would happen if they knew the truth. I already got a lot of that as a kid, being teased because I was an orphan. Can you imagine what would have happened if the truth had been out there? Maybe it was a lie, but I can at least thank Gram Arnold for trying to protect me from that."

She opened the locket and showed him the photo on the left. "That's me and my mom right after I was born. She loved me, Jax. Maybe she made mistakes, maybe she got caught up in addiction, but she loved me. I'm not ashamed of her anymore. I'm also not her. Look, you know the truth and you're not running. Abby knows too, and she's been a wonderful friend. At some point I have to trust that the people who really love me won't care, and the ones who do care, don't really love me. Not everyone has to."

"Only if you're sure."

"I'm positive. I know time's short—"

He smiled at her. "Actually, it's not. I've extended the project so we can do this properly. The island filming will wrap up soon, but everything else we can manage over the months ahead. It will mean a delay, but I don't care. We're going to have a ton of footage to edit and create the story I want to tell."

"But your job... You have to be back at the university in September."

"I do, but I'm going to manage what I can remotely. As someone reminded me recently, I need to trust my crew. I don't need to be up their ass every minute of every day."

She laughed, feeling lighter than she had in days. And then the reality struck. He did have to be in Pennsylvania in September, a little less than a month away, and the summer fling she'd insisted she wanted was not a possibility now. She wanted all or nothing, and as much as it scared her, she knew she had to stop playing it safe all the time.

"Jax, did you mean it when you said you loved me?"

He squinted against the sun as he looked down into her face, but a smile lit his lips as he cupped her chin in his hand. "Love. Present tense. I love you, Summer."

Without hesitating, she took the leap. "I love you too, Jax."

He kissed her then, not the soft reacquaintance from before, but a contact so all-encompassing that she lost herself in it, letting the sensations wash over her. The bite of the wind, the heat of the sun, the plaintive cry of the gulls, the taste of his mouth, so familiar. The feel of his body against hers, calling to her.

She needed him, more than she'd ever needed anyone, and here he was, saying he was hers.

With shaking fingers, she reached for the buttons on his shirt, revealing his taut chest with the sprinkling of light hair. His gaze blazed into hers as she slid the shirt down off his shoulders, and then he grasped the hem of her T-shirt and pulled it over her head, leaving her standing in the white pants and a light pink bra. Desire took over. They were protected up here, in their private refuge from the world, away from eyes and opinions and reasons why this couldn't work. It was just them, and this moment, and she reached behind her back and unhooked her bra, letting it fall to the platform.

"Here?" he asked hoarsely.

"Here," she confirmed. "I don't want to waste a single moment longer, Jax."

She unbuttoned her jeans and slid out of them as well as her panties, all in one go, until she stood before him utterly naked, utterly vulnerable, and, miracle of miracles, trusting in him. Trusting that whatever they had, they'd find a way. "Touch me," she said, leaning against the inner railing of the platform.

He did, pinning her hands on the rail and kissing his way down her neck to her breasts, making her gasp and writhe against his touch. He slid a hand between her legs and she called out, surrendering to him completely. She loved him. Loved him! The knowledge made his touch hotter, his kiss sweeter than she ever could imagine.

"You, too," she murmured, reaching for the button on his shorts.

They didn't waste time. Didn't even bother going horizontal. Instead they made love against the rail, in the wind and salt air and brilliant sunshine, until Summer cried out with pleasure and Jax followed close behind. Only then did they collapse on the deck with his shirt providing a thin barrier between their bodies and the floor of the platform. Sweat clung to their skin, and Jax leaned over and treated her to a long, luxurious kiss.

"I missed you," he whispered. "So damn much."

"I missed you, too." He laid back and she rested her hand on his chest. "This wasn't how I anticipated today going. It was vetting your doc."

"I had to get you here somehow," he joked, running a hand over her hip. "Now I don't want you to leave."

"Okay."

He sat up, leaving her balancing her weight on her hand. "You mean that?"

"If you can trust me, Jax, I can trust you. Otherwise we don't have anything. And that's not what I want. Not when I've waited this long to feel this way."

They kissed again, long and slow. She wasn't sure she'd ever have enough of him, if she were honest with herself. But at some point they would have to move. They were naked and without a single drop of sunscreen, and it was coming on the hottest part of the day. Still, maybe just a few more moments...

"Summer, about what comes next..."

She kissed his nose, the crest of his cheek. "Hmm?"

"I was thinking of asking to extend the lease here, at least for a little while. I can come up on the weekends. At least it would give us time to sort out what we want to do, you know? It wouldn't be so bad."

Summer pondered his offer for a moment. It would be lovely, escaping up here during the autumn, when all the colors were vibrant and the fall air crisp and clear. But she also knew why he'd suggested it: she had told him in the beginning that she never wanted to leave Jewell Cove. That this was her home.

She'd been hiding here for over twenty years. Wasn't it time to stop?

"Or," she began, "I could spend the week with you. We could drive up sometimes... my lease on my apartment isn't up until January. I'm not sure I'm ready to leave Jewell Cove behind completely. Not yet, anyway. But this could be a good start."

"What about school?"

"My classes are remote. I can do them from anywhere."

His eyes lit up with hope. "You'd do that? Come with me to Pennsylvania?"

She put her hand to his jaw. "I'm willing to give it a try if you are. You shouldn't be the only one to compromise, Jax. You have commitments to keep, and I need to stop hiding. We want to be together. Yes, I'll do this, and we can figure things out as we go along."

He crushed her to him, her breasts smashed against his chest, and she laughed into his shoulder. "I'll take that as a yes?"

"You're damn right. And until September, you're gonna stay right here. I don't want to lose another moment with you."

"I hope you don't want me to take my old job back."

"You don't want it?"She shook her head. "That's not what I want to be for you. I just want to love you. Besides, three days a week at Treasures leaves me lots of time for other...pleasures." She grinned cheekily.

"Promise?" he asked.

"Promise." And despite the blazing sun, they stayed at their private refuge just a little bit longer.

Epilogue

One year later

Summer stood at the point, looking out over the water, the lighthouse rising proudly to her right and the house behind her. The morning breeze was fresh and cool, with the promise of perfect August weather later. This afternoon Jax was premiering his documentary at the church, a rather modest launch for something they'd worked so hard on together, but one he said he wanted for his adopted community.

Her grandparents would be there. Just now their rental car was parked in front of the house, and they were staying through the weekend. His parents, too, were staying at the house and making for a lovely family celebration. Abby and Tom would be in attendance with their little daughter, and Jess and Rick with their two in tow. Josh and Lizzie, who had found the island treasure in the first place, and Summer—all the Jewell Cove descendants of the original three founders. Plus many others, who were excited to see their little town become just a bit famous.

The story that Jax told in the hour-long film was one of hidden treasure, scandal, and betrayal, but also of bravery and love. Summer had seen it and cried when it was over, she was so proud of it.

She turned and looked back at the house, so lonely here on the point of land jutting into the Atlantic. But it wasn't lonely, not when there was love inside its walls. Now she and Jax split their time between Penn State and here in a different way. During the school year, they lived in his house. And for Christmas last year, Summer had given up the lease on her apartment and Jax had surprised her with the deed to the house at Refuge Point. Now holidays and summers were spent here, by the ocean. After wrapping the documentary, Jax decided to take a break and try his hand at writing a non-fiction over the summer. He was making progress, but planning a wedding had eaten up some of his time.

It was all happening soon.

Summer heard a noise and turned. Jax stood by the lighthouse door. She sent him a wicked grin and started in his direction, the wet grass making her legs itch. She didn't care. While today was the premiere and Saturday was their wedding, right now all Summer wanted was to sneak away with him and repeat the promise she'd made to him a year ago.

To love him. That was all, and for always.

He smiled back, and opened the door.

Thank you so much for taking this journey with me—from Abby Foster arriving in Jewell Cove to solving the very last piece of the treasure puzzle with Summer Arnold. The little town I made up now holds a special place in my heart, and I hope it does in yours, too!

I love small towns, so I hope you'll join me in my Darling, VT series! Meet the Gallagher family and be swept along as they fall in love and find their own happy ever afters – and maybe discover there's something to the legend of the Kissing Bridge.

The first book is called SOMEBODY LIKE YOU, and you can turn the page to read the first chapter.

Happy reading,

Donna

CHAPTER ONE

Every single terra-cotta pot was smashed.

Laurel Stone blinked quickly, annoyed at the sting at the back of her eyes as she stared the mess. She was angry. Furious. Most people would rant or turn red in the face. But not Laurel. When she got mad, she angry cried. And right now she was so infuriated that she could barely see through the hot tears.

She'd come in early to do some watering and deadheading before starting the weekly stock order, but discovered the gate hanging limply from its hinges, its lock busted. She immediately took out her cell and called the cops, working extra hard to keep her voice from shaking. Falling apart was not an option. She'd made it through a lot of life changes lately and had kept it together. This time was no different.

Now, as she waited for the police, she swiped at her face and bit down on her lip. It was only six thirty in the morning and she hadn't even had her first coffee yet. The brew sat cooling, forgotten in her ladybug print travel mug. Normally she hummed away to herself, unwinding the hose in the cool morning air. Not today. Today she had to deal with the fact that crime actually happened in quiet, idyllic Darling, Vermont.

And that left her shaken.

The Ladybug Garden Center was her pride and joy, her foray into building a new life for herself. There'd been little incidents in her first few weeks of opening, but she hadn't thought much of them. The parking lot had been messed up a bit where someone had pulled doughnuts with their car. Two lilac bushes from the bed by the store sign had been stolen. She'd sighed at the inconvenience but chalked it up to simple mischief.

This time the intent was obvious. Deliberate. And it felt personal.

All the pottery was in shards on the floor. Six-packs of annuals had been pushed off their tables, spilling dirt and crushed blossoms. Hanging baskets had been carelessly dropped, so that the planters cracked and split. Tomato and pepper plants were strewn everywhere, broken and wilting. The lock on the little safe had been smashed, and they'd taken the small amount of money set aside for a float.

Laurel was sweeping shards of pottery into a dustpan when she heard the gritty crunch of tires on gravel. She stood up and braced her hand on her hip as the cruiser crept slowly up the drive and into the parking lot. Might as well get the report over with, and then get on with the cleanup and the call to the insurance agent.

The cruiser door opened.

Damn, damn, damn.

She'd forgotten, though she wasn't quite sure how she could have since Darling was such a small town. Aiden Gallagher. One of Darling's finest, complete with a crisp navy uniform, black shoes, and a belt on his hip that lent him a certain gravity and sexiness she wished she didn't appreciate.

The last time she'd seen Aiden, she'd been home from school, barely twenty-one, and he'd flashed her a cocky take-a-good-look grin, all the while parading around the Suds and Spuds pub with some girl on his arm. Not that she'd expected any other sort of behavior from him. But still. Ugh.

Aiden approached the gate and she took a deep breath. He was a cop answering a call. Nothing more. And that was how she'd treat him. She definitely wouldn't acknowledge that they'd known each other since they were five years old. Or that he'd once had her half-naked in the backseat of his car.

"Laurel," he greeted, sliding through the gap in the fence. "Looks like you've had some trouble."

She would do this. She would not cry again, especially not in front of Aiden. She had too much pride.

"A break-in last night." She opened the gate a bit wider so he could get through. He passed close by her, his scent wafting in his wake. She swallowed. After all these years, he still wore the same cologne, and nostalgia hit her right in the solar plexus. He took off his cap and she saw his hair was still the same burnished copper, only shorter and without the natural waves, and his skin showed signs of freckles, but nowhere near as pronounced as they'd been. He wasn't a boy any longer; he was a man.

He looked over his shoulder, his gray-blue eyes meeting hers. Definitely a man.

"Wow." He stopped and stared at the carnage. "They made a real mess. Was anything taken?"

She shrugged, focusing on the issue at hand once more. "Inventory-wise, I won't know until I get things cleaned up and do a count. But I doubt it. The float for the cash is gone, but that's only a few hundred dollars. Mostly they just made a mess."

Laurel bent over and righted a half-barrel of colorful begonias, purple lobelia, and million bells. Her gaze blurred as she noticed the crushed, fragile blossoms and pile of dirt left on the floor.

"Laurel?"

She clenched her teeth. If he saw her with tears in her eyes... Today was upsetting enough without adding humiliation to the mix.

"Laurel," he said, softer now. "Are you okay?"

"I'm fine." She bit out the words and pushed past him, going to the counter area. She could stand behind it and the counter would provide a barrier between them. "You don't need to worry about me or take that soothing-the-victim tone. What do you need for facts?"

She sensed his withdrawal as he straightened his shoulders, and she felt momentarily sheepish for taking such a sharp tone. But she was angry, dammit. Hell, she was angry most of the time, and starting to get tired of hiding it with a smile. This was truly the last thing she needed.

"Do you have a slip or anything with the amount of the float?" Now he was all business. It was a relief.

She took a piece of paper from beneath the cash drawer in the register. "This is our run-down for what goes in the float each night. It's put in a zip bag in the safe. Like a pencil case."

He came around the counter, invading her space, and knelt down in front of the cupboard. "This is the safe?"

"I know. It's not heavy-duty—"

"It looks like they just beat it open with a hammer."

Great. Now she was feeling stupid, too. "It's Darling. I didn't expect something like this to happen here."

He stood up and gave her a look that telegraphed "Are you serious?" before stepping back beyond the counter again. "Something like this happens everywhere, Laurel. What, you didn't think crime happened in Darling?"

Well, no. Or at least, not until today. The fact that she'd already come to this disappointing conclusion, and then he'd repeated it, just made her angrier.

Coming home was supposed to be peaceful. Happy. The town was small, friendly, neighborly. Even after years away, many of her customers remembered her from her school years and recalled stories from those days. Darling even had a special

"Kissing Bridge" in the park. There were several stories around how the bridge got the name, so no one really knew for sure. But the stone bridge and the quaint little legend to go with it brought tourists to the area and made Darling's claim to fame a very romantic one. In a nutshell, those who stood on the bridge and sealed their love with a kiss would be together forever.

She should know all about it. Her picture—and Aiden's—hung in the town offices to advertise the attraction. Just because they'd only been five years old at the time didn't make it less of an embarrassment.

"I'm not naïve," she replied sharply. "Is there anything else you need, or can I get back to cleaning up?"

"Can you think of anyone who might want to give you trouble? Someone with a grudge or ax to grind?"

Other than you? she thought darkly. This was the first time they'd actually spoken since she'd poured vanilla milkshake over his head in the school cafeteria in their senior year. "No," she replied. "I can't imagine who'd want to do this."

"I don't suppose you have any video cameras installed."

She shook her head, feeling inept and slightly stupid. Maybe she was a little naïve after all. She hadn't lived in Darling since she was nineteen. Things had changed in her absence. New people, new businesses.

"I'll have another look around. It looks like a case of vandalism more than anything. Probably some teenagers thinking it's funny, or after the cash for booze or pot, and smashed some stuff for show." His gaze touched hers. "Kids can be really dumb at that age."

Her cheeks heated. He hadn't had to say the actual words for her to catch his meaning. "You never know. They might have been dared to do it. Or some sort of stupid bet."

He held her gaze a few seconds longer, and she could tell by the look in his eyes that he acknowledged the hit. He'd kissed her because of one of those bets...more than kissed her. They'd been parking in his car and he'd rounded second base and had been headed for third. And then she'd found out about the wager and lost her cool. Publicly. With the milkshake.

The only thing she regretted was saying yes to going on that drive in the first place.

"So you still haven't forgiven me for that."

Laurel lifted her chin. "To my recollection, you haven't asked for forgiveness."

Aiden frowned, his brows pulling together. "We were seventeen. Kids. That was years ago."

Which didn't sound much like an apology at all.

"Yes, it was. Now, I have a lot of mess to clean up. Is there any more information you need or are we done here?"

He stared at her for a long minute. Long enough that she started to squirm a bit at his continued attention. Finally, when she was so uncomfortable she thought she might burst, she turned away and retrieved the broom and dustpan from where she'd left them.

"Do you want some help with this?"

She didn't want him to offer. The idea of spending more time with him was so unsettling that she immediately refused. "No. Don't you have to get back to work? Besides, I have someone coming in at eight. You go do what you need to do, Officer Gallagher."

"Officer Galla—oh, for Crissakes, Laurel. Is that necessary?"

She pinned him with a glare. He was standing with his weight on one hip, accentuating his lean, muscular physique, one perfect eyebrow arched in response to her acid tone.

She wasn't the kind to hold a grudge. Not generally. Heck, she'd forgiven Dan months ago, and that was for something far bigger than a silly teenage bet. Why did Aiden get under her skin so easily?

Maybe it was because he'd been so callous, even after the fact. If he'd shown any remorse at all... But he hadn't. He'd taken the paper cup the milkshake had been in and fired it across the cafeteria floor before charging out. And he'd never once spoken to her again.

Until today. And despite the change in circumstances, she felt much the same as she had that night in the backseat of his car. Out of her depth, over her head, and at a distinct disadvantage.

She looked away. "Sorry. I just want to clean this up and get ready to open."

She picked up the broom and began sweeping the little bits of broken pots and dirt into the dustpan. She saw his shoes first; big sturdy black ones that stopped in front of her. Then his hand, warm and reassuring, touched her shoulder. She'd been rude and brusque, and he was being kind. Damn him. Emotion threatened to overwhelm again. Couldn't he see that gentle compassion was harder for her to handle than cool efficiency?

"Are you afraid to stay here alone this morning?"

Her throat tightened. "No, of course not."

"I'm on duty until this afternoon. I can check in from time to time."

"I'm fine." She looked up at him and set her jaw. "I can take care of myself. I'm a big girl."

He stepped back. "All right. But if you think of anything or anything else happens, call right away."

"Okay."

She kept sweeping and listened to his footsteps walk away across the concrete floor. The building always smelled delicious thanks to the flowers, but this morning the scent was even more pungent because many had been crushed and mangled. She sighed and rested her weight on the broom handle. He was just doing his job. And she was pissed off—at the state of the garden center and the fact that the one person in Darling she didn't really care to see was the one who'd been sent to help.

"Aiden?"

He turned when she called his name, but his expression was neutral. She wished she could be that way. Unfortunately, she always seemed to wear her emotions all over her face.

"Thanks for your help this morning."

He nodded. "Just doing my job."

He walked to his cruiser and got in while Laurel stood there with a flaming-hot face. Once he'd turned to exit the driveway, she kicked a plastic bucket that had been abandoned in the middle of an aisle, sending it spinning away with a loud clatter. No sooner had she decided to extend an olive branch than he came back with a line that deflated any sort of possibility of amity. He was just doing his job, like he'd do for anyone else. She was no one special. Never had been. The knowledge shouldn't have cut, but it did.

Anyway, the bigger issue was the problem at hand—getting the store ready to open in just a few hours. The Ladybug Garden Center was her baby now. She'd invested all of herself into it, and she was determined to see it succeed, not only this spring and summer but into the fall and winter. In order for that to happen she would have to take steps to ensure this sort of thing didn't happen again.

Just as soon as she cleaned up the mess.

And stopped thinking about how Aiden hadn't changed that much, either. In good ways and in bad.

Keep Reading SOMEBODY LIKE YOU

About the Author

Since 2006, *New York Times* bestseller Donna Jones Alward has enchanted readers with happy ever afters and home-comings that have won several awards and been translated into over a dozen languages. She's worked as an administrative assistant, teaching assistant, in retail and as a stay-at-home-mom, but always knew her degree in English Literature would pay off, as she is now happy to be a full-time writer. Her new historical fiction tales blend her love of history with characters who step beyond their biggest fears to claim the lives they desire.

Donna currently lives in Nova Scotia, Canada, with her husband and two cats. You can often find her near the water, either kayaking on the lake or walking the sandy beaches to refill her creative well.

You can find her at www.donnaalward.com .

www.ingramcontent.com/pod-product-compliance
Lightning Source LLC
Chambersburg PA
CBHW032011310726
48972CB00002B/366